Also by Mark Hudson
Gordan Hudde Fiction
A Deep Purple Hue
An Angry Orange Sky
A Hint of Silver
An Emerald Abyss

Nonfiction
A Retail Investigator
Sitting With Jimmy

Authored and published by Mark Hudson owner and operator
of ONE FLYER PUBLISHING.

Romans 13:4

for he is God's servant for your good. But if you do wrong, be afraid, for he does not bear the sword in vain. For he is the servant of God, an avenger who carries out God's wrath on the wrongdoer.

An Angry Orange Sky

A GORDAN HUDDE NOVEL

Mark Hudson

© 2017 Mark Hudson

All rights reserved.

ISBN: 0999006614

ISBN 13: 9780999006610

Chapter One

Approximately one hundred and twenty miles northeast of Mazatlán, Mexico, in the mountains of Durango, two black Land Rovers picked their way carefully on what could only be called a goat trail. This pass was purposely kept in a poor state to discourage the *federales* or other cartels from attempting any mass frontal assault if the location was ever discovered. The lowland desert sage, agave and rocky brown, gave way to Mexican *piñon* and Apache pine, a mountainous green land. Back on the coast, even in September, it was most likely near 80 degrees today, but the temperature dropped as you headed inland to higher elevations, and, when the sun set, the temperatures here would drop into the low 40s. Sunset was several hours away. Yet you could still be in near-total darkness travelling in and out of the heavily wooded valleys; both vehicles traveled with the headlights on.

In the first vehicle, the driver was Raul Hernandez, the right-hand man to the man who sat directly behind him, Luis Fernando Calderon, head of the crime family that controlled the state of Durango and most likely the third-strongest cartel in all of Mexico.

In the front passenger seat was Piero Campos, second in the Aztec Mafias Peruvian drug cartel, run by Daniel Herrera, who was seated behind him, very relaxed, as this mountainous terrain was nothing new to them.

In the vehicle behind were four very hard men, two men each from their respective outfits. The men were heavily and well armed, more for protection from rivals than from the federal police. The men in charge of the police and military were well paid by all the cartels, and seldom did anyone from the government take action against them.

Arriving at their destination, the two vehicles pulled into the tree line near a small shack, mostly a roof, to protect the two AK-47-carrying guards from light rain. A 55-gallon drum was being used to burn wood for heat, and two beaten and older trucks were parked further under the trees. The two guards snapped upright when they observed the two vehicles. They were used to the old pickups that carried men and supplies, and they knew that this was something unusual. One of the men recognized Luis Fernando and called out,

"*El Jefe!*" He tried to stand tall for the dignitaries.

"My men, how goes the tedious watch? Is all well?"

The guard knew very well what the answer should be.

"*Aye, El Jefe.*"

"Very good, very good. Carry on." He dismissed them with a wave of his hand.

The group of eight men began walking two by two up a well-maintained trail until they reached a flat area covered in poppies, planted in a ten-foot-wide swatch that extended one hundred yards in length. *El Jefe* pointed this out to his guests,

"We have many more. As you walk, these trails are very difficult to see except from directly overhead and, even then, seldom found."

Daniel Herrera looked at the field of future heroin.

"As wonderful as this is," he said, "as lucrative as our business arrangement has been in the past, and as beautiful a drive as this was, what brought us here was the percentage of losses that seem to have plague our shipments over the last six months."

Herrera was a thin man, approximately 5'5" tall, with brown, short-cropped hair. He had been successfully running the Peruvian cocaine business for about twelve years, and he was not accustomed to anyone attempting to humor him.

"I have agreed that a 10% loss would be acceptable, with a goal of zero. But there has 35% in losses over the last six months — this is unacceptable," said Herrera.

Luis Calderon replied, "Yes, I agree, and I have brought you here to show you the cooperation with the Mexican government and to point out that my losses over the same time have been just as considerable, if not more."

Calderon was closer to fifty than his Peruvian counterpart. His salt-and-pepper hair melded in with his full and closely trimmed beard; at near 6'2", he was the tallest man in the group. He carried himself with poise, power, and elegance; he moved in this environment as if walking through the palace grounds instead of a remote wilderness. Calderon, unlike so many of the other drug czars throughout the southern hemisphere, did not think himself as some kind of military wannabe and never wore camouflage or any other military clothing. He wore crisp Armani suits, and, even though they were hundreds of miles from civilization, today was no different.

The group turned and began walking between some low, long buildings with activity taking place inside. The path widened as they left the canopy of the trees, and the temperature went up a few degrees as they re-emerged into direct sunlight.

"As to our mutual concerns over product losses — due mostly to American criminal enterprises across the border — this is what I wanted you to observe," said Calderon.

The group found themselves standing directly in front of a large hole in the ground. Three dirty, tired men looked up from the bottom of the pit, while two men with Uzis stood at the ready at either end of the dig.

"You see, Mr. Herrera, we have found the person who is responsible for the leak in information." Calderon waved at the hole in the ground with a sweeping gesture.

"The *person* or the *people*?" Herrera looked down at the condemned men.

"We have here Rafael Torres, along with the brothers Rojas, Juan and Diego; at least one of them is responsible for the last month of losses we have experienced," Calderon said.

Calderon stepped to the edge, looking down at the first man. "Rafael, tell me: Why are you here?"

Rafael Torres looked up from his potential grave.

"El Jefe, I am in your service near the border, but I have served you faithfully, and you have treated me well." He looked down in deference to the powerful man above him.

"But I have treated each of you well. Is that not so, Juan Rojas?"

Juan Rojas did not look up. "*Si, si,* It is true, *El Jefe,* I don't know why I am here!"

"Is this how you feel as well, Diego?" Calderon took a half-step closer to the far side to get a better look at Diego Rojas.

"I have always done my best, Mr. Calderon." Diego Rojas said, without much enthusiasm.

Rafael Torres suddenly scrambled as close to the side of the dirt hole as he could get, to place distance between Juan Rojas, directly under Calderon. The men with Uzis jerked their weapons into a ready stance and took direct aim at him as he as he attempted to crawl into the dirt wall.

"Wait!" *El Jefe* yelled out.

Calderon knelt at the very edge of the nearly six-foot-deep hole. He reached in and grabbed Rafael's chin, pulling up to make him come into eye contact with him.

"Rafael, why do you look for safety in the corner of this hole?"

"*El Jefe,* as the sun sets, and we are done digging, I am now freezing cold."

"Yes, and what?" Calderon asked.

"*El Jefe,* look at Juan. He is sweating like we have been running," Rafael Torres said.

"Rafael, you are very observant. Congratulations!"

Calderon pointed at his men with machine guns, who both fired a short burst of bullets into Juan's torso. Juan made a few gurgling sounds as he crumbled to the ground and died in a fetal position.

Suddenly, Diego screamed out in terror, "I — I did not know!" reaching skyward with both palms up.

"And this is exactly why you are of no use to me."

And then Diego died much the same as his brother.

Luis Fernando Calderon reached down into the blackness at the cowering Torres.

"We found that Juan had been selling information to our competition across the border. Mr. Torres — you are observant. You did not beg for your life, and you have shown great courage. I believe you may have potential that has been missed by others. You could be of great service if you wish to come with me now."

American CIA agent Rafael Torres reached up out of the pit, taking the hand of Calderon, and scrambled to his feet.

Calderon stood eye to eye with the 28-year-old Oklahoma native Rafael Torres and said,

"Go get a blanket and get some warmth by the guard-house. You will come with us tonight."

He turned back to Herrera.

"Now you see that we do fix our problems here. I know that, due to our former issue, your organization has lost millions of dollars. I would like to offer you an opportunity to have us deliver your goods to America at a 5% reduction in cost, or I would like to offer you 5% in our heroin business."

Herrera knew that heroin had become the new "cool" drug of choice for American youth and thought that this would be his best chance for future additional income.

"And what exactly do you wish in return?" Herrera asked Calderon.

"Ah, very astute. As you know, my organization is not as large as the Sinaloa group on the Pacific or the Gulf group on the East coast, but we are a very strong third-largest operation. We have watched our competitors along the coasts fight over the Colombian product, and we couldn't help but notice that the Colombians take some delight in their discourse. We would like to ensure our future success without a need to fight amongst ourselves by making a mutual, explicit contract — where you and I do business only with each other."

He paused, watching Herrera very closely.

"This will save us all from dealing with conflict. While the two bigger groups fight between themselves, you and I will grow and prosper. I propose that we check back in a year to see how successful we have been, and renegotiations can take place then, if needed."

Herrera nodded his head in agreement. "I accept your proposal in theory but would suggest 10% of your heroin trade would be acceptable."

"Why not say 8% for the first year? You may send some of your trusted men, who can participate with the growing and production to understand that my word is golden and that this deal will be fruitful. Now," Calderon placed his arm around Herrera and began the journey back to the vehicles, "you can mull it over as we drive to my cabin. I have some fine tequila ready to celebrate what will be a very beneficial business."

Chapter Two

At the La Playa Hermoso Grande in Mazatlan, it was, indeed, still in the high 70s. Floating in the pool, still in direct but slowly fading sunlight, Gordan Hudde enjoyed another Corona. The pool water was about the same temperature as the air; this sure beat the hell out of shoveling snow. He'd spent the last week trying to even out the farmer tan he'd gotten from military operations in the Middle East. This was actually the first time in his life that he was not working over any three-day period, and he was beginning to enjoy it. Work would have consisted of being shot at anywhere in the world that the United States may have been in conflict. Anyone looking at him in the pool could think he was in construction or something requiring physical labor, as here was a man in obvious great shape and good health. Hudde's arms and shoulders rippled with heavy muscle; his belly was flat, and his strong legs dragged in the water as he pushed himself on the floating lounger.

He was amazed at the beauty of the place and how easy it had been to overlook so many things while he had been working for the government. Suddenly a palm tree in front of a bright blue backdrop of cloudless sky was a thing of beauty. When he had seen the same thing before in foreign lands, he'd never even noticed. The pool at the resort was a huge, vast expanse of water and things to look at. On one end was a swim-up bar with a thatched roofed overhanging the water, where you could look in at patrons eating or drinking inside. There, a small group was mingling and laughing; a large, pink man in his mid-sixties seemed to be the center of attention. Hudde first guessed *a businessman with his wife and daughter* but then the way he reached down to grasp the younger woman's pert behind, he had to rethink; they were of no concern so he looked further west and north.

The pool narrowed at the north end into a meandering slow stream, which, if followed, took you to another expanse of a pool catering to younger kids, complete with a toddler pool. It was surrounded by fountains of water that you could walk through. They seemed to be on a rotating timer, which some of the smaller children were trying to figure out. On this side, an array of water slides were set up at the deeper end, and some of the older kids were screaming and hooting it up, enjoying the fun. The tile surrounding the pool was a clay-pot color, with imprints of pyramids and birds and dinosaur bones in bright colors of red, yellow, and orange on them. The pool itself was lined with a bright-blue pebbly texture that felt good on Hudde's toes and made the water a brilliant blue color if you looked down from your room. Hudde pulled his floating lounge chair out of the water so that other guests could use it if they liked, and then he threaded his way through the chairs and thatched, shaded privacy cabanas toward the lobby, taking the time to give a beer salute to anyone who made eye contact.

The hotel lobby was vast and just as colorful as the outside. The girls behind the counter wore rainbow-colored shirts covered by bright aquamarine jackets. There were two doormen dressed like conquistadors, complete with halberds. Hudde went to the elevators and took a ride to the top floor, the ninth, to his room.

The room had clay-colored tile floor similar to the tiles near the pool. It opened immediately to a king-sized bed on huge wooden beams that seemed fit for a king, overlooking floor-to-ceiling windows that allowed you access to the patio. The bathroom consisted of dual sinks and a giant tub that Hudde wouldn't use. The shower was a walk-in, surrounded by large glass-tile blocks. The showerhead was high enough that a large man could shower without hitting his head, and there was a built-in seat where you could sit and soak if you desired.

Hudde showered quickly and dressed in some tan-khaki cargo shorts and an army-green polo. This was about as fancy as he would get. He stepped out onto the patio and looked down at the Pacific, just 300 yards from the pools, the sea turning from a light blue near the white sands to a gradually deep and foreboding navy blue off in the distance. This certainly was something that he could do for a few more months while he decided his next course of action. Did he want to head back to the States and the dangers of being a CIA operative? Was the director going to make him a desk jockey because he was afraid to let him back in the field making decisions on his own?

Nope, whatever lay in his future, he was not going to decide today, so he headed down to the bar to grab a late lunch. He skipped the formal dining area as he had found a waitress on his third day here so completely intoxicating to look at that he ate at the bar every day. He knew it bordered on stalking but couldn't help himself. He wouldn't think of hitting on her, as he pictured she most likely fought off thousands of men every year; he didn't want to add to a problem. He knew he was just passing through and just enjoyed her beauty like someone who enjoyed fine art.

Isabella Santiago was both hostess and waitress during slower times at the Carne a la Parrilla. The hotel was one of the biggest and best tourist attractions on the Pacific coast, and she was happy to have a job. At 5'1", she often wore heels that were a little too high, not too good for standing all day. But she wore them just like she wore her blouse, which slid down her shoulders, displaying a large amount of cleavage. She could use all the good tips she could get. If a little flirtation got her an extra few percent — well, like her mother told her, "You are only young for a short while. Use your looks while you can." So she donned her gaudy, festive clothing and went to work every day, hoping for better things to come for her.

A customer arrived — the American who had been coming in for almost a week now. He was a ruggedly good-looking man. With huge shoulders and hands, maybe just shy of 6' tall, he had a short, heavy black beard covering his face, but his hazel eyes twinkled like he knew something that you didn't.

He seemed nice enough and hadn't done or said anything that made her suspicious of him, yet there was something not quite right about him. He didn't act like a man on vacation — no cell phone or constant emailing, no wedding ring, always by himself, and always very observant. He was always watching everyone and everything. Isabella made up a story that he was working for giant American oil or mining company and waiting for an important meeting. He smiled a polite smile and followed her to a table; she made sure that her right leg remained outside her wrap-around skirt, her high-heeled foot pointed like a runway model when she turned to seat the gentleman.

"Is this seat OK for you, sir, or are you expecting others?"

"It's just me, and this is fine, but maybe you could call me 'Gordan.' I'm not all that comfortable with 'sir.'"

"Yes, sir." She shook her head and smiled. "Gordon."

"It's 'Gordan' with an 'a,'" he said, "probably a typo when I was born." He smiled up at her as he took a seat. "I have been here more than a week now. Hearing my first name once in a while would be nice." She smiled back, and he knew that he would have to extend his trip until this woman would at least take a walk or have dinner with him.

Chapter Three

The Sinaloa cartel was run by Eduardo "The Cowboy" Gonzales, a nickname coined by the *Sinaloa News*, and Gonzales liked it. What Gonzales did not like was reading in the paper about his competition expanding into North-Central Mexico. The Gulf cartel was attempting to gain greater access to the American border than they already claimed. He slapped the table and yelled down at the paper, "Carlos, you greedy bastard! You already have the entire Texas coast and border. I will cut your throat if you try to move West."

He had met once with Carlos Morales early in his career in an attempt to tamp down violence along the border. Better not to attract the attention of the American population, who might then demand action from their government. Morales, always the businessman, was quick to agree, and they maintained an uneasy peace between New Mexico and the Texas border. After all, it was difficult to reign in dangerous and desperate men when they were attempting to get noticed and move up in the cartel. Gonzales knew that any given action on the border might not have been sanctioned by Morales, but he could not let an attack on any of his men go unpunished. He risked losing the respect and fear of his own men. High up on the third floor of his mansion just North of the city of

Culiacan, nestled in the hills, The Cowboy screamed out for his lieutenant, Lopez, who was never far away,

"Miguel, get your ass up here."

Miguel walked quickly onto the patio where Gonzales was taking his breakfast.

"Why are you not here speaking to me about Puerto Palomas?" He folded the newspaper and slapped it down onto the table. "Why do I read of such things in the newspaper first?"

"Eduardo, I didn't want to upset you before breakfast. It was news that I thought could wait."

"I don't pay you to make those decisions. Now, what was the problem — or don't you know?" Patience was not one of The Cowboy's virtues.

"It looks like one of our pigeons was keeping an eye on one of the Gulf-group operations in Juarez, and he was seen. When they chased him down and killed him, they dumped his body in Palomas and dropped him off at one of your bars there. There was a brief shootout. I don't know who did it, but a couple of kids got killed."

"Palomas is our town, Miguel. Severe punishment is necessary. What do you think, then? Maybe five for one, plus burn down one of their buildings in Juarez for the kids?" The Cowboy nodded several times. "Our men must understand that we will avenge them with much anger; the people of Palomas must know that we do not take this lightly. Those men singled us out by dropping him off at our bar; this was no accident. So make it happen. Let the Gulf boys know that the death of one Cowboy will not go unpunished."

"It's done, then." Lopez spun out of the room to make the proper calls. He exited the vast 20,000-square-foot home and walked across the cobblestone driveway and turnaround with a large fountain at the center, past the six-car garage complete, with The Cowboy's own mechanic, who lived over the garage. Past the servant quarters, a 3,500-square-foot home for the cooks, maids, and nanny. Down to the two large barns, one which actually housed some horses and the final one, something like a WWII army barracks which always held a minimum of twenty men. Rows of bunk beds ran the length of both sides of the barracks, and these the lower-ranking soldiers took. At the end was a large, open bathroom with open showers and rows of sinks and toilets. Upstairs, there were two 800-square-foot apartments, and Miguel called one of these home. The other was available if any of the other lieutenants needed to stay and was not invited into the main home. Lopez enjoyed being in the barracks, as he was the highest-ranking person and therefore in charge out there. He also liked being away from the main house, except during dinner, when the food there was five star while the food sent to the soldiers was, well, much like army chow.

Chapter Four

Three weeks later, Carlos Morales, head of the Gulf cartel, was sitting in his office just blocks from Universidad Autónoma de Tamaulipas, located in the city of Ciudad Victoria. He was close to 6' tall, thin but tough. He liked to dress like the main heavy in an episode of *Miami Vice*. Here he had built a small office complex just for his cartel business. His father had used incredibly violent tactics to take over the cartel, but Carlos wanted to show that he could be loved as well as feared. It didn't work in reality, as, at the low end of the drug business, you cannot get away from addicts and dealers or the crime and victims that result. But Carlos told himself that this dream made him a better person than his father. He also did give much of his wealth to the people of Ciudad Victoria in some public works, like a new water-purification plant at nearby Vicente Guerrero Lake. His lieutenant, Marco Vargas, was explaining how seven of their men were found at a fire-bombed warehouse where the Morales cartel staged drug- and human-trafficking runs into America.

"So what did this note say?" Morales asked.

"'Cowboys take revenge seven to one,' senlor Morales." Vargas walked over to a bronze statue of a large stag standing on a rocky outcrop on a table at the window. "I am sure this is for the stool pigeon that our men killed several weeks ago."

"Yes, but that was not sanctioned by me, but this, obviously, was sanctioned by The Cowboy.. We cannot allow this to continue along the American border. Let's look for some opportunities inland and see what we can find that will remind Mr. Cowboy that this behavior is unacceptable."

♦ ♦ ♦

Meanwhile back at the La Playa Hermoso Grande in Mazatlan, Gordan Hudde was about to grab a bite to eat. He had told himself that today was the day he would finally ask Isabella if she would have dinner or something. He was mad at himself for allowing so many weeks to go by.

Hudde smiled up at Isabella as she seated him at what he was starting to believe was "his table." "May I tell you something?" he asked her politely.

"If you feel you must." It was sarcastic, but she was still smiling at him.

"I have been working since I was very young, always busy and going forward. I joined the Army and, again, just work on top of more work. I never really thought about where I was going, but as long as I was moving, I felt comfortable."

He paused, looking up at her light-brown eyes with little yellow flakes.

"I was totally immersed in all things fast and dangerous. I never saw anything that made me want more out of my life, but then I suddenly stopped here, and *Boom!* Like explosions in my mind, I am beginning to see things I never noticed before — things that are interesting and things that are beautiful."

"So you are saying I am beautiful." She raised an eyebrow and seemed a little disappointed as if he hadn't brought enough.

"Listen, Isabella: You are *Hollywood* beautiful — OK? So, don't get me wrong. But I mean to say everything seems different to me. I want to experience good things, enjoy life more, and I would like to get to know you, maybe spend some time together."

"I understand, and I think "Hollywood beautiful" is a pretty nice compliment, but — "

He cut her off, "But you have been hurt by someone you met here before, a vacationer. You were younger, yes?"

"Go on." She slowly slid into the bench seat across from him. When she sat, she allowed her breasts to be pushed further up and out of her blouse by pressure of the table, and Hudde almost lost track of his thoughts. When he regained eye contact, she smiled mischievously back at him.

"Well, I would guess that working here, where there is much wealth and men who are used to getting their own way, you have come into contact with many men who disappoint you. I had no intention originally of even speaking to you. I just enjoyed watching you move about the bar. A big part of the reason I am here is that I pay attention to my surroundings. I watch and surmise what people are thinking. It is a gift that has kept me safe." He allowed himself a deep breath and glanced about the bar before looking back into those big eyes.

"I know the assistant manager is in love with you. He comes in three times during your shift to check on the restaurant. while, when you are not here, I have never seen him."

She rolled her eyes and sighed.

"The busboy is in total lust with you, as he trips over himself and walks into walls whenever you are near."

She smirked a little and shrugged her shoulders in a "So what?" kind of gesture.

"Now, I saw you flirt a little extra with one of the college guys in here a couple of days ago. You know — the guy about 6'5", blonde hair with a group of partiers, but when he made an official pass at you, I think you stopped him cold."

He had her total attention, and she was beginning to look a little surprised at these observations.

"Again, there was the group of business folks in last week Thursday night, and I saw several of the ladies giving you the once-over, but I doubt you even noticed, so I don't think that's an issue."

She couldn't help but interrupt: "No, no, that's not an issue."

He put his hands up in a surrender sign. "OK — just using my gift of observation. Your mom lives outside the city; you wear jeans and t-shirts and are not afraid to get dirty, and you enjoy the outdoors."

"Yes, but how? Are you stalking me?" She furrowed her brow and looked a little worried.

"You changed here the other day, and I saw you leave. You looked very comfortable, and your jeep looks like it has been off-road, with the dirt and mud caked on the side. It hasn't rained here in several days, so I guess you have maybe been a little further off road. I told you I have been paid to be observant."

"Just what do you do, Mr. Gordan?"

"Well, just now I couldn't tell you, but I have started to think that I may not go back to my job."

"So, what are you going to do? Beg for money on the side of the road?"

"Ha! No, recently someone close to me died and left me a large amount of money, enough that I may not need to work. This is why I vacation here now; otherwise, I would not be able to afford this place." *Not really a lie.*

"I am sorry; I didn't mean to hurt your feelings."

"It's OK. I got over it. So, what do we know: You are a beautiful, hard-working woman, determined to do what is right for yourself, tough enough to deal with the assholes that probably frequent this place as well as nice enough to have all your coworkers seem to really like you."

She seemed genuinely happy about his assessment so far.

"I, too, am hard working, eager to do what is right, have not dated a woman in almost three years, and find you absolutely captivating. I just negotiated another month's stay here just so that I could get to know you. I am asking: Is that enough to take you to dinner?"

Isabella was really studying his face, her left lip curled up in maybe a one-quarter smile.

"Well, the assistant manager is about 42 years old and has a child from another woman who used to work here; he is nice enough, but, no thanks. The big man was very handsome — big and strong — but you were correct that a very similar thing happened to me several years ago. I will not allow that to happen ever again; I will not be a vacation fling to tell his friends about back home. I am much more than just passion, Mr. Hudde, and beauty will get one only so far. I will have you know that I flirted extra to let him know what he would be missing, not for giving me a bigger tip. I did not notice the women, but it still is flattering. Now, as to our busboy" and she wagged a finger out in front of Hudde, "he has very bad thoughts about me, that one has. I think I am sorry for his first girlfriend."

Hudde tried desperately to stop his own "bad" thoughts.

"I know a man is not supposed to talk about a woman's age, but I would guess you are twenty-five to twenty-seven? I think you are completely comfortable with the way you look, but I assure you, I would not be interested if your co-workers did not also like you so much."

She began to interject, but he stopped her with a hand up.

"Sure, some are jealous or envious, but they all like and/or respect you, and that means a lot. I see many people search you out during your work here. They like your company."

He got a full smile and knew what the answer was going to be.

"OK, Mr. Gordan. You get to take me to dinner, but not here, and you must tell me why this took you almost a month before asking me this question."

"Well, because I have been brave in the face of danger in the past doesn't mean I still do not fear rejection. To be very honest, I was afraid of you saying 'No,' as this would ruin my continued stay here, and I would be forced to leave." He shrugged his shoulders and smiled a bit sheepishly. "See, I daydreamed about meeting you outside your work, and if this dream cannot happen, I do not think I could stay."

She rubbed her chin, mimicking how Hudde sometimes rubbed his beard.

"So now the man admits to dreaming about me." She smiled a huge grin and slid from the table, heading back to her station. "This could be interesting, Mr. Gordan."

Hudde thought she shook her ass a little extra as she walked away from him, and it was confirmed when she suddenly stopped and looked back over her shoulder, catching him in the act.

"Stop that, Señor Hudde!" and she waggled a finger in his direction.

Chapter Five

CIA agent Rafael Torres was entering his second full year undercover in Mexico. He had never been deployed overseas, but he knew that the Taliban had nothing on the cartels in Mexico when it came to propensities for violence. While the *El Jefe* Calderon was known to be reasonable, his men meted out quick justice when a thief was found at the growing and processing locations. Since being saved from death by Calderon, Torres had identified two men who were stealing from his Durango mountain distribution facilities. The two men had been chopped into torsos and all the parts put into a single box, which was sent back to the village they grew up in, allowing their loved ones to sort out which part belonged to who as a warning for future applicants.

Torres would never fear getting caught stealing, but being an undercover agent would certainly get him something extremely grotesque and painful. He had very loose orders to infiltrate and learn everything he could from the Calderon cartel. He did not know what the CIA ever did with the information that he forwarded and, honestly, was a little disappointed at the lack of action by the agency or DEA. His only return contact with his handler was always "Good work. Keep it up."

Torres now reported directly to Raul Hernandez, Calderon's right-hand man and most powerful lieutenant in the Durango cartel. Torres had now worked his way up from being a mule, to setting up distribution across the border in America, to his current position of overseeing growing of the heroin fields and rough production. This was actually a safer job, and, for the first time, he slept a little better at night. There had been a few incidents where some local bandits, fueled by their own drug use, attempted misguided attacks on the mountain facilities. Each one of these had resulted in the entire attacking force being wiped out, with minimal injuries to the Calderon men.

Torres had been invited to the Calderon home for meetings and parties, and, each time, the fear of being found out was so great, it nearly froze him. Torres wanted to be successful but was wondering what "successful" meant. Almost two years ago, when he'd begun this operation, he would have felt his current position would have been the greatest achievement. But, as no Mexican federal police or Army had raided any compounds, all of the Calderon lieutenants still walked freely. It appeared that the drugs ran fairly smoothly across the border and cash came back; he was not sure why he jeopardized his life so. He had risen well inside the cartel to the point that he had been put in charge of two tough young men eager to raise themselves in the cartel: Piero Campos, a young, tough Peruvian lent to the Calderon cartel as a sign of cooperation, who had been working in the mountain growing regions, and Jose Sanchez, a local who was smart and quick witted and had impressed Torres when he had met him working some of the border-trafficking jobs. Jose and Piero now stood together outside the door to the room that Rafael and Hernandez occupied.

Rafael was pitching his idea to Hernandez: "So day-trip deep-sea fishing boats from Mazatlan delivers the product to actual American tuna boats in deep waters away from the coast. The tuna boats take the product back to San Diego, where they always have been. We lose less product, pay off fewer officials, and bring back larger profit."

Hernandez shook his head "No."

"These things have been tried before, Rafael. First the coast is controlled by the Sinaloa Cowboy's men, and, second, our distribution would need to be added to the San Diego area, increasing risk if we still need to deliver to Vegas and Phoenix. If we try to begin actually selling in San Diego, the Tijuana boys will give us no peace. They are a small but very dangerous operation."

"I have two tuna-boat captains that need the money, Raul. I need some help finding some fishing boats in Mazatlan, but if you try this, I guarantee that we successfully take more product with less loss than you do every week on the border."

Raul Hernandez was looking at his boots.

Rafael continued, "The first couple of trips, me and my boys will meet the boats and personally deliver the product to Vegas. Then, with your approval, we will set up some more men to continue in the future."

Risk was what this job was all about, and, if Raul had a man willing to put himself out there, well, that suited Hernandez.

"You may try this one time, and we shall see." He shook hands vigorously with Torres. "We will either start a war with our neighbors, or we will become very well liked and most favored by Señor Calderon."

Rafael turned, obviously happy, and his men smiled back into the room at him. "Tonight we celebrate!" Torres called out to his men. He placed his hands on the back of the necks of both Piero and Jose, pulling them into to his comfort zone, whispering so that they were the only ones that could hear. "Look around, men. Follow me, and we all live like this one day."

They nodded in agreement and grabbed a drink, taking it out onto the veranda.

The Calderon estate was a real, working Spanish-style ranch and farm. The home was open and large, exquisitely built with brick and rock from the local mountains. Calderon's bedroom was the only part of the home on the second floor. Upon entering the front doors, you saw a vast, open sitting area leading out to a courtyard complete with a life-sized statue of Cortez entering from the outside, coming in past two huge iron gates. Large reddish-brown stone tiles covered the courtyard, a large round fountain was the centerpiece — a life-sized statue of Christ carrying a large cross surrounded by palms and decorative plants that must have taken an army to prune and maintain. The wood used on the cabinets and furniture was heavy and dark; it conveyed a rich earthiness that was much like Luis Fernando Calderon himself.

Calderon entered the courtyard and walked through, greeting his men warmly. He approached Torres and placed his right hand on his left shoulder.

"Mr. Torres, you have not disappointed me after our first meeting. You have ambition and courage, which I admire a great deal." He pointed at Cortez. "It appears that, like my ancestors, you look to the water as a new conquest."

"Si, Señor Calderon. I believe we can increase the traffic and lower our losses, and I hope to prove this to you; my men and I will not fail you."

Calderon studied the face of Torres and then looked at each of his men.

"Yes — I believe you will do this. Now, enjoy my home and food, think of the success we shall share in the future, and have no worries tonight!"

Calderon then walked about his men, sharing stories of working his ranch and starting in the cartel many years ago; he was a sincere and gracious host.

Chapter Six

Heading north from The Cowboy's estate in Sinaloa, Mexico, Route 24 headed into a mountainous vast wilderness that was the heart of the Sinaloa cartel's growing and production area. It was currently being reconnoitered by four Gulf Coast cartel men in an army-green Jeep Cherokee. Marco Vargas was riding shotgun, literally, looking out the window at the dirt road as they turned, heading North near Soyatita. They were to let the Sinaloa cartel know that no action could be taken against Gulf cartel men without retribution, and they were doing so closer to The Cowboy's home to deliver the message that he was not impervious to violence.

There was also an effort to keep the violence from approaching the border or the tourist areas — both very wise business practices. Deaths of members of the teams that worked for the cartels in the mountains caused very real delays in production, as it was sometimes difficult to find workers after they had experienced an attack and observed violence. It was far more glamorous to work on the border — or across the border, for that matter — and it paid better, as well. Vargas, a former soldier, knew that they needed to get in and out without being observed, as there were only two ways in and out by vehicle, and he didn't feel like hiking back to the Gulf Coast from here.

After heading several miles North on the dirt road, they turned back to the West and picked their path, slowly four-wheeling through the brush and stones carefully as no one wished to be stuck in the heart of Cowboy country. A stream stopped their progress — not because the Jeep would be unable to ford it, but because the opposite side of the creek was too overgrown and wild to make it through. Vargas got out and walked upstream to look for a better location to make the crossing. After walking approximately 500 meters, Vargas observed that the creek's Western bank would be easily traversed and headed back to the jeep. He noted that the creek was shallow and boulder free; he felt it easiest to just travel the distance directly upstream, as no major barriers were preventing them from doing so. They made it easily and continued almost a mile further West before finding the way blocked by trees and steeper canyon walls. They backed up into some trees to get overhead cover and then settled in until the morning to walk the final five or six miles to the Northernmost extent of The Cowboy's territory.

It seemed to Vargas that the jeep got colder during the night than the air around them, but they slept inside anyway, although somewhat restlessly, and got up at first light. He divvied up a supply of Chinese-type 69 Bounding Mines to the men, and he took some white phosphorous grenades and a single American Claymore. They headed West through the difficult mountainous terrain. At approximately 1000hrs, Vargas checked his map and compass; he felt they were now approximately two miles North of the Northernmost poppy fields, and they began to pick their way South. When the group was approximately 500 meters from their destination, Vargas had the group halt and make a camp with a strict zero-noise order. He whispered to them that they could rest and eat with one of the men on watch at all times. Vargas found a game trail and headed on to see if he could get a visual on their target.

He continued on the relative easy game trail right down to the first poppy field. He stopped under a pine and listened and looked for workers or soldiers and found none. He stepped into the open and scanned; this area had dropped a little lower than the surrounding fields and was not a good vantage point. To the West, a rock cliff stood out amongst the top of the trees, and Vargas headed back into the brush to make his way there. When he arrived at the base of the cliff, he took special care to look at each place he was reaching or setting his foot down so as not to find a sunning snake.

As he neared the summit, he took out his binoculars and began to scan the area. South, he could see some huts with some small smoke contrails spiraling up into the sky. In the fields, some workers were either cutting the poppies or gathering the sap. He imagined that each field was at a different stage of readiness, so that the workers could rotate each week. This plan of retaliation that he had helped devise with Carlos Morales would hurt The Cowboy and allow his own people not to get hurt in the process. It would also be a personal slap at The Cowboy for not keeping his people safe within spitting distance of his own home. Vargas had nothing against The Cowboy's employee's, but he despised The Cowboy himself — Carlos Gonzales, that fat little bastard going around in camouflage, as if he'd served in the military. He actually argued with Morales to take out Gonzales himself, but he'd been denied.

Returning back to his rally point and his three men, Vargas cleared off a 1-meter-by-1-meter flat spot in the dirt and created a relief map of the team's target area. From his vantage point in the rocks, Vargas could make out 5 strips of poppies growing in approximately 100-meter strips 5 meters wide, all running South and North. He designated the entire East strip as a no-go area for his men so they could travel up its Easternmost edge without fear of tripping one of their own mines. Each man was given a strip of poppies of their own to travel 50-60 meters in and then work their way back, placing the mines as they go. The mines the men were planting were similar to a large can of beer. On the top, a three-pronged pressure detonator would be screwed onto and into the mine. Once the mine was placed into the ground so that only the prongs were visible, the pin would be removed from the detonator. Once armed, pressure on the prongs would set off the blasting cap. On the mine, a smaller explosion from the bottom of the mine would send it skyward. The rest of the mine would then explode approximately 1 meter off of the ground. It was quite capable of killing anyone in very close vicinity but usually just injured anyone else. They would head out at 0100hrs and attempt to rally back at this point at 0300hrs.

Vargas had other plans but would regroup with his men no later than 0315hrs, and they would make the hike out to the Jeep. None of them would feel safe until they were back on the Gulf Coast.

It was 0100hrs, and the team headed out and down the trail. They made it to the edge of the Westernmost poppy field and split up to do their work. Vargas crept carefully South, down to where he had seen the huts earlier. He could smell wood burning, and voices were carrying up to him from some lower elevation, but nothing gave him any great concern about being caught. He had personally selected this area, as he was unaware of anyone ever disrupting The Cowboy's operation here, and this lack of action had led to relaxed guards.

The first hut he came upon was very small. Upon entering, he clicked on his headlamp, equipped with a red lens, and observed nothing but tools and shovels. He removed his pack and took out an American M34 white phosphorus grenade — the Americans called it "Willy Pete" — and a roll of fishing line. He tied the grenade to a corner post at floor level, straightened the pin to make it more easily removable, and then placed a line to a shovel handle; anyone collecting tools might set this off. He snapped off his lamp and snuck back out into the night.

The next hut was really just a long low thatched roof that covered the processing of the poppies; it looked as if they were conducting purification here. There were two 55-gallon drums of hydrochloric acid standing near the Southernmost end. An old diesel generator that was probably used to run lights or to pump water sat quietly by a five-gallon fuel tank. Vargas kept low and made his way to the drums. The drum farthest inside was approximately 1/3 full. Vargas could see the deep grooves dug into the dirt — evidence that the large plastic drums were moved regularly by tipping them on edge and rolling them. Vargas dug underneath the drum just enough that so that he could slide a WP grenade underneath the drum. After ensuring a perfect fit, he pulled the pin completely from the grenade. Now, if he were to allow the spoon to flip free from the grenade, the timer would begin, and an explosion would occur within 4 seconds. Very carefully, Vargas forced the grenade, spoon side up, under the royal-blue plastic drum. Once he was finished, he pushed the dirt back and smoothed it over till no one would have been able to detect that it was there. But if anyone lifted the drum, it would set off the grenade, which would cause a fire no one would be able to put out — water would just aggravate it and spread it.

On the opposite end of the hut was a wheelbarrow with the front wheel tight up against the Northernmost corner post. Vargas tied a grenade to the base of the post and then repeated his earlier process, tying the fishing line to the wheelbarrow's front frame. Glancing at his luminous watch, he found that it was near 0245hrs, and he started making his way North to the game trail that he and his team had been using, keeping to the Easternmost edge of the fields. He made it back to his men by 0300hrs and told them to start heading North and not to stop until they made it to the Jeep. Then, he turned back about 50 meters to a very narrow and steep portion of the path they had used. At the top of the path, a tree had fallen, and he anchored his Claymore to the base, covering it with some debris. He set up the trip wire, and, then, when he was satisfied, he connected it to the mine. Anyone following them would be greatly surprised.

In just more than an hour, Vargas caught up with his team. In half the time it took them to travel to the poppy field, they made it back to their Jeep and picked their way back to Route 24. There was no way for them to travel East from here They had to head back South and West, driving right past The Cowboy's grand estate gates of his home between Pericos and Culiacan. But they traveled it easily and without delay, making it to Mazatlan before being able to head back to the East. They had to travel through the Durango cartel land in between, but there were no beefs between the two cartels at this time, and Vargas was very comfortable that they were home free.

Chapter Seven

Rafael Torres closed his eyes and turned into the stiff ocean breeze. He took a deep breath and tried to relax. He was confident that this second trip by his team and the first by the second tuna-boat captain were going to be successes. The sun would be coming up soon, and he wanted to be out of San Diego before rush-hour traffic. He gave Jose Sanchez the universal hand sign for "Speed it up" by spinning his finger in the air. Sanchez and Piero Campos were using hand jacks to wheel their cargo from the tuna boat to a waiting U-Haul in the parking lot on Tuna Lane near N harbor drive.

Standing there looking over at the *USS Midway*, Torres was in awe. He never could understand that something so huge could float. It reminded him of the first time he had seen a jumbo jet taxi down a runway, and he thought it would never fly. Many boat captains and crew were coming and going, preparing themselves for time out on the ocean looking for fish. So early in the morning, and so much activity! Yet he and his crew were completely ignored by the fishermen preparing for their day; the only one seeming to pay any attention to him was a seagull resting on top of a quad parking lot light. Campos tapped Torres on the shoulder, bringing him out of his thoughts: "Hey, boss and Sanchez — shotgun!"

"Yeah — my turn" Sanchez shot back and climbed into the covered bed of the 15' U-Haul that they had been using. Campos pulled down the roll-up door and latched it, banging on the side as he headed for the passenger seat. Torres fired up the truck and headed to R5, meeting the I15 straight to Vegas. Once there, they would head into an auto-repair shop where the drugs would be distributed, just like they always had coming in from Phoenix. The two loads that he and his team had brought in would have less overhead, as they had paid no bribes and had fewer people to bring in 10 times more product than overland; Calderon would be very pleased. And that was odd to Torres that he was feeling so satisfied with pleasing Calderon — the man he thought he was here to help bring down. Ever since Calderon had pulled him from that muddy hole in the ground, he felt a growing respect for the man. He knew that, as long as the agency was telling him to work for the man, he would do just fine. As he was going to make Calderon even more money, he was more nervous about the other lieutenants, whose jealousness could be the end of him before any major action was taken by one of the governments.

Torres was even beginning to like the two men working for him. He was sharing all the money he was making equally with them; they knew it, and he made sure to help with any dirty work so they understood that he would get dirty with them. He knew that his safety might depend on the loyalty of the men he surrounded himself with, and he hoped that nothing he would be required to do in the future would be too detrimental to these two men. He started thinking about how his CIA funds were being directly deposited into an account in Washington while he was now making six figures a year here — in cash, tax free. Maybe it was good that no actions had been taken against the cartel. A man could set up a nice retirement in a few years of working here — if they could stay alive, that is.

When they arrived at Big Jim's Auto repair in Vegas, there was no rest for the wicked. The three pulled the truck directly through an overhead bay, and the door was dropped behind them. The three men took a set of keys from a hook on the wall and walked to a second bay, where a silver '97 Cadillac Deville sat waiting, gassed up and kept in mint driving condition. It was completely legal and not visibly tricked out at all — no low-rider effects or anything to draw attention to it. It did, however, have a trunk that was inaccessible from outside the vehicle. The trunk was welded shut from the outside; any officer stopping this vehicle for minor infractions would not be able to force the owner to open the trunk. If you removed the back seat, the trunk contents could be slid forward on rails; today, the content was large stacks of US currency; other times, it was weapons.

Sanchez adjusted the front driver's seat and settled in for a shift of driving. They would immediately head South through Kingman, Phoenix, Tucson, and then Douglas before crossing the border into Mexico. This would take them almost a full day of driving, each man taking 4-hour shifts worked great; each man could take 8 hours' rest before returning to behind the wheel. Sanchez could get them to Phoenix before changing, which suited him because he hated the trip on the I10 from Phoenix to Tucson — nothing to look at except desert and cops, as this was the major thoroughfare for traffickers from every cartel. This was the leg that Torres drove, and he hoped they would never be stopped and risk having his cover blown. But they were not stopped, and they headed into the relative safety of Mexico.

Chapter Eight

Hudde stood before the full-length mirror in his room in nothing but his under-armour boxer briefs. Even with only swimming and some push-ups and sit-ups in his room, he rippled with almost superhuman strength. His shoulders, neck, and arms would have fit perfectly on someone with a much larger frame than his. His neck size of 22 inches, along with massive shoulders, made it necessary for him to wear 3X or 4X shirts — they often looked like dresses because of their length. He had fooled several the carnival weight-guesser gamesmen when they guessed his weight closer to 200 lbs., many pounds beneath his actual weight. His beard, freshly trimmed, looked similar to how Ulysses S. Grant wore his, although Hudde allowed the chin area to grow a little longer; he liked to pull down through it when he tried to think. He was confident that he could be dropped into any room in the world, filled with the most dangerous people, and he would come out unscathed — yet, here he was, fretting over a single 5' tall, 115-lb. woman. He realized that he had no pants, only a single pair of blue jeans. He grabbed a bowling shirt with some blue and grey stripes that was baggy and comfortable and finished it off with some light boat shoes he'd bought especially for this occasion. It was going to have to do.

Isabella was just outside the hotel lobby, seated near a fountain. She hopped up when she saw Hudde exit and smiled and half-waved. She had chosen a mid-length skirt that seemed light and cool. It had a couple of layers that gave it movement — and Hudde had a difficult time forcing his eyes not to linger longer. The skirt also added to the difference between her hips and waist. Her top was something akin to a halter, tying behind her neck, and one thick strip went around from her mid back — hiding a bra strap, Hudde thought. Even with this incredible physical presence, it was her hair that drew his attention. It was thick, rich black, maybe with blue highlights, and was like the mane of a lion. Waves and flips around her head made her hair seem to have a life of its own. Hudde fought the urge to plunge his hands into it on either side of her head and pull her close for a kiss. Instead he looked at his feet and said, "Hello, Isabella."

She teased him. "What? Are you afraid to look at me?"

"You know what they say about the eyes." He smiled into her beautiful face; her skin radiated a golden sheen. His green eyes met with the dark-cocoa brown of her gaze.

"Come on. Are you hungry?" She turned South and pulled at his left hand with her right hand, stopping short when he didn't move. "I'm going to need some help here" She smiled up at him and pointed down at his feet. She pulled again, trying to get him heading in the right direction.

He finally started moving, with her tiny hand in his massive grip; he was happy. "Where are we going?"

"Well, you said money was no issue, so I made some reservations at the hotel down the beach. They have a famous chef, and, as the restaurant is on the roof, I hear they have a spectacular view." She stopped and looked up at him. "That's not too forward, is it? Is it OK with you?"

Hudde lifted his face to the sky and let out a belly laugh. "No, no. That's great; I had no idea what you would like and totally froze, so I made no plans." He squeezed her hand a little in his and said, "Thank you for saving me."

"Oh, you just jumped into the fire!" In a deliberately exaggerated Spanish accent, she said, "Meeester Hoood!" And she kept her hand in his as they walked along the resort road. It became natural; she made him feel as if they had known each other a long time, and he relaxed.

When they entered the top-floor restaurant, Hudde immediately liked it; he felt like he was walking into a 16th-century Spanish galleon. The hard, dark woods were not imitation, and Hudde had to fight a feeling to jump up on the bar, take one of the antique-looking rapiers from the wall, and scream out, "Evast, ye curs!"

Seated near a window with a spectacular view of Pacific coastline, with the Isla de Venados appearing to float nearby, Isabella spoke in Spanish to the waiter. "I need you to try something other than the Corona you always have, so I ordered you a Negra Modelo. Give that a try. I think it goes especially well with good food, but let me know." She continued, "So have you decided what you will do next?"

"I haven't given it a thought." Hudde replied. "I mean, maybe being in a hotel for months isn't going to continue to be an option, but, for right now, it will do. What about yourself? Somehow I'm guessing that the hotel work is temporary for you; how much longer will I be able to enjoy watching you walk me to a table?" His eyes and smile gave off a mischievousness that she seemed to enjoy.

"Is that it? I am just a piece of meat for you to look at?" She narrowed her eyes and tried to look stern.

"I do enjoy the fine arts," he replied, furrowing his brows and pursing his lips in an attempt to appear fastidious; he picked up his water glass — pinky extended — to add to the act.

"Well, just what part of me is like art, Mister Hudde?" She looked up at him, suddenly serious.

The waiter saved him when he brought the beers with some seriously frosted mugs.

"Man, that looks good!" Hudde grinned ear to ear, not wanting to have that conversation this early in their new relationship.

"I'll grill you after a few beers." Isabella raised her glass of frothy amber liquid.

"Oh, absolutely delicious." Hudde exclaimed after clinking glasses and taking a deep pull. "Although I'm afraid that I have been trained to be able to withstand a good grilling... depending on your technique" Hudde turned at the hovering waiter. "More of this, ah ... um ... *muchas gracias*." And he accentuated it by pointing at the beer.

Isabella looked at Hudde and shook her head vigorously "No." "Don't do that! Leave the Spanish to me." She smiled a brilliant smile and then added, "But you get an 'A' for effort."

"I knew that, sometime in my life, I would get some 'A's.' I'm glad it started with you."

They ordered — Isabella, a twelve-ounce strip steak with a side salad, and Hudde, a twenty-four ounce porterhouse, a baked sweet potato with a side of roasted scallops, and a dinner salad.

After the waiter left, Isabella chuckled. "A little hungry?"

"No lunch," Hudde winked, just before taking another large swig of his beer. He reached for some crusty bread and butter that the waiter had just dropped off with the second round. "I'm glad to see you're an eater, not a bird ordering just a salad."

"Oh, no — I believe in eating. I was a bit surprised that you ordered scallops," Isabella said.

"Yeah, I don't even know what they are — just that I had some years ago, and I remember that they were really very tasty. I guess I always thought they were like shrimp or something."

"Well, a scallop is a marine bivalve mollusk. You eat the muscle that opens and closes the shell. A shrimp or prawn are decapod crustaceans and are very different," she said.

"OK, that's more than I needed to know. Back to our earlier conversation: What is it you do beyond seating me at the bar?" he asked.

Isabella smiled ear to ear. "Actually, I am about to graduate from veterinary school. I have a full-time job lined up with a shelter near my home."

"Wow, that's tremendous news! And I get to celebrate with you here!" He raised his mug again to meet hers across the table. "Looks *and* brains make you a very dangerous woman."

"Just don't forget it." She smiled some more. "Now, on to what you do, Mr. Hudde…"

He interrupted her. "I have to admit the 'Meester' thing does do something for me, but really: Just call me 'Gordan.'"

"OK, Gordan. The girls and I were talking at the hotel, and we are torn between you work for an oil company or possibly something more sinister." She furrowed her brow to show her concern.

He, however, just grinned. "So you and the girls were talking about me. Interesting." He nodded while looking up at the ceiling and pulling down on his beard.

"It was meaningless, idle gossip, and, well, I was just listening anyway." She waved it off before continuing, "Anyway, what is it you really do — *if* you can say, that is?" It was a joke, but it hit a little close to home before Hudde remembered that he had quit the CIA months ago.

He didn't feel like starting this relationship with some of his preconceived stories, so he started with the truth. "I joined the army right out of high school and found a new home and family." He grabbed his beard. "I was good at it, and there is always something out there to get ready for."

"Have you been in combat? You know..." Isabella trailed off, asking with her eyes the question everyone wants to really know the answer to.

"Yes, I have been in a lot of situations, and it meant I had to kill people to survive," he informed her.

"I'm so sorry to bring it up," Isabella started.

"No, it's OK." Hudde smiled at her. "This is what many civilians can never understand, and I will put it to you this way. What if you forever continued to train for taking care of animals — nonstop, every day for years and years — but you never got to do it? Wouldn't you want to know? Wouldn't you want to get out there and try to help? That's what it is like for most of us in combat jobs: We know it's crazy to want to go to fight, but you can't stop wondering if you can carry out your training."

Isabella turned and looked out the window; she took a sip from her beer. "That makes sense; I can understand what you are saying. It's just that you could die. Honestly, I try not to think of things evil and terrible."

Hudde saw a small tear roll down her cheek. It was very powerful for someone he hardly knew to be so moved by the thought of his loss.

Hudde felt a lump form in his throat; he reached out and wiped the tear with his thumb. "I have no plans to go back." He smiled and nodded at her.

"But still, all that terror out there makes me sad," she added.

Hudde shook his head and told her, "No, no, no! I will have none of that tonight. I'm currently sitting with the most beautiful woman I have ever been near, who is graduating from veterinary school shortly, and I have no worries tonight!" He stood, as if giving a rousing speech, raising his beer: "Tonight the men of the US military salute you, the thing we all hold most dearly when away from home." He raised his beer high. "Salute!"

The waiter hurried over to see if there was something wrong. Other guests were obviously not amused.

Isabella belayed any fears of the restaurant staff and hushed Gordan. "I can't worry about the US military right now. If this was really our first meeting, I would run away. Now, sit down, ya big oaf."

"Hey, that's how most of my first dates ended." And then he added, "Trust me: I'm more than enough for you to worry about!"

The food came and was delicious.

After the meal, the two strolled back to the La Playa Hermoso Grande at a snail's pace, enjoying the cool breeze coming in off the ocean, the slowly darkening summer sky, and the simple contact of two intertwined hands and fingers.

They walked straight to the parking lot, stopping at Isabella's Jeep. They stood at the driver's side door, still holding hands. When they stopped, face to face, they found both hands and held them like some kind of ceremony.

Hudde broke the momentary silence. "I have so enjoyed everything about tonight. I hope we do this again soon?" A statement, a question, his hope hung in the air.

Isabella slightly closed her left eye and cocked her head as if in deep thought. "I think I like you a little. You can try again, if you must." She smiled slyly.

Isabella was making decisions about whether she should allow a kiss or if she should flirt a little and then go. There were still games to be played when Hudde suddenly reached around with his right arm and pulled her close to him.

Isabella instinctively placed both her hands on his chest to push away but stopped when she realized he was not pulling her close for a kiss.

He whispered lightly in her ear, "Nothing in this world would make me happier, Isabella Santiago."

It was a brief moment, but she felt the strength in his arm, totally wrapped around her waist. As he took a brief moment to breathe in deeply the scent in her hair, his barrel chest expanded, pushing against her upheld palms flat against his ribs. She felt the warm, moist breath as he exhaled near the nape of her neck; she enjoyed it. She felt heady, and she was about to lean back and let him kiss her when he released his hold and stepped back.

Hudde felt he could reach around her waist twice — there was firmness and softness at once. He pulled her close, feeling first her small hands come up onto his chest and shoulder and then her breasts, softly pushing into his upper stomach. He took another deep breath, smelling her hair and skin — vanilla and spice. He exhaled and told her he wanted to see her again. He used her name so that he could hear it himself. He had a brief moment where he wanted to pick her up, throw her over his shoulder, take her to his room and ravage — no, worship — her. He shook the thoughts from his head, and, as quickly as he had grabbed her, he released her.

"Good night, Isabella. Please drive safely. Will I see you tomorrow, or are you at the shelter?"

She took a moment, catching her emotions. She couldn't stop her heart from beating faster. "I guess some of us work for a living. I will see you tomorrow."

He stood tall near the back of her Jeep, and she knew he was not going to move until she had left. She jumped into the vehicle, turned it over, and started out, making a small wave as she passed him.

On the way to his room, Hudde's thoughts raced with his beating heart. *Of course, she was beautiful, she was smart, friendly, and he liked her — who wouldn't?* he thought. But there was something more, maybe chemical, hormones? He burst into his room and dropped to the floor, doing pushups until he felt he could no more, hands spread wide, hands in close, fingers turned inward and then out. His arms, shoulders, and lower back quivered with the burn, lactic acid building in the muscle tissue. He forced his body down, until he was, as if hovering, just an inch off the floor. He told his arms to hold him there, back rigidly straight, a plank of hardwood, not a living being. He had always been the master of his own body, and now he beat it into submission for 30 minutes before heading into a cold shower.

Chapter Nine

Thomas woke early. Funny that a young man who'd run away because he didn't want to work on his family farm was now working for The Cowboy growing poppies — still a farmer. He threw his feet over the side of his army cot onto the plywood that was the floor to his tent. Well, it was not really a tent but a tarp with some mosquito netting, but, currently, it was home. He ran his fingers through his dirty, greasy hair; showers weren't really an option here. He thought he would go to the stream later today and wash up.

He yawned and rolled his shoulders before he reached for his boots that he'd placed onto 4-foot branches that had been driven through cracks in the floor, thus allowing the boots to remain dry as well as snake and bug free. Of course, it was sparse and not easy living, but one day he would gain the attention of someone more important, and they would use him for greater and greater projects — of this he was sure. He had zero interest in drugs, and, so, his brain was not addled, like some of the others' that had not made it to date. He liked all his parts attached, thank you.

Knowing his job, he walked up to the Northernmost fields, chewing on an oatmeal bar that he had bought the last time he'd had the opportunity to go into town. The morning sun filtered down from the canopy of trees. Small birds flittered between branches, calling their morning calls. It was much cooler here than down in the valley, and Thomas stopped in a beam of the morning sun. Closing his eyes, he turned his face toward the sky to soak in the sunlight; feeling his cheeks warm, he smiled. He turned and looked back down from where he'd come. Yes, this was just temporary.

Thomas had not the slightest idea how they turned the paste they took from the poppies into a drug that people around the world would kill for and die taking. He looked at the big, blue plastic drums and seeping tables in the large hut and shook his head. He didn't know anything about chemistry, but he was sure he wanted nothing to do with that part of the process. He stood before the small hut that contained the tools and stretched; he would take a shovel and a machete and head into the field, first ensuring that the forest did not creep into the growing area and then checking the bulbs of the flower to see if it was time to score them. As a worker who needed no instruction, it wasn't so bad, he thought. He reached into the shed and removed a machete from a nail higher up the wall. Grabbing the handle of a shovel, he dragged it behind him as he headed toward the field.

Behind him, Thomas heard a popping noise. Turning, he saw that the shed was on fire. In this predawn light, there appeared to be a large, glowing ball at the center of the shed and a great deal of bright white smoke billowing upward into the sky. He stood, mesmerized at the growing flames. The dry surrounding brush was beginning to catch fire. Flames quickly spread from the base to the top of the shed, and it groaned its displeasure and listed slowly, falling toward the processing shed. Unsure what he could do, Thomas grabbed the wheelbarrow, not wanting to lose that as well. He lifted the handles and ran to an open area. Again, the loud *Pop!* and he turned to see the post of the shed go up in flames. This shed, while open, still contained fumes from the HCL, and they ignited, rolling under the thatched roof. In seconds, the whole thing went up in flames. Other men now ran to save the giant blue barrels. Seconds later, another ball of light lit up the area. One of the men's clothes caught fire. He ran a few steps before falling to the ground, blood-curdling screams escaping before he fell silent. The diesel generator caught fire and the five-gallon can as well. It was chaos. Dry branches and debris that had been moved to make the camp caught fire. The entire area could become a blaze, as the winter had been drier than normal.

Thomas broke from his trance. He ran down the hill, toward his tent. Running up the hill was one of the armed men.

"What is going on?" the guard screamed at Thomas, grabbing his arm and halting his progress.

"I think we are being attacked!" Thomas screamed into the man's face, spittle flying. Thomas did not care; he pulled his arm from the man's grasp and continued his retreat, not stopping until he'd returned to his home.

Off in the distance, a mine was tripped, a large explosion echoed through the treetops, and another Cowboy employee died in the dirt and poppies.

◆   ◆   ◆

"Now is not the time to question me, you cowardly bastard!" the Cowboy screamed into his phone. "You are to send men into my mountain retreat and clear the area of any enemies!"

Colonel Sanchez was not used to being screamed at, but, considering who he was speaking to, he wanted to keep his head. "Señor Cowboy, I assure you that I have men moving already. I was not questioning, Señor. Please be assured, I merely suggest that —"

The Cowboy interrupted: "I am not paying you for your mind, moron!" and hung up the phone. "That bastard better have some men up there soon, or he will find someone else to play army," he said out loud, to nobody. After all, he owned people higher up the food chain.

Chapter Ten

Carlos Morales called Marco into his lavish office, offering him a drink. It was just after lunch. Morales pointed at a comfortable chair and waited for Vargas to be seated.

"I have heard some rumblings of chaos happening in the fields of The Cowboy."

Vargas smiled at Morales, swirling his tequila around his glass before downing it.

"If it worked as I envisioned it, it will be more costly to operations than in lives. I still think you should allow me to remove him altogether."

Morales shook his head "No."

"Marco, we can never allow the cartels to devolve into total anarchy; taking out a *Jefe* is not to be tolerated, and every cartel should be called to action if that ever happens." Morales walked to the window, gazing out at the park below. "Marco, reach out to your contacts in The Cowboy's operations. Now that we have reminded him we are willing to fight just as hard as he does, see if we can set this ugliness aside for now."

"Sir, you are tough, our operations are strong, but you must know that The Cowboy will never stop this; that psychopath will never allow you to have the last word," Marco said.

"Let's see what he has to say before we go to war. In the meantime, tell our men to be on the highest of alerts."

Vargas stood sharply and exited the office, walking with purpose through the halls. He did have a small office here on the third floor so that he could be available whenever Morales needed him. But Vargas despised being indoors. His shoulder-length brown hair and good looks made him perfect for the Morales cartel, right out of central casting. But his was no television show; lives hung in the balance in most of the decisions that Vergas made. His driver flipped a cigarette away and hopped into the Land Rover, cranking it up and stopping before Vargas. Vargas never needed anyone to open a door for him, and he hopped into the passenger seat.

Vargas was deep in thought. He looked at his driver and said, "Let's head to the mountains."

The vehicle shot forward, heading North and West. Vargas returned to his thoughts. He knew this was going to continue to escalate until one side or the other could take no further damage, this bullshit referendum by the cartel *Jefes* to keep themselves safe from direct attack. Meanwhile, all the men were at a much higher risk — like their lives weren't difficult enough without two bosses getting into a pissing match over a shitty town on the border.

The next thing Vargas realized, they were pulling into one of their growing operations. Two security men acknowledged them as they passed slowly by the ever-narrowing dirt road. The vehicle came to a stop in a shaded area with much overhead cover. Vargas changed into some camo khakis and combat boots that he kept in a duffle at all times with him. He slid a Colt .45 into a holster and clipped it onto his belt, accessible to his right hand.

He strode with extreme confidence into the camp. The head of security for this operation hurried over to meet him. The man's name escaped him at the moment, but Vargas had learned that this did not matter for men of stature. He spoke very forcefully, standing straight and tall.

"How go the security matters?"

"Lieutenant, everything is quiet. Is there anything I can do for you?" This was professional code for "What the hell are you bothering me for?"

"Show me."

They began walking North and West from their current location. "Ah, here is one of my men," the security chief pointed out.

Vargas violently grabbed the man by the front of his shirt, pulling him in close. "Where is your weapon, soldier?" he asked.

The young man was shocked, looking at his supervisor for assistance. He wisely said nothing in case it would get him into trouble for pointing out that he had not received orders to carry at all times.

"Lieutenant, nothing of importance has happened here — well, in years, I think — unless that is why you are here." He paused.

Vargas released his grip on the young man.

"So, if something were to happen here, right now, you would call time out until you were able to get to your weapon? Boy, did you ever serve in the army or police?"

"No, sir. I am sorry. This will not happen again!"

"It better not!" Vargas accentuated it with a pointed finger. "Look, we are expecting trouble soon. Please, for your sake as well as for the sake of the people and property you are here to protect, do not let this happen again."

Vargas turned back to the man in charge. "How many men work for you now?"

"Nine and myself."

"And how many men are on duty right now?"

The man looked inward for whatever answer would be correct.

Vargas snapped his finger. "Now!"

"Well, three: The two you passed on the road and one man in the North field."

Vargas stepped into the man and placed a hand on his shoulder, taking him into his confidence. "We do expect trouble. You need everyone to be on high alert. You and your men should be, at a minimum, at 50% security. Do you understand? Your life may depend on it."

"*Si*, lieutenant. Right away. Count on me."

"I do."

Vegas walked away with as much vigor as he had approached the man in the first place. He whipped out his phone and checked the signal strength. Good enough. He contacted the man who recruited for him from the army ranks, a captain in the infantry.

The captain picked up at his end. "*Si.*"

"Captain, I am going to need fifty more men, quickly."

"As always, I can do this. Time frame?"

"Yesterday." Vargas paused for effect. "And captain, if another farm boy shows up into my operations, I will hold you personally responsible."

The captain knew better than to respond; they both hung up.

Chapter Eleven

Hudde stood before the beachside shop, looking up at a sign he really could not read, but he knew exactly what merchandise he would find inside. He remembered a team member once paying him a compliment that he would have done well on the "teams." He had thanked the captain and moved on, but, deep down, he would never — no one ever — admits their fears in the military, at least not out loud.

Hudde was afraid of deep water.

He was a strong swimmer — it was just the thought he had looking in the most peaceful goldfish bowl: If you were to drop any fish small enough into the bowl, the friendly looking goldfish would eat them. There were many things much bigger than him, probably just a hundred yards from where he stood. So he headed into *"Todo Agua,"* a giant wood-and-steel replica of a spear gun hanging outside up over the door.

A bell dinged overhead as he walked through the threshold. Nobody rushed to him, and he scanned the rows of fishing rods and lures, hats, and sunglasses. He saw where he needed to go — snorkeling and scuba equipment. Fins, knives, boots, and full-body wet suits: This place had everything he would need. He understood that it would be pricier than if he had purchased the equipment back in the States somewhere, but he didn't care about that right now. A man approached him and eyed him up. He ripped off some Spanish so quickly that Hudde laughed.

"American," Hudde stated matter of factly.

The man just nodded, and Hudde wondered if maybe he did not speak English. The man stepped back. He was about the same height as Hudde, and his skin was leathery, the color of a tobacco leaf. He was approximately fifty years old, in Hudde's best estimation. He wore some cutoff khaki pants and a tank top. Throw a patch over his eye and Hudde thought he would have been perfect for the next pirate movie.

"Ex-military?" the man asked.

"Oh good, English," Hudde stated. "I should have tried to learn Spanish before I came here, but it was a spur-of-the-moment trip."

"Were you in the navy?" There was an accent, but Hudde could not place it.

Hudde asked, "A real Spaniard?"

"Ah, no! I am from Portugal! Angelo Santos Rodrigo Cristova at your service, sir." He placed his feet one in front of the other, bowed deeply at the waist, and, using his right hand, he rolled it in the air laying it finally palm up with great fanfare out in front of Hudde. Hudde knew that this had been repeated many times, but it still worked. Hudde grinned ear to ear, feeling like he'd just met royalty.

"Pleased to meet you, sir," Hudde responded. "Gordan Hudde"

"Ah, Gordan the Hood," Cristova said.

"Yes, I imagine, in some lifetime," Gordan replied.

"So now you wish to swim with the fishes!" He appeared to be a man who found humor in everything. He smiled broadly, and Hudde thought he caught the glimmer of gold.

The two men walked the small sales floor, and Cristova helped Hudde fully equip himself for some snorkeling.

"You have chosen well, my friend." Cristova retrieved a box for Hudde to carry his treasure back to the hotel for further inspection.

Hudde had chosen some fins basically based just on the name: "Escape" fins. Hudde appreciated that thought. They were open heeled, and Hudde purchased some boots or neoprene socks so that he could walk without fear of stepping on something and to stop chafing from the fins. He had a good mask and snorkel, and he couldn't help but buy a dive knife with a calf strap.

"Be careful, my new friend," Cristova yelled out as Hudde was walking toward the door.

Hudde turned to nod his head goodbye and saw that Cristova was pointing up at the wall where an 11-foot-long hammerhead was mounted.

"You will not be alone!" Cristova warned.

Hudde wondered if he should keep his receipt in case he never used the items.

He entered the lobby and saw Isabella heading in his direction.

"Buying me things will not help you," she said, smiling broadly.

She made a big unhappy face after Hudde gave her the opportunity to glance down into the box.

"Want to go snorkeling?" Hudde was serious.

Isabella made a dismissive gesture with her right hand as she walked toward the bar. "I don't even go to the beach." And off to work she went.

Hudde spent a moment trying to decide if he enjoyed seeing her coming or going more. He shook his head vigorously to try to remove those images and headed upstairs to further inspect his new gear.

After removing tags and sizing the straps of the fins and facemask, Hudde grabbed a towel and headed for the beach. Hudde dropped the towel on the sand, not yet too hot to be walking on it. He looked out into the Pacific, thinking every ripple or wave was caused by some monster of the deep. He sat on the towel and wiped his boots clean of any excess sand. Glancing about, he observed some younger kids splashing around in about three feet of water. It gave him confidence that nothing evil was in the immediate area. He slid on and strapped up his "escape" fins. Then he strapped his knife to his left calf and flopped out into the currently gentle waves, walking backwards once in the water, until he knew that he could swim. Spitting into the mask, he added some ocean water and swished it around. He donned the mask and slipped into the water, biting down a little onto the snorkel.

He quickly began to get the hang of it and enjoyed the feeling of looking about. He quickly realized that the waves helped create an environment that made visibility more difficult, and he began getting further and further from the beach. The visibility began getting clearer and clearer, until suddenly Hudde realized that he had been swimming away from the beach for about thirty minutes. His visibility was now somewhere close to fifty feet, he gathered, and he realized that he could just about see the bottom at this point. He got vertical and, bobbing with the swell, he could see the beach 1/2 mile away — then the water would drop, and it was gone. He let himself slip under the water and saw some bright-blue little fish swimming near the bottom. A few smaller coral-like structures were here, spreading and reaching for the sun. Looking further West, the water just became darker and darker, like a curtain moving before a stage, and he envisioned a form — a large Great White Shark — swimming straight at him. He made it back to his towel way quicker than he imagined he could; the fins did work well. Leave the waterways of the world to the navy; he had a newfound respect for the seals.

Later, while he was sitting comfortably at the cantina and enjoying a burger, Isabella stood near his table, hands on her hips. "Did you find me some treasure, my frogman?"

Hudde glanced left and right. "Don't tell anybody, but that scared the shit out of me!"

Isabella tilted her head back and let out a hearty laugh. She was still chuckling as she headed back to the front of the bar to greet new customers.

Chapter Twelve

The Cowboy was conducting business on the phone as usual at his vast home third-floor office. This consisted mostly of screaming at the top of his lungs at everyone. Currently, Army Colonel Sanchez was getting an earful — the Colonel wanted to drive an anti-mine tank through his poppy fields.

"I have seen those things on the news working over in Afghanistan, you stupid bastard — have you?" He didn't wait for an answer. "If one of those gets anywhere near any of my fields of product, you will be buried there, in each and every field. Do you understand me?" It wasn't a question.

There was a brief silence for the servants downstairs until the *Jefe* started up again. "I don't care if you lost three men or three dozen — you get them up there and have them walk my fields. I am losing time and money every second." There was another brief moment of respite, followed by a more sinister threat, as it was spoken in a normal tone of voice: "Fine, Colonel. My good friend Miguel will join you to oversee your operation. Understand that he is in charge. Yes, yes — *that* Miguel."

The Cowboy redialed and spoke: "Miguel, I need you to head up into the fields and put the fear of God into the people up there who are supposed to be working for me. And Miguel, spare no feelings when it comes to the Colonel!" He listened for a moment. "If you need to — I don't care. Just motivate everyone to get to work."

The Cowboy screamed out for some ice, and the staff literally ran from room to room. His man servant carried a bucket quickly up the last flight of stairs. The rumors that were swirling around the house staff was that The Cowboy had once shot and killed a servant who'd brought him a drink with too much ice. Now, he added the ice himself.

Gonzales set the phone down on a large, light oak table before him. He drank a soda and rum drink, perfect for the early afternoon, he thought. This room was the only part of his home that was three stories high. It was his office and was square — twenty by twenty feet — completely surrounded by a deck, in case he wanted to have a private meeting outside. The office was completely enclosed in bulletproof glass capable of stopping a fifty-caliber bullet. Steel shutters could be dropped down as well for shade as additional safety — his fortress of solitude. It was simply furnished, but there was a comfortable chair and ottoman in the corner that he plopped down into now. He began thinking about a large piece of military equipment with chains or discs flailing at the ground, tearing up everything in its path, including his precious crops. He began to get angry again and needed to close his eyes and slow his breathing. *That stupid bastard.* He began to picture Miguel cutting out the Coronel's heart, and he relaxed.

Chapter Thirteen

A little more than three weeks since their first date, Isabella had invited Hudde to her graduation ceremony from her veterinary school. The shelter that Isabella would be committing her time to was headed by a sixty-five-ish gentleman about two inches taller than Isabella, making him five-foot-four, tops. His energy level was amazing for an older gentleman. Hudde grew tired moments after meeting him just watching the man walk the floor, speaking to people and looking after the care of animals at his place of work. The doctor, Gutierrez, forgot about Hudde as soon as they stopped shaking hands and disappeared into his work.

Isabella showed Hudde to a dog with a cast on a front leg. "I helped the doctor set this leg yesterday. Some kids brought him in. Not sure if he belonged to them or not, but we fixed him up and fed him. He's doing well." She beamed with accomplishment and good thoughts. Hudde was impressed with how much this place seemed to accomplish with so few assets. They walked the grounds, and Isabella showed him the animals currently in her care. She sincerely wanted to make the animals healthy and happy; her enthusiasm was inspiring.

"And then, one day, hopefully, I will start my own practice, and maybe there will be enough paying clientele so that

I can also help some of the strays and poor people in the area." Isabella turned into Hudde, her small hands pressing into his chest, their bodies making contact from the waist down. "Well, what do you think?" She made a pouty face, and Hudde could see what she looked like as a little girl.

"It's amazing, Isabella, and it's sad. I have a hard time looking at the suffering of animals."

She smiled up at him. "Big army man has a soft spot for animals — that's cute."

"Animals, children, women, and the elderly in general," Hudde continued. "Anyone who is unable to defend or take care of themselves." Hudde looked deeply into her eyes. Reaching into her hair with his right hand, he grasped a handful and playfully pulled her head back until he could kiss her deeply.

"If you do not get off of me, *you* will not be able to defend yourself."

Isabella laughed and pirouetted away from underneath him, grasping his hand as she stepped away. "Come. I promised my mother that she would meet you today, and she has prepared her specialty just for the occasion. I hope you enjoy spicy food."

She climbed into her Jeep, top down. Hudde grasped the roll bar and swung into the passenger side; the Jeep rocked back to the right. She drove too fast, she stopped too late, and Hudde found himself stepping on an imaginary brake several times. That lion's mane of rich black hair danced and flew about her face as she drove. Hudde found it erotic whenever she had to reach up and slide some strands out of her mouth.

She headed out to the East of Maztlan, the roads changing quickly from single-lane pavement to single-lane dirt. Hudde was momentarily taken back by the level of poverty there, in the small village they had entered, compared to the tourist area he had become accustomed to. And, then again, he thought it wasn't much different than the difference between the tourist areas of Vegas or Hollywood or Atlantic City, which gave way to poverty just a block from the main strip.

Homes were amazing, built right at the edge of the road in many places, and children were playing outside with lean-looking dogs barking at them as they kicked balls or rode bikes. Isabella took a smaller dirt road to the South. The road deteriorated even further, passable in most places only by a single vehicle at a time in only one direction. In a few low places, mud was still present even though it had not rained in days. Hudde realized he had gotten that one right when he first observed Isabella getting into a muddy Jeep.

They pulled into a low, tan-colored adobe home. "Mama's!" Isabella said as she jumped from the Jeep before it stopped moving. "Bring the cooler in the back, would you?" she asked as she walked him into a living room.

There was some knotty pine furniture covered with some colorful throws. The wall, Hudde noticed, had an obligatory crucifix and a picture of Christ descending from the heavens, the clouds parting in front of brilliant light.

Isabella began speaking in Spanish, and Hudde turned to see Gabriela Santiago enter the room. Hudde immediately saw the resemblance; Isabella definitely got her mother's thick, rich hair, the high but chubby-looking cheeks, and ample bosom. She filled out her apron with the tie tight across her waist so that it gave her a very voluptuous, hourglass figure. The two women were like opposing machine-gun fire with the speed and staccato of the Spanish being spoken. Hudde immediately realized that he may never learn the language well enough to follow these two.

"Pleased to meet you, Mrs. Santiago." Hudde tried his best to be unimposing and happy, smiling; he wasn't known to be the most cheerful-looking fellow.

She stepped into and hugged him warmly but then stepped back and wagged a finger at him, probably repeating something that every loving mother says to their daughter's newest boyfriend. She stepped into and hugged her daughter.

Isabella fired off another volley and then turned to Hudde. "Mama understands English but pretty much never speaks it since... well, I told her you are not like that, anyway." She smiled and encouraged him to follow into the kitchen.

"The best enchiladas in all Mexico!" Isabella waved the smell up into her face as she stood over the stove.

Gabriela stood at the stove, shushing away her daughter, pointing at the small dinette table.

"Sit — get a beer," Isabella said, pulling out a seat for herself. "One for me, too."

Hudde reached into the icy cold water of the cooler. He twisted the caps off of two bottles of beer and carried them back into the kitchen, setting one in front of Isabella and taking a seat himself. The women were still going back and forth, and Hudde could not make out the tone.

Gabriela turned to Hudde and began speaking. Isabella, moments after, began the translation: "Forgive a mother who so loves her daughter, but she thinks you should say whether..." Isabella paused, and the two began going back and forth again. Hudde realized that Isabella didn't want to ask whatever question her mom had posed.

"It's OK, whatever it is. I'm an open book — really," Hudde said as he looked earnestly at both women. He sipped at his beer and waited.

"My mom wants to know if you are in love or just 'in lust' for me — what your intentions are, Mr. Hudde. There is no man in the house, and, before she feeds another American with bad intentions, she feels it necessary to ask. I'm sorry."

"Wow — that's to the point! I mean *we* (and he pointed back and forth between the two of them) haven't even had that conversation yet."

Isabella looked at her mother and began to protest.

Hudde stopped her with his hand and said, "No, no. I understand, and it's OK. I am not embarrassed or unsure of myself." Hudde looked at Gabriela and continued, "The moment I laid eyes on Isabella, I was 'in lust.' How could that be a secret? I have now known Isabella about two months, and we have been seeing each other almost a month of that time.

Isabella is smart, friendly, kind-hearted, hardworking, and very beautiful; I fell in love very quickly. So what I say for the first time out loud is what Isabella and I are currently doing is finding out how *she* feels about *me*."

Isabella looked to be getting a little choked up. Hudde paused, looking at her to gauge her reaction.

"I am a patient man when it comes to Isabella; I will wait for her to get to know me better." He then directed his next comment directly to Isabella: "As a matter of fact, I was going to ask you to help me find a house or condo that I could rent longer term if you were, or are, interested."

Her answer was to leap up and jump into his lap. "You're a fool! Of course, I want you to stay."

Hudde smiled. "I guessed you would have protested to your mother more if you didn't want to hear my answer."

Gabriela began speaking. Isabella translated: "Mama believes you are telling the truth and are a good man. She was going to trick you into having some of her hot salsa, but, now, she will let you choose."

Isabella jumped up to grab a bowl and the homemade chips warm from the oven.

"I can't let a challenge go without responding," Hudde said. "Bring the hot."

Gabriela let out a short burst of Spanish that ended in *"gringo!"* Mother and daughter laughed.

Hudde didn't wait for a translation. He scooped some of the salsa onto a chip and began eating. His taste buds picked up the tomato and sweet onion, and the hot began hitting him as he chewed and began to swallow. Funny that he first felt it in his scalp. Sweat began to run down near his ear, and his nose began to run.

Mother and daughter sat nearby, both ready to laugh some more, but Hudde did well washing it down with his beer before having some more. Like a doctor asking a nurse for surgical tools, Hudde said "tissue," and the tears now began to stream down his cheeks as well.

Isabella jumped up and returned with a box of tissues. "Hey, you did better than a lot of people we know."

"OK," Hudde said, "my turn to ask your mother a question. You are about fourteen or fifteen years older than your daughter?"

This immediately took the focus off of anything Hudde was going to do or say.

After her mother spoke for several minutes, Isabella jumped up and began loudly speaking back to her mother. More back and forth. Hudde was thinking about asking when Isabella yelled out in English, "You always said, 'twenty two,'" and she really over-emphasized the number.

"Years and years she yelled at me and always said 'twenty two. Wait, Isabella, wait!' I always thought she wanted to raise a nun, and now she tells me 'sixteen'! Mother!"

Gabriela spoke slowly and in very good English: "For the sake of Señor Hudde, I want to be honest." She shrugged her shoulders and continued in Spanish.

"She said, 'I am old enough to know myself now, and that what a good daughter I am.'" Isabella shook her head as she translated.

Gabriela stomped her foot, clapped two times, and said, "Food!" She began preparing some plates.

Hudde thoroughly enjoyed the food, and, though the language barrier was sometimes difficult, he felt at ease. He thought you could do worse in life than telling a beautiful woman that you were in love, and proclaiming it to her mother seemed honest and honorable. He shared stories of his days in the Army, and they told how Isabella's father and mother had met and fallen in love and how he had been killed during a cave-in at a mine on the Gulf Coast when Isabella was just a baby, as well as the story of how the two women had grown together into a strong family unit, protecting each other as much as they could. It was a nice evening, and Hudde hoped there would be more times spent there in the future.

Hudde noticed when Isabella said, "Time for us to go, my friend," and touched his shoulder. "I have to work tomorrow."

The two women said some goodbyes, and Gabriela grabbed Hudde warmly and pulled him down and near so that she could whisper in his ear. "Take care of my daughter, and she will take care of you." She kissed his cheek and sent him on his way.

"What did Mama say?" Isabella asked.

"I think that was just for me," Hudde teased. And then the wind from the open vehicle was too much for casual conversation. When they arrived at the resort, Isabella pulled into a side lot, away from employee parking, and Hudde knew that she wanted to speak.

When they stopped, Hudde jumped out and met her as she got down from the slightly raised vehicle. He quickly jumped down onto one knee and stated, "Isabella, I've wanted to ask you a question all night…"

She smacked his forehead and said, "What was that 'go slow' stuff?"

Down on his knee, Hudde, in turn, interrupted her: "Isabella, will you be my girlfriend?"

"What? Oh, you are a fool!" She smacked his forehead again with the heel of her palm as she dropped down, straddling his leg, sitting on his thigh, wrapping her arms and legs around him, "I've been your girlfriend for about a month now, you ass!" She kissed him long and deep — the most passionate moment they had shared yet.

"About that 'going slow' stuff," Hudde said, coming up for air. "In a few seconds, I'm carrying you all the way to my room and giving you no choice."

She responded by kissing him yet again, harder and longer, finishing by moaning softly into his neck, "Maybe that's what I really want."

Hudde hoisted her up over his shoulder and stood up in a single motion.

Isabella let out a short loud yelp. "Put me down, you big ape!" slapping him in the back. He flipped her over, setting her down gently onto her feet. She turned and hugged him again. "Thank you for tonight — my mother loved you."

"Well, now that we know your mom's true age, if you mistreat me, I have options."

"Oh!" Isabella wasn't expecting that. "That's awful! You shouldn't joke like that." But she was grinning.

"Who's joking?" Hudde said over his shoulder as he started to walk away. "I have a cold shower calling my name. Goodbye."

Isabella kicked him in the ass before he was out of reach; she turned and jumped into her Jeep, speeding away tooting the horn while waving.

Chapter Fourteen

At Ciudad Victoria, in the lavish glass-and-steel conference room at Carlos Morales' Gulf Coast cartel headquarters, eight men sat around the long, highly lacquered oak table. As in any worldwide sales operation, there was much discussion about product development, warehousing, and distribution. Every one of the individuals in the room was dangerous, shrewd, and someone to be taken seriously. Only one had close ties to the American DEA.

Ricardo Cruz was a Mexican-born American citizen. His father, brothers, and uncles all worked for the cartel. His mother just happened to be an American who fell in love with a dark, mysterious man who was his father. Ricardo had only ever worked for the cartel as well, but through some difficult times about a dozen years previous, someone from the American agency had recruited him for information. After delivering some of his enemies to the Americans, he had negotiated an official status with the agency. Through the years, it had developed to the point that he believed his information would bring down Morales himself. One of the bastards in this room had killed his only son, and the bastard at the head of the table had "OK'd" it. Morales' hair was slicked back, a nickel-plated .45 slung beneath each arm, trying to be James

Crockett. One coast *Jefe* a *Miami Vice* wannabe and the other a Cowboy. Fucking ridiculous. Cruz shook his head, deep in his own thoughts.

Morales broke through Cruz's internal conversation, "So now The Cowboy seems to want to discuss our current problems." He stood from his head-of-the-table position and walked the length of the table.

"It seems the work of Marcos has brought him to his knees, and now he needs to have a meeting." Morales gestured over to Marco, who nodded his head, basking in the moment.

Cruz was about to interject his belief that this would be a good idea when Morales continued.

"He has suggested that we meet in Phoenix and discuss our options to end the violence between our two businesses." Obviously Morales had observed Cruz's movement to make a comment; he turned to him. "You have something to say on this?"

Cruz was conducting the lightning-quick type of strategy and thinking that had made him valuable for so many years to both sides. It must not be remembered later that he supported this idea.

"*El Jefe*, I would not agree to this meeting, even in a neutral territory. I would agree with Marco, who we all know has been supporting removing The Cowboy from the business altogether." He pointed at Marco and gave him a thumbs-up; Marco returned the compliment with just a nod of his head.

"I bring you all here to listen to your opinions and hear your counsel. Let's hear it now," Morales said, throwing out an open-ended statement.

Back and forth the arguments went all afternoon, until it was finally decided that Morales would go to Phoenix. No one in the room was happier than Ricardo Cruz, who now had the date and location of a meeting of two of the world's biggest cartel heads, and they would be right in the Americans' own city, ripe for the plucking. How many of his adversaries or competition could he have removed from the chessboard that was his world with just a single call to his contact! For, while he had grown important, surely he would not be traveling to Phoenix.

Chapter Fifteen

"Oh, my lord!" Isabella made a slow turn in a modern, open second-floor living room that Gordan and the real estate woman were walking through. You could see straight through — living room, kitchen, to a second-floor floor balcony. Hudde liked the stainless-steel kitchen appliances and the straight, clean lines.

The agent continued filling them in. "As you noted, this area was part of a big boom that the developers thought was coming, and then the floor fell out of the market. The American renters just completed renovation with the newest everything. Please feel free to finish on your own. You can find me out front when you are satisfied." She smiled at the happy young couple and walked out the front doors.

"It could use come color," Isabella noticed out loud, as everything seemed to be white or off white except the appliances — a giant television hanging on the wall and the kitchen cupboards that were stained light brown.

Hudde was in the master bedroom. A giant bed filled the room, and, when Isabella entered and walked in under his arm, there was quiet, as both thought about the possibilities.

"It will do," Hudde noted, continuing to the master bath. "Now this is what I'm talking about," he said with enthusiasm.

A huge bathroom counter with two sinks and four hanging silver-emblazoned light fixtures overhead were immediately visible. A highly decorative vanity chair sat in the middle counter space, obviously designed for a woman to apply makeup. Even better, Hudde thought, there was a giant, completely-tiled walk-in shower. The wall separating the shower from the rest of the bathroom was made from large glass blocks. The interior tile was a light muddy-brown color with rough-looking texture, flecked with yellow or golden color when the light hit it right. Above, there were several shower-head fixtures, and several more protruding from the sides as well. There was a bench made of tile that ran approximately five feet across the side wall; this, clearly, had been designed by someone who enjoyed soaking in a shower.

"Wow — a water park!" Hudde looked at the levers and controls on the wall. "I hope it comes with instructions."

Isabella nosed in under his big right arm. Suddenly, with her in the picture, his whole train of thought was temporarily disrupted. "What do you think?" he asked as he walked back out to the vanity area. Looking back at the glass-block wall, he saw the fun-house mirror images of Isabella as she inspected inside the shower. The bright-colored outfit she was wearing to go to work in flashed and turned like a kaleidoscope, creating a unique and different image in each glass block. Hudde imagined her naked body in the shower and the 100 different images that would provide.

Isabella brought him out of his erotic daydream by placing both her palms against his stomach and saying, "That could be fun." She smiled mischievously up at him.

"Stop it; you have to go to work." He worked his right hand up into her hair just behind her ear, his thumb tracing the outline of her jaw. "The question is, 'Would you come here to hang out?' You won't let me come to your apartment, so you have to like it."

"I tell you: It's for your own safety. The people in my neighborhood don't appreciate the *gringos* as much as I seem to." And she added, "Against my better judgement."

"You guys supply the drugs, and we buy them. Why the hate?" Hudde said. Before letting her go, he bent and kissed her quickly. "Come on. Somebody has to go to work."

She took his hand as they exited the home. In the street, Hudde marveled at the area. One block North of his hotel and two blocks East was this "gated" community. It was designed to be a simple square block; a ravine with a stream flowed to the ocean, cutting East-West straight through the middle. The interior streets consisted of four cul-de-sacs, with the dead-end circulars each stopping at the ravine. The wall surrounding the area was beautifully crafted, and the streets were as good as anything in private drives across rich communities in America. The land, which Hudde could imagine as once freshly bulldozed now was being overtaken by local hardy fauna and cactus. Only two homes had ever been built. The one they were standing at in the first drive and one across the ravine kitty-corner to where they were standing. Several cars were parked in front of the other one, so Hudde guessed that the other home was occupied. Trash littered the landscape with light papery things getting caught up in the prickly pears.

Broken glass and cans were sprinkled liberally throughout the unused property — litter ruining a beautiful area.

They approached the real estate agent, and Hudde commented, "I'm sorry, but it looks like somebody built a home on a working landfill."

Isabella had to be nice. "But inside, it is beautiful!"

Hudde went straight to business. "Do the owners have an idea of rental increments? Are they going to be here during specific periods, or will they want to be here off and on?"

The agent cleared her throat. "Well, the American trust-holders both still work, so they planned on returning in November, and they are open to renters from now till then."

"So, they have a six- or seven-month opening. How many renters have they lined up to date?"

"Well," the agent shuffled some papers, "they just finished the renovations, and you are one of the first so far to actually review the property."

"OK — nobody yet. So I will pay their asking price for the complete six months. No need for them or you to look any further, but they have to give me two weeks' notice before they need the property, and they have to allow me to stay longer at no cost if they do not return in the six-month time frame."

The agent looked at him, seeming confused.

Hudde added, "I pay through the end of October. If they don't show until November 20th, I get to stay at no cost, except utilities. OK?" He raised his hands palms up looking for a response. "They don't need to worry about months without a renter or that some unruly rich college kids are ruining their property. They also save whatever they are paying you." He thought a little about that and then shrugged his shoulders, adding, "I will pay you $500 up front if they take the deal."

"OK, Señor Hudde, I will forward your proposal. Nice to meet you, Isabella." They all shook hands, and the agent got into her small, yellow Honda civic and took off.

"Wow!" Isabella exclaimed. "What just happened?"

"I think I just got a house!" Hudde was excited by the prospect.

Chapter Sixteen

There were no big meetings at the Sinaloa cartel, there was no boardroom, and there was no executive meetings; there was just The Cowboy. Eduardo Gonzales made decisions, gave the orders, and people/subordinates had better scramble. You could imagine his confusion when something he requested was not followed through on. Like now, when nobody could tell him who had mined his farm in the mountains. Weeks after he'd demanded answers, he still did not have a name. He screamed his displeasure at Miguel Lopez, the lieutenant in his command he trusted the most and the man most responsible for most of the deaths The Cowboy had ordered.

"*Jefe!* Please, a few more days of patience. Someone will talk to my informers, someone will brag at a bar; soon you will have a name." Lopez thought how difficult it was for him to preach patience when he had none himself.

"You should get Colonel Sanchez and 100 men and just go level that pussy's building. I mean — building an office building so he can pretend to be a businessman." He rubbed his forefinger several times across the bridge of his nose trying to calm himself.

Miguel knew best how to handle The Cowboy during these tirades and was one of the only men capable of spending much time with him. "Cowboy, if you desire it, the Colonel and I will make it so; however, you understand that no others will hesitate to openly kill a *Jefe*. Who knows if your name may be on another's list?" He smiled, knowing full well that Gonzales' name was on many lists, even within his own cartel.

The Cowboy open-palm slapped the bulletproof window of his study. "Motherfuckers!" This time he was yelling at no one but fate.

"No. We wait," was all he said, staring out the same window for several minutes before asking Miguel to pour them both some drinks. "How goes the Phoenix trip plans?"

"All set, *Jefe*. Both sides will honor the rules."

"Good, good. Well, then, tell me: How goes the farm that was attacked?"

"Good news, *Jefe*. It is back functioning at 100%. They have checked the fields for additional mines and rebuilt the sheds and shacks that were lost. I sent money to the survivors and families of the dead and have hired the additional men that we needed; it is good." He sat down in one of the simple chairs, ensuring that he did not set his drink down on the highly finished table. "The Colonel made some noise, but some additional cash shut him up."

The Cowboy dropped his forehead into the palm of his hand. "What could I ever accomplish without men of the caliber of Colonel Sanchez? He would sell his mother to fuck all his troops if it made him some extra money."

Both men got a laugh at that one, but, of course, everyone *always* laughed at The Cowboy's jokes.

Chapter Seventeen

Isabella looked at the A-bag, duffle bag, and large box in the back of her Jeep. She looked at Hudd., "You can tell you're rich by the way you travel."

Hudde laughed heartily. "I still don't know I'm rich." He smiled down at her. "We should go. I'm moving in."

He threw the A-bag over a shoulder and grabbed the duffle with his free hand. Isabella picked up the box, looking in as she did. "You gonna keep this stuff?" she said, referencing the snorkeling gear.

"I don't give up. You, of all people, should understand that." He walked the stairs to the front door. He stopped to look at the view. To the East, it was not all that exciting — the back of some large hotel complexes and the barren landscape of the unsold lots. Hudde opened the door and walked in. He took the bags straight back to the bedroom. Isabella set the box down in the corner.

"You need to get your own sheets and towels."

"Never thought of it," Hudde acknowledged. "You going to help?" he said with a grin.

"Stop it right there. This doesn't mean I become your personal plaything just because you got your own place."

"Oh, why so serious? It means you can stay with me and watch some movies, eat, fall asleep, and not worry about your coworkers seeing us together. It means you can hang out whenever you want. Is that so bad?" Hudde hesitated a second. "You're two blocks from the hotel and about two blocks from the shelter. Maybe this will be nice for you — unless, of course, you don't trust yourself all alone with me."

"Now you're irresistible?" She started pushing him back toward the kitchen, two hands on his chest, pushing at a 45-degree angle with all her might.

"No, now I can put into effect my evil plan," Hudde announced. He picked her up into his arms like a child and carried her over to the bed. He held her there, above the bed, and began nuzzling her neck and ears. "Say the words, and we can end this tension and get on with being a couple."

Isabella screamed as if she were in need of rescue, and he dropped her very unceremoniously onto the middle of the bed. She bounced twice before coming to a rest, looking up at him. Her t-shirt had slid up to her lacy tan bra; her flat, golden belly, now exposed, moved with her quickening breathing; her "innie" belly button begged him to kiss it. Her lion's mane of mid-back-length black hair fell about her face and shoulders, framing her perfectly. She was seductive even without trying.

"I guess there could be worse," Isabella said to him, reaching up to pull him down to her without making any attempt to pull her shirt down.

Hudde placed a knee onto the bed and began kissing her. She kissed back; he bit her lip a little and then kissed and playfully bit at her jawline. She turned her head, exposing more of her neck, giggling a little. Hudde used his teeth to pull at her earlobe, and he whispered softly how beautiful she was and how much he wanted all of her. She moaned an acceptance; he continued kissing down her neck and across her bra. His kisses followed down her stomach to that belly button. She smelled of vanilla and musk, and his mouth watered.

She put her hands into his short hair and pulled up so that he was looking at her and said, "I don't know — I don't trust myself."

He stopped and placed his bearded chin into her belly button, looking up through her cleavage at her unsure but smiling face. He exhaled deeply; his jeans needed adjusting.

He smiled a big smile. "Yeah, it could be worse," he said. He hopped up, pulling her with him to the kitchen. "I'm hungry." She followed him closely and wrapped her arms around his waist, hugging him strongly when they got to the counter. There was heat coming off the two of them. He placed his hand on the side of her head and held her so that he thought she could hear his heart beating.

"Don't worry. It will be right when you think it is. I am not that other guy. You don't have to worry."

She spun from his grasp and thanked him for understanding. She stopped at the open refrigerator, contemplating the meal and enjoying the cool air.

He slapped her ass hard enough that it stung through her jeans. She let out an "Ouch! That smarted!" She rubbed her backside with a small hand.

He dropped his head near her ear and said, "You just need to know that it is getting harder and harder."

"Oh, I noticed!" she said with a big, evil grin.

"It's so wrong that you're actually enjoying this. It's just mean," Hudde said. He couldn't help but smile back. "You have a future career as a dominatrix."

"Mama always told me to do what I'm good at!"

Chapter Eighteen

In the Phoenix offices of the FBI, a flurry of activity was taking place. Information provided to them by the DEA from an informant in Mexico stated that a meeting of the top two cartel leaders in all of Mexico would take place somewhere in the area. Agents were visiting and making calls, contacting all the best hotels, looking for possible links to this meeting. FBI agent Kurt Hoskins had flown immediately to Phoenix from Washington. Meetings were taking place between the FBI and the Justice Department to determine if Eduardo Gonzales, aka "the Cowboy" or Carlos "Don Juan" Morales could be detained via international law; neither had been charged by the United States for any crime.

The Canyon Suites at The Phoenician had been identified by the tip, but Hoskins understood that every possibility should be checked out. Once rooms were identified and confirmed, they would send in tech teams to bug the hell out of them. No conversation would go unrecorded; not even the shower would be safe when they were done. The FBI and DEA would clear and occupy the rooms directly surrounding the rooms designated for the *Jefes*. Special-weapons and tactical- action teams would be standing by in complete combat gear, staged as they did to enter rooms and take down tangos.

Hoskins' phone rang; he pulled it from the center console of the pool car he had signed out from downtown Phoenix.

"Hoskins. Go." He listened intently and then said, "OK, notify all units that we meet two blocks North of the hotel in two hours — all equipment and teams standing by, 100% at the ready."

The two Mexican crime bosses didn't even bother to use aliases; the brazen attitude of men like this amazed Hoskins even after 15 years.

Two hours later, behind a shopping plaza just off of Scottsdale Road, Hoskins stood before 20 men and women representing all the departments and teams that would be participating in this operation. A dozen dark vehicles and three panel vans were parked nearby.

"OK. Welcome to the desert, people," Hoskins began to address the group. Several nodded, commenting to their buddies on the heat of the day. "I have two teams at the hotel now conducting recon; we cannot rule out that the cartels would have advance teams here casing the area. This means once we get the "go" call, you will take your positions and do so in one trip; that means you, too tech guy. No back and forth to your vans — got it?" He pointed at the tech leader, nerds with guns.

There were nods and murmurs of agreement.

"Right now this is an "observe and report" operation, but, if I get the right call, it will become an arrest." The tactical team leaders smiled at the thought. "The most famous detention since Ole Pineapple Face." Hoskins had the attention of everyone there. "Word is that, tomorrow afternoon, two separate flights will arrive at the Scottsdale airport. Limos will pick up the 'dignitaries' and take them to the hotel. I have two teams waiting at the airport to pick them up and follow them to the hotel. By that time, nobody should even be able to *guess* that a federal agent is in Arizona, let alone Scottsdale. Roger that?"

Hoskins received affirmatives from each team leader. "You all have your missions. Stand by, because we should receive the go from the hotel any second now. The advance teams will meet you and walk you to the suspect rooms. Roger that?" Getting no response, he called it out again: "Roger that?"

"Roger" everyone spoke out in unison.

Hoskins headed out to check the lay of the land at the Scottsdale airport.

Just a few miles North of his meeting, Hoskins received an "all clear" call from his advance teams at the hotel. He called the highest-ranking member of the tech team and said one word, "*Go!*"

Chapter Nineteen

Hudde brought a box of tissues out to the kitchen dinette table at his place. Isabella was sitting, head down, both hands over her eyes, sniffling.

"I can't believe she would kill herself," she started to sob. "I mean she was so nice and smiled all the time. I thought she was happy!" She was talking about a young woman who'd also practiced at the animal shelter and who had suddenly taken her own life.

"I'm sorry, Isabella. I know that you just started there. Maybe the others knew something that you didn't. Maybe she was sick or had serious troubles. Lots of people hide things like that very well."

She blew her nose into a tissue. "I thought maybe she was somebody that I could go to for help and to learn more, but I never got the chance." She broke down a little more.

Hudde walked behind the chair and lightly rubbed her back.

"That's OK. Get it out. We can't do anything for her now but pay our respects."

Her sobs subsided, and she said, "Yes, I know, she wasn't much older than me. It's, it's…'shocking'…I guess is the right word." She took a swig of bottled water that Hudde had set before her and then rubbed her nose with the tissue, throwing it out and yanking out another with a flip of the wrist. She practiced some deep-breathing exercises in an attempt to stay calm.

Hudde ran his hands over her head, pulling the hair from her face. He bent at the waist and kissed her forehead. "Whatever you need from me, you only need to ask, OK?"

"I know; I knew you would be wonderful." She smiled up at him and took his hand. Holding it to her face, she kissed it and held it close. "I'm suddenly very sleepy; would you hold me for a while?"

"Oh, absolutely."

She took his hand and led him to the bedroom. He laid down on his back, and she crawled up from the end of the bed. Any other time, it would have been so sexy that he would not have been able to control himself, but, today, he fought those thoughts. She lay in the crook of his arm, her head on his chest; her hair was everywhere about his face, and he reached with his right hand to take it from his mouth and nose.

She rolled her left leg up over his, draped across one side of his body; her head rose and fell with his breathing. "Is this OK?" she asked, without looking up at him. She sounded almost out already.

"Wonderful. Get some sleep." He pushed her hair back from her own face, and she slept for hours. Him, not so much.

The sun set, and Hudde watched its fading light creep across the bedroom wall and ultimately lose to the darkness.

His eyes adjusted to the dark; the glow from the alarm clock became brighter and brighter.

Isabella stirred, rubbing her face on his shirt. "Oh, I needed that so much. Wow — what time is it?"

"It's almost nine. You took about three hours off. Why don't we grab a beer and watch some TV?"

Isabella swung her feet over the edge of the bed, running her fingers through her hair and then fluffing it up. She yawned, throwing her arms high above her head and arching her back. Hudde watched her chest expand, pushing hard against the t-shirt she was wearing. Isabella stood and leaned left and then right, finishing by stretching down to touch her toes.

Hudde observed, "Reminds me of a cat I once knew."

"Let's raid your fridge. This"...she paused..."kitty is hungry." She smiled and grabbed his hand as she walked by.

Chapter Twenty

She had to take Hudde shopping to get something present-able for a funeral service. They ended up getting a pair of kha-kis that were close enough to dress pants and a dress shirt; Hudde picked out a suede blazer that he thought was cool. While waiting for Isabella's approval on the blazer, Hudde looked out the front window and saw that a camping and out-door equipment store was across the street.

"We aren't going to take up camping," Isabella said, mat-ter-of-factly, as she handed him the bags. "This is OK on short notice."

"Yeah, but I need something more like a boot because I refuse to buy dress shoes." Suddenly Hudde was a small boy again.

She shook her head. "Yes you're right. Let's see if some-thing is suitable over there for you."

Hudde started to toss the bags into the Jeep's open top, and Isabella stopped him.

"They won't be here when we come back." She kept walk-ing, and he carried them with them.

Hudde found himself looking at the equipment in the store. He loved looking at camping, hunting, and fishing items, even though he'd never done those things outside the military. He did find some military-tan desert boots that, with his longer pants on, would look almost like he was wearing shoes.

"Hey" Hudde said to Isabella, "it's way better than wearing sneakers, and I may still get some use out of them elsewhere."

Isabella shook her head in defeat. "Whatever, Gordan. Good enough."

Hudde smiled at the small victory.

They went back to his place, and he changed, looking as good as he could. He didn't want to make Isabella feel out of place due to her goofy American "boyfriend." She was dressed in a black dress that was sleeveless. The top portion, over her shoulders, was made of lace; matching lace protruded from the hem of the dress, making it knee length. It was hard for Hudde to imagine Isabella in anything that didn't somehow make her look sexy. He was trying different outfits on her in his mind when she grabbed his hand and said, "Let's get going."

There were many sad faces, and people seemed to be very sincere as he watched Isabella interact with the people at the funeral. Hudde was introduced over and over. He thought he noticed that Isabella seemed to take a proud stance when she did so, and that made him happy in these sad circumstances. Hudde was very familiar with death — even thinking about his own. There were almost no atheists in foxholes, as they say all the time. Hudde had a personal relationship with the Lord; he was of no denomination, no fixed faith, but it was there nonetheless. The Lord had need of soldiers, too — they were all throughout the bible.

Finally Hudde met an elderly American couple who had retired in Mexico and had brought their dog into the shelter to get some veterinary help. "Oh, she was so nice. You could just tell how much she loved animals," the American wife was saying. "Our boy "Trickster" is just outside if you would want to meet him."

Suddenly Hudde wished he were the only English speaker present. "No, some other time. Thank you." He shook hands and moved along, looking for Isabella.

She found him as much as he found her. She grabbed his hand and said, "I have had enough sadness for one day. Let's go."

They drove straight to his place; she asked him if he would take a walk with her. He changed into some shorts, a baggy tank top, and sneakers. He looked at the sun's position, wondering if he needed some sunscreen but decided against it, thinking that, about the time he started to burn, the sun would be going down.

Isabella hopped out onto the front deck wearing black yoga pants, a bright yellow sports bra covered up with another of his tank tops tied neatly at her waist. Her hair was tied loosely behind her head in a big, bushy tail. He whistled one long low note when he saw her. She zipped right past him, hitting the street and heading South. "Come on, Romeo. Keep up."

Hudde realized that she was burning up some energy, while thinking that he sometimes would do the same thing; some of his best ideas seemed to come after heavy exercise.

So he fell into stride and walked in silence. She led them two more blocks to the South before turning to the West and heading to hotel row and the beaches. They didn't slow down for anything, and she was beginning to breathe deeply.

"Nobody had any idea why she would take her own life," Isabella said out of the clear blue. "Her supposed best friend had no idea that anything was that bad." She breathed deeply a few times, arms pumping and a determined look on her face. "It's not right that you wouldn't have anyone to talk to." A few more steps. "My dad died, and my mom is alone. Your parents died, and you were alone. It's not the way we were designed to go about, Gordan."

She led them down into the sand and headed North. Walking in sand — especially trying to go faster — is always a little more difficult. Even Hudde began breathing a little harder at this point.

"I guess feeling bad at a funeral is just normal. I don't know." She huffed a few times. "Have you lost a lot of friends?"

"Sure. It's something that, in combat, you must put aside momentarily, and, then, often, you just try not to think about it later, too." He looked down at her as they marched. "Military guys get over it by drinking too much and then trying very hard to get payback. It gets harder the more the enemy digs into the civilian population. You can't find them, they hit with roadside bombs, and we don't ever feel satisfied. It's a vicious cycle."

"I'm sorry," she said. "I shouldn't have asked you."

"It's forever part of me, Isabella, just like today is forever a part of you: You don't win a race with bad memories. You just come to find peace with the sadness and then move on with your own life." He smiled and stopped. They came to a large outcropping of rock and a natural rise of the land up and over to the next street that ended in a long jetty, which protected a nearby marina. It appeared to Hudde to be one part natural and one part man made. "What next, there, drill sergeant?"

The first part of the obstacle was about five feet high, and Isabella took Hudde's hand. He helped her climb onto the rock. The next three large boulders were laid just so that she leaned and stretched, making it up each level until they stood about 15 feet higher than the beach; only two more levels needed to be climbed for them to make it to the top. Hudde admired her tenacity to continue but not as much as he admired her shape as she crawled up to the next rock.

"Wait one," Hudde called out.

"What — can't keep up?" she said, turning to look down slightly at him as she was now about two feet taller than him. With both hands on her hips, she made an exaggerated disappointed face. "Army man tired?"

"I could carry you and do this all day," Hudde said nonchalantly. "This may be the wrong time, but I just have to go on record to protest."

She made no movement; she just stared unapprovingly at him. "It's gonna get dark."

"Look, those pants should be outlawed. I've been staring at that taut, heart-shaped ass all afternoon, and I just have to point out how good I have been."

"Any other complaints?" Isabella kept a straight face but pursed her lips like the beginning of a smile.

"Yeah, now that you mention it. You slept on me the other night, and all I could smell was that soapy, vanilla musk; now it's everywhere in *my* room." He continued, "And when we watched TV, I think you were teasing me by letting your top slip down, and every time your foot moved, you rubbed my crotch." She started smiling broadly. "It's not funny. Do you know how hard it is to hide an erection half the night?"

"Wait, wait, wait!" Isabella waved her hands in front of him. "First" — she used two fingers to point at her own eyes and then down at her breasts — "the way I lost your eye contact all the time at the hotel, I thought you were a breast man!"

He shrugged his shoulders. "I'm an everything man when it comes to you."

"Well, good answer." She paused and then held up two fingers. "Second, flirting is a woman's God-given right, and I can't help it if I am good at it. So maybe I was toying with you a little. And *last*" — she now held up three fingers — "you didn't hide that erection very well the other night." She started giggling and then laughing out loud. She turned a little away from him, sticking her ass out toward him, bending slightly at the waist, looking back over her shoulder. "You like it, huh?"

He didn't answer her, but he reached out and grabbed her hips, holding her in place, and bit her in the cheek, playfully, but he earned a scream.

"Ouch, that hurt!" she said, extra seductively rubbing her behind in the process.

"You're killing me."

"I'm sorry. Come here," she ordered.

He stepped as close as he could to the rock she was on; she pulled him in and tilted his head up so that he was looking at her.

"I know that I'm in love with you now. I just had to be sure it wasn't something else; a woman can find lust almost anywhere — love is much harder." She kissed him deeply. The sun was dropping slowly into the ocean; waves crashed nearby. This was something Hudde was completely a novice at. He just hadn't had the time to be in love before, and he allowed her to hold his head against her breasts while she ran her fingers through his hair. He had to admit it that felt good. His hands found her bare back, and he let them slide casually over the soft smooth flesh; he started thinking about baseball — to keep the blood flowing to his brain.

She suddenly push back on his shoulders, creating a gap between the two. "Why don't you take me back to your place and get me some food. Then I will take a long shower, and, afterwards, you can show me all the things you have been thinking you will do to me."

Hudde's eyes narrowed, and his brow furrowed.

"You heard right: Take me home and love me."

"We are taking a cab," was all Hudde said, and he sprung past her, leaping over the single steel-railing fence heading down the sidewalk at the top of the jetty, now heading East back to the street.

She called out for him after crawling under the railing: "It will be better with me — wait up!"

Chapter
Twenty-One

Each *Jefe* had left Mexico and Mexican airspace at approximately the same time. Kurt Hoskins had his FBI teams wound up and waiting in the rooms surrounding the future guest rooms of the *Jefes*. Review of the CCTV surveillance and sound checks in both rooms led him to believe that they had prepared all they could. He had cars with two agents in each of them standing by at the Scottsdale airport to pick up both men upon their arrival. This was the time for agents to check and double check their weapons, adjust their body armor, and stretch. Nervous ticks became apparent.

On the car radio, a DJ stated that Phoenix was experiencing partly cloudy skies. The agent behind the wheel of the car tasked with following The agent craned his neck to look at the skies above. He could see one lone cloud drifting Southwest to the Northeast, and he smiled. He wondered what "partly cloudy" looked like right now in DC.

He looked at the sleek, small jet coming in from the East and used his binoculars to read its tail numbers. He keyed his mic: "Unit Two, this is Unit One. I have eyes on your tango. Over."

"Roger that, Unit One. We have eyes on the flight now," came the response.

A small propeller craft came in low and slow, seeming to just miss the Northeast fence that bordered the street — definitely not the aircraft he was looking for. Again using the binoculars, the agent read the tail numbers on another jet making a pass. He keyed his mic: "All units, this is Unit One. I have eyes on the second tango aircraft. Stand by for movement."

A large agent ran out of the small terminal. He jumped into the passenger seat of the FBI vehicle known as Unit Two,. "OK. They are in a large, blacked-out Cadillac Escalade, and they are moving," he said to the driver.

The security gate began to open, and the big black Cadillac thumped twice as it hopped over the rail and an immediate speed bump. Unit Two keyed his mic: "Delta on the move. Unit Two in position." They slipped out moments after the Caddy, barely catching the turn arrow to head South on Scottsdale road. The FBI driver let everyone know that they were heading in the proper direction.

Unit One keyed the mic: "Charlie moving, also heading South now on Scottsdale road. Looks like the party is right on schedule." He turned and looked at his partner. "Looks like we got the easiest job. We know right where they are going." He relaxed, not worried about losing his target.

Unit Two broke the temporary silence: "Be advised — target Delta has pulled into a furniture-store parking lot."

Hoskins came on. "Anything suspicious? What are they doing?"

"Nothing, team leader — just sitting in the Southernmost part of the parking lot right now."

Unit Two pulled in down the street at a fast-food restaurant, fully expecting their target to pull out and continue heading South.

Unit One announced, "OK. Our guy's in the same spot. We're pulling in just North of the location."

Hoskins keyed his mic: "Just keep eyes on; let me know when they are back on the move. Maybe there is a third party we are not aware of. Units One and Two — be on alert."

Two "Rogers" let him know he had been heard.

Unit One called out, "It looks like 'Charlie' and a second are moving; I think they are going into the furniture store." Then he added, "That's a roger — 'Charlie' plus one body in the store."

Hoskins called out on his radio: "Tech Two — somebody get me everything there is on that store. Any Mexico connections, all employees and owner info."

"Tech Two — Roger that, team leader."

Wearing jeans, a simple white dress shirt and his cowboy hat, Eduardo Gonzales and his man Miguel Lopez felt the cool air-conditioning flow over them as they entered the furniture store. Glancing about, it looked like bedroom furniture spread out to the North, while the center of the store had some dining-room furniture. Gonzales headed deeper into the store and to the South, where he observed some living-room items.

A woman fighting 60 approached the two men. Eduardo felt she was dressed too young, in a tight pencil skirt and ruffled blouse. He thought she was fighting the height of her heels, trying to fit in with the ultra-rich, the only ones who could shop in a place like this.

"May I help you, gentlemen?" Her feeble smile and her avoidance of introducing herself or shaking hands gave away her feeling that these two Mexican men were probably in the wrong place.

"I am looking for a new sofa," Gonzales said, heading further into the store. "Ah, this is what I am talking about, Miguel. Would you look at this?" A huge, dark-wood, real-cowhide sofa sat there, taking up a huge space. "This I could use!" Miguel just nodded his approval.

The store employee now grew interested. "Well, my name is Beth. Maybe we should go fill out some credit applications. It can save you 10% if you make a purchase today." She held out her hand.

Eduardo ignored the hand; he chuckled about the credit application. "Miguel, pay the lady."

Beth only then noticed the small satchel that the other man was carrying. She walked over and started operating the computer-based register.

Miguel asked her, "Beth, can you deliver this to a Mexican address?" He smiled broadly at her, but she didn't feel any warmth from it.

"Who cares? I will send my own men," Eduardo responded without looking at them.

"That comes to $7648.48" Beth said to Miguel. "Will that be a charge?"

"We don't believe in charging." Miguel reached into the satchel and brought out a roll of $100s. Beth believed the roll was $10,000 and was sure when Miguel counted out $7,700 and told her to keep the change.

Seeing the men flush with cash, Beth suddenly turned on the charm. She tried to place an arm around Eduardo and pointed out some heavy coffee tables.

Eduardo turned away from her and said, "No offense, woman, but you wear too much perfume. My eyes are watering."

"Aw, what the hell?" the only other employee in the store said out loud as a "roach coach" — local slang for a Mexican food truck — pulled into the parking lot right in front of the building. It stopped there and looked as if it were going to set up shop. "They can't do that!" the man said to everyone.

Eduardo walked to the front of the building, almost all glass. He saw Don Juan and his man Marco getting out of their vehicle. He turned to the two employees and a new man, most likely the manager, who'd come out of an office in the back.

"Do not worry, my friends. I will ask them to leave — OK?" All three employees seemed content with that. From behind Eduardo, loud mariachi music began permeating the air. The manager appeared angry and kept moving forward. Eduardo stopped him by putting his hand up before him.

"Sir, if you would be so kind, please allow me to handle the food truck. It will just be a moment, as I would like to get a taco," Miguel said as he stepped into the manager's personal space. Suddenly, the store manager felt somewhat unsettled.

There was a moment when their eyes met, and the manager knew this was not a request. Miguel reached into his bag and handed the man $500, just like that.

"OK," was all the manager said.

Eduardo and his man began walking to the door but stopped short. Miguel came back and got the receipt for the sofa, telling Beth, "Our men will be here in two days to take possession."

"You probably hear the mariachi music from my mic," Unit One was saying. "Microphones will be of no use, I don't know what's going on."

Unit Two chimed in: "We can hear it half a block away."

Team leader confirmed, "Yeah, Roger that. Units One and Two — I'm getting it from your radios." Hoskins bent his head and squeezed his nose with his thumb and forefinger. "Just keep your distance, and keep me up to date."

"Look who it is — Don Johnson!" Eduardo held out his hand keeping up appearances of civility.

"Yes, Eduardo. I know what they say." The two did shake hands. They needed to stand close to hear each other over the music.

Carlos Morales seemed tired. "Look, Eduardo. Why don't you just tell me how we can work without being at each other's throats. This hurts both our businesses equally."

"You know what hurts my business, Morales? People blowing up my buildings and mining my fields, destroying millions of dollars of future profit!" The Cowboy could not keep the anger off his face.

"A response to you for murdering my men and burning down a building, also destroying product and morale," Carlos pointed out. "We could do this for months; in fact, we already have." He took a deep breath and leaned in close once again. "Just tell me: How does it stop?"

This was exactly what The Cowboy thought would happen. "Why don't you let your boy Marco ride back with us? Then we call an end to this. My people tell me he was the mastermind behind the ugliness at my farm."

Morales looked down at The Cowboy. "You know this will never happen. What about a dollar amount?"

The Cowboy locked eyes with Morales. "Maybe I just kill you here, myself."

"If you wish to die also, go ahead. We are both getting older. Life holds little mystery for either of us now." The cowboy understood that Morales truly believed this.

"Ah, fuck it. I will think about money."

Morales shook his head, disgusted. "We flew thousands of miles for this?"

"I'm getting tacos, and I bought a new sofa." Gonzales smiled. "Nothing wasted about this."

"Stick to the plan, you crazy bastard." Morales stuck a finger in The Cowboy's face to drive the point home. Then he turned and headed back to the Caddy, Vargas in tow.

Gonzales ordered up two-dozen tacos and had Lopez give the illegal Mexican at the mobile grill a thousand dollars before they loaded up and headed South. "Tell him we appreciate him moving his business today to care for us. He can return to his normal haunts."

The two Cadillacs, following all traffic laws, suddenly turned and headed back North, straight to the airport. Driving through an open gate onto the tarmac, the vehicles headed to the freshly topped off jets awaiting their return.

Kurt Hoskins barged into the hotel room with a tactical team from Phoenix. He yelled, "Three guys with me" and then turned, running through the high-priced five-star hotel. Agents running in full gear through the hall and lobby caused a few screams. Hoskins threw his keys at one of the agents and yelled, "As fast as you can — get us to the airport!" He jumped into the back seat and got on his phone. Hoskins speed-dialed his contact with the Justice Department. "I don't care if he's in a meeting with the pope!" he screamed into the phone.

FBI Units One and Two were both parking in the Scottsdale airport. The four men jumped out and ran in unison into the small terminal. They went to the rear, Western-facing wall and looked out the windows there. Both Mexican *Jefes* were loading up; the Morales plane was the first to begin moving to take off. The agents walked out to the tarmac. Eduardo Gonzales knew they were there — he had seen them the moment they landed. He turned and blew a kiss as he ducked his head and walked into the small jet.

Hoskins and his team screamed to a stop just as the other four agents were coming out of the terminal, walking casually. Hoskins' phone rang. "Hoskins. Go" He looked down for a moment before shaking his head. "Well, are you prepared to shoot their planes down? Yeah, nice work!" He wished he could slam his phone. "Stupid fucking wastes of oxygen!" He screamed and walked in a circle, not knowing just how to explain this one to his superiors.

It turned out that the only person on the planet more discomfited by the news of the botched American operation was Ricardo Cruz, back at the Gulf Coast cartel.

Chapter Twenty-Two

Hudde lay on his back on the left side of the bed, his arms behind his head, propped up on a pillow. He breathed deep and slow, trying to just enjoy this moment as long as possible. Light was just beginning to fight in from behind the vertical blinds of the sliding glass door leading back to the patio. The large ceiling fan rotated slowly, creating the slightest breeze across his naked body; he slept without a cover. On his left, Isabella was on her stomach lying across and hugging a pillow, a light sheet draped kitty-corner across her back, starting at her left buttocks up to her right armpit. Her hair was a beautiful mess, and her ample bosom squeezed out from under her chest. Her legs were spread; the sheet pressed across her naked bottom and legs, creating an image that stirred his own groin. After last night, he knew not to disturb her. It would have made a beautiful, seductive painting. Hudde allowed it to burn into his memory.

Hudde padded barefoot out to the kitchen and started the coffee maker. He cracked the vertical blinds near the dinette set, and the sun's light began warming the air immediately. Hudde went in and took a quick shower without turning on any bathroom lights. He grabbed a cup of coffee, looked in to admire Isabella again, and sat contemplating about what the rest of his life would be like. It was amazing to him that this the first time he had thought of his own life in terms of what it would be like at 50 or 60 years old. He always thought he wouldn't make it into his 30s with the way he had lived his life so far. He stared at the box of snorkeling equipment and said aloud, "I'm not done with you yet."

On his third cup of coffee, he heard water running in the bathroom, and, after a more few minutes, Isabella came out, her feet slapping loudly on the tile, wearing one of his tank tops, which, while it covered her down to her knees, did very little to cover her chest.

"Oh, coffee!" She poured herself some into a plain brown mug. "I think I will see if Mama will cook for us today. What do you say, my lover?" She ran her free hand through his hair and kissed his temple, plopping down in a chair near him.

"Won't get any complaints from me, but if she still is refusing to use English, it makes it difficult."

"I'll talk to her. Don't worry." She reached for her phone, on a nearby counter.

Hudde just shook his head as his tank top nearly fell off her shoulders when she did so. "Maybe I'll go for a quick run to the beach."

Isabella was already speaking very quickly in Spanish. Hudde went into the bedroom, changing into some compression shorts, baggy cotton gym shorts, and another tank top. He sat on the edge of the bed, put on some socks, and slipped on a pair of cross-training sneakers he had brought with him.

When he returned to the kitchen, Isabella was saying goodbye. Hudde stood over her as she told him her lunch plans. She did that thing where she rubbed both hands in her scalp and then bent over, allowing her hair to cascade over the top of her head, before flipping it back in a fluid movement.

"You sure you're going for a run?" she looked at Hudde through some strands of hair. "I thought maybe you could help me shower."

"Oh, I'm your man!" And, just like that, it was nearly impossible for Hudde to remove the compression shorts.

When they pulled into Gabriela's dirt driveway, she was standing outside, watering a hanging planter on her small front patio. She was wearing a red blouse with a plunging neckline and a flowing black skirt; she padded about barefoot.

Before he said anything, Isabella slapped his face playfully. "No comments — or you won't get anything from me for a while!" She wagged a finger at him.

"*Viva la Mexico!*" Hudde replied.

There was some interesting back-and-forth between the two ladies, in Spanish; Hudde knew his job: he grabbed the beer cooler and headed into the living room.

He was summoned into the kitchen by Isabella. There he was confronted by Gabriel, who placed one hand on his face and kissed the other side; he managed to maintain complete eye contact with Isabella the entire time; she was grinning from ear to ear.

Gabriela said, "So you believe Isabella has a hot mother?" She smiled mischievously. "You play with much fire, saying such a thing to my daughter."

"Your daughter's been toying with me for months. It was the only way I could pick on her." Hudde tried his best to appear sheepish.

"Oh, I know how my daughter can be, but you didn't answer the question." She placed one hand on her hip and then tilted her hips, placing all her weight on one side, a pose Isabella had struck before. She stood still, looking expectantly at him.

Hudde stole a glance at Isabella; she was smiling, waiting to see how he was going to manage these difficult waters.

"First, let me say thank you for using English. And, of course, you're attractive. How else did Isabella get so beautiful?" Hudde continued. "I was really trying to figure out how you have remained unattached so long."

She kissed his cheek again and then patted his chest before stepping away. "Thank you. You're a good man. I've been telling Isabella that I would take a cruise and meet a wealthy foreigner who would whisk me away to Europe and treat me like a queen."

"And yet, here she is, year after year, slaving away at a crummy garden, working odd jobs, and keeping me fed." Isabella said.

"Well, don't tell me you plan to go with her; I'm afraid I would never see either of you again."

"That's right. Keep on your toes, buddy." Isabella smiled at him.

"Here is the final test to see if you are good enough for my daughter." Gabriela was holding a rough bowl with what looked like meat and gravy. "If that mongrel out back doesn't bite you, you can continue to see my baby."

"Mama!" Isabella said forcefully.

"I'm good with animals — well, four-legged ones anyway."

Hudde took the bowl and headed out the back screen door. He didn't know if it was a German Shepherd mixed with a wolf or what, but it was a big animal, probably near 120 lbs. It immediately began a low, throaty growl that Hudde recognized as "What are you doing in my world?"

He was wondering how he had missed meeting him on the last visit when Gabriela called out, "He's not mine, and I just feed him occasionally, if he comes around."

Hudde began talking to the animal in as non-threatening a voice as he had, telling him he was just here to feed him. Without moving forward, he found a piece of meat and said, "Here ya go."

He flicked the meat to the dog. The animal snapped at it but missed it in the air, finally gobbling it down after his nose found it on the packed and hardened dirt. Hudde did not advance any further; he just set the bowl at his own feet and didn't move. The large dog came closer, sticking its neck out, sniffing at Hudde. The dog took a final step and wolfed down the food. It sniffed at Hudde one last time before turning and trotting off the property.

"Do you know who owns him?" Hudde asked, handing the cleaned bowl to Gabriela.

"I don't think he belongs to anyone" she said. "I see him around. I guess others give him some scraps when they can, and the rest he makes up with rabbits and gophers that he keeps out of my garden."

"So, have I passed?"

"I didn't think he liked men that much — maybe some unknown history. But you did good."

Gabriela ushered Hudde to the table. "It is not like he is a vicious killer, and I just knew he would growl at you. I didn't really expect anything else; I would never have done that to you." She patted his cheek.

They ate good food and enjoyed maybe a little too much beer. It was a nice evening. Both women were relaxed and seemed to enjoy the banter and back and forth movement of the conversation. Gordan asked Gabriela if she knew much about the family history. He said that, with Spanish, French, Inca, and Navaho all having history in the area, he wondered if there were any tales she was willing to pass on.

"Poor people here — all of them," she said. "Foreigners coming here, searching for riches, leaving with little, if anything. Conquering the natives for slave labor or worse. Who needs that history?"

Gabriela looked at Gordan, tilting her head in a way he had seen Isabella do, and asked, "What about you? You are here basking in our sun, and it is expensive for you to do so. Have you rich relatives from Europe that you want to tell us about?"

"Mama," Isabella started.

"No, that's fair." Hudde raised his hand in acceptance. "I do have some money. I often tell people that I inherited it, but I actually earned it, fair and square."

Isabella said, "Hey!"

"I know — it's part true and part not all the information. Understand, my money is my money. Nobody lost it or is looking for what I now have; but to be honest, I took it from someone."

Isabella looked a little shocked; her mother was smiling, getting something out of him that her daughter obviously did not know.

"Understand that not a single living person knows this — OK?"

Both women shook their heads in unison.

"A bad man tried to bribe me, tried to trick me; his plan was to kill me and take the money himself. It did not end well for him."

Gabriela placed a hand on her chest and gasped audibly, Isabella placed a hand on her mother's knee.

"It was nothing illegal. I am not wanted for any crime; I assure you I am still an employee in good standing in America. Matter of fact, my old boss has sent me several messages, asking me to return soon." He scrolled through his email on his phone and showed one such message to both ladies. He was unsure why he was telling them this. He realized that he was not planning on returning to his job; he switched topics as quickly as he could.

"Now, as to my heritage: My parents died so young, I only have some stories they told me in the foster homes; I can't attest to their accuracy, and, by the time I was old enough, I didn't care, as the Army was my family. They said my mother was Scottish and my Father from Germany or the Netherlands; poor people, I assure you. There is no throne waiting for me to ascend and accept my rightful place."

Gabriela moved over and sat on the sofa near Gordan. She looked very intently into his face and eyes. "Poor people are everywhere. We can only do what God has given us the ability to do and hope that it is enough."

Hudde smiled warmly. "Your family is very rich, Gabriela, and I have been blessed to be near both of you now."

His eyes twinkled, and Gabriela could see the beginnings of laugh lines at the corners.

"Ask your daughter: I am so very happy to be a part of your lives. I feel born again, and my life has never been so full of amazing possibilities."

"I see that you do not lie about this, and my daughter is happy. A mother can't ask for any more than this." She rubbed his cheek before getting up and heading into the kitchen to finish cleaning up. Isabella jumped to help, and her mother pleaded with her to sit and enjoy the evening.

"Do you miss your work or friends?" Isabella asked him, moving over to the sofa after her mother had started on the dishes.

"I've missed that for years now." Hudde said, matter of factly. He saw the confusion on her face and elaborated. "I've been working quite a bit alone for the last several years. When I was operating with a team, well, it's something you never can quite describe — the respect and love you feel for the guys willing to give it all, willing to put themselves out there." He smiled at her, sat back, and pulled her feet up into his lap, beginning to rub them while he continued.

She leaned back, smiling and enjoying the attention.

"The work I have been doing is very much, I think, like mountain climbing or sky diving. There is a thrill and a fear that you are foolish to continue to do these things without keeping both." He pulled her foot closer to him, pressing upward with his thumbs from her arch to her toes.

"I will pay you not to stop what you are doing now," Isabella said to him.

"I just can't stop touching you." Hudde smiled at her.

Isabella fired off some Spanish, and Hudde frowned. "I don't ever want you to stop." And she beamed a brilliant smile back at him, sliding further onto her back, closing her eyes.

"You want to know another secret?" Hudde asked her. "My secret with the snorkeling was that I was very afraid, but a part of me wanted to keep swimming out. I wanted to see what was out there. I wanted to know that feeling that makes me want to go further into danger, to confront my fear; it sometimes scares me even more."

Isabella sat up, pulling her foot away from him. "That is enough, then. No more swimming in the ocean for you. I will not have you eaten by a shark because you're too stupid to stay on land with me!"

Chapter Twenty-Three

The Cowboy eyed his new couch. It went well with the heavy furniture and decorating that he already had. He did like the trip North. They had gotten this thing, and he had confirmed that Carlos Morales had ordered the attack on his cartel and that his man Marco Vargas had carried this plan out. Miguel Lopez, never far from Gonzales, sat at the bar, eyeing his boss.

"OK. So, now we know these things as fact. What is the next step?" Vargas was hoping to take a trip to the East coast to deliver a message.

"Morales wants to pay me for the damages," Gonzales stated, matter of factly. He walked over to the bar and pulled down a bottle of tequila, pouring out two shots; he gulped one down and then looked at Lopez. The Cowboy wasn't drinking alone.

Gonzales patted Lopez as he walked by. "So what dollar amount would we put on this thing, anyway?"

Lopez had thought it out already but pretended to be in thought. "Maybe 100,000 to 120,000 legitimately. The hurt morale and scared villagers — what price do you place on that?"

"Exactly, exactly right." Gonzales, beginning to walk about, was in thought. "But any price we give him, he will come back at a 50% reduction. My problem is that I keep thinking about that greasy bastard Vargas sneaking around in my world, killing my people, destroying my things. His head is what I think I want." He nodded to himself.

"It will have to be so painful to Morales that he would not want to answer you, *Jefe*; otherwise, it will just escalate the violence further. It will have to be an epic response." Lopez didn't turn to watch Gonzales pace; he sat with his chin in his hand, thinking about possible attack scenarios. Vargas was the chess piece directly across the board from him; if he were removed, Lopez felt he would be the most powerful and dangerous player left.

Gonzales poured two more drinks and sat down on a stool near Lopez, downing his. "Yes, I will think some more about this. In the meantime, contact Morales and tell him '$500,000.' We will forgive.. No need to hurry; let him sweat."

Chapter
Twenty-Four

Gordan Hudde sat drinking coffee at his kitchen table, gazing out at "his town," with only two homes in the entire block; this was how he thought about it. Isabella was getting ready to go into the hotel to work. He could hear the water running and the blow dryer. Occasionally, she would break out in a song, usually in Spanish; she had banished him from the bedroom or bathroom while she prepared because he was unable, it seemed, to control himself. There was something so sexy about watching her primp and prepare for work.

The thing was, he felt an odd sense of something was not right, and loose ends were something that he could not have. He searched his brain, trying earnestly to come up with something; what could possibly be wrong? After she had kissed him and grabbed her keys, running from the house, it dawned on him; one word popped into his mind: "Temporary." He had a home in the USA; he had this home for six months and a girlfriend, which was new. He felt like he had to do something to make it feel permanent, not temporary. Was this just a fear that it could end? She could change her mind at any time, and it frightened him.

He laughed out loud; maybe it was better that he'd never really done this before. He had friends who'd dropped out of the military when they got families. The stress of losing them, from the service member's death or from the incredible difficulty of long deployments, was too much for them. Those people lost their edge, their ability to maintain the high level of readiness that was needed for his kind of work. And then it dawned on him: If, while at work, he did not understand something, he would find an expert to explain something to him, and he would learn.

Two hours later, Gordan sat sharing coffee with Gabriela at her home. She was surprised but happy that he had searched her out.

"I've never been too embarrassed to admit when I don't know something." He was explaining his visit to her. "I'm no monk — don't get me wrong — it's just this feeling I can't get away from that I have to do more...I just can't explain it."

She laughed at him, taking his hand in hers over the table. "My daughter has you tied up in knots."

"I quit my job, my house is temporary, and I don't want Isabella to be temporary." He shook his head and scratched his right eyebrow, pondering.

"I imagine your job has been very stressful. I imagine you plan and plan to make things go right."

"Oh, yes — plan, train, and prepare," he acknowledged.

"Well, you can't plan for Isabella, Gordan. I think the more you plan, the more difficult it will be for both of you. Listen, I know she loves you. She hasn't said as much, but I expect her to soon. You must understand that, as a very young girl the attention from men started; she was somewhat of a free spirit when she was younger. I can tell you all the attention from men every time she turned around was difficult for a while, but about three years ago, she took time off and refocused her life — looking after animals, working. You are the first person she has brought here since then. This is how I know , after all I am her mother; I see how she looks at you." She smiled. "Don't plan for my daughter, Gordan. Love her every day, and just see what happens. If you need to tie up things like your work, you can do that — but not Isabella. Understand?"

"Yes, I think so."

Gabriela continued to hold his gaze. "I can see that you are a serious and passionate man. Focus your energies on enjoying each moment. You will never get any of them back." She stood up and walked behind him. Dropping her small hand, she pressed on his chest. "Breathe, child; I think you were once consumed with your job. You cannot allow Isabella to consume you the same way. You will lose both of you that way." She bent and kissed his cheek. "My daughter said you tried snorkeling; do something — have more passion than just Isabella, and it will help you. You will see."

"You have helped a lot. Thank you." He hugged her, very thankful for the insight.

"Anytime. You are welcome." And she waved from the front patio leaning on a support post, a beautiful picture in his rented rear-view mirror.

Chapter Twenty-Five

The next few weeks, Gordan took the sage advice of Gabriela Santiago. He searched out Angelo Cristova at the dive and bait shop and discussed the ocean. He brought liquor as payment for the knowledge Cristova gave him. He took up exercising again in a regimented way. He called out his own cadence in his head, and he wondered if every ex-military person did the same thing. He ran a four-mile route that took him over beach sand and road, and he could swim or do pushups and pullups off of his own balcony. He felt more alive and surer of himself than he did before; this is exactly what he needed.

Cristova set up a small group that he was willing to take to a reef where, he told Gordan, he would be able to enjoy the ocean and see many great things. Gordan jumped at the chance and found himself sitting at the bow of a 16-foot wooden craft bouncing in the chop, smiling ear to ear at four other foreign tourists, two men and two woman, with their own snorkeling gear. When they arrived at the location, Cristova dropped an anchor fore and aft and then stood, speaking to the people he had selected for this personalized trip.

"OK, my friends. When it is time to go, I will blow this horn." He held up a common air horn and gave it one quick blast. If I see a shark, I will blow this whistle," and he placed a whistle into his mouth and blew it several times. "No need to panic: Just take deep breaths and return to the boat. If you are frightened, I will pull you up first." He looked about. "I have never lost anyone to the sea in nearly 47 years. I won't today." He grinned. Hudde couldn't help but see this man as a pirate from the 16 century. It was just impossible, as he handled himself so self-assuredly and walked easily in this small boat, taking waves as if he were comfortably in his shop.

Cristova continued his safety speech. "Please do not touch the coral. It is sharp, and, if the current pulls you into one, we will soon see our shark friends coming to the party." He wagged his fingers at the five waiting to get into the water.

Hudde looked down into the light-blue clear water; he guessed they were in 16 feet of water, which was amazing as they must have been a mile from shore. Hudde slipped into his "socks" and fins. He felt self-conscious about the knife but, well, he couldn't help it. He strapped it to his leg and slipped into the water. Spitting into and allowing ocean water into his mask, he dumped it out and slid it over his eyes. Taking the mouthpiece firmly into his teeth, he turned horizontal and swum easily around the boat.

Gordan quickly learned that, after diving, if he turned his head to the surface and blew out hard through the snorkel, it cleared any water, and he wouldn't take in a mouthful when he tried to take his first breath after returning to the surface.

He thoroughly enjoyed this experience — way different from his first attempt off of the beach.

The other swimmers were off doing their own thing. One was an older couple, and the woman was in a one-piece swim suit. The man floated more on his back. His big belly looked like a whale breaching. The other couple, closer to Hudde's age, swam past. The woman was in a two-piece that was nothing extraordinary. However, when she swam under Hudde, she used both of her legs at the same time, like a mermaid — it was a sexy movement in the water. Hudde wondered what Isabella was doing at that moment.

♦ ♦ ♦

Isabella had just gotten out of her Jeep. Several miles from town, she was making one of her first-ever solo "barn calls" for the veterinarian service. The long, low ranch home had good cover from some large pinion trees. There was a barn close by, but Isabella could not see any animals. A woman in her fifties came out to meet her. One look at Isabella, and she shook her head sadly.

"I'm so sorry, honey. I am sorry." She wrinkled up her face and began walking in the direction of the barn. A warm engine clicked as it cooled from a '70s dark-green Chevy impala parked nearby.

"Well, this is what I do, ma'am," Isabella tried to assure the obviously upset older woman.

The woman wouldn't make eye contact as she held the door open for Isabella to walk into the barn. The door shut behind her. The woman did not enter with her. The bright daylight turned to immediate darkness for Isabella; she stopped quickly, allowing her eyes to adjust to the sudden gloom.

"What?" was all that escaped her mouth before someone struck her in the face, knocking her to the ground.

"Oh, my God! Why — what's going on?" Someone grabbed her by the hair and pulled her head roughly so that she was looking up. Her eyesight wasn't helped by the tears in her eyes.

"Wow, this is a tasty looking piece of ass!" someone said over her, roughly shaking her by the hair.

"I'll take a slice," somebody said behind her. Rough hands began pulling her pants down, and fingernails scratched her back. She turned onto her back, trying to kick with all her might.

The man who was holding her hair slapped her two more times. She could see him glaring at her now. He had short dark hair and a goatee. She thought she saw a glimmer of gold in his mouth.

She screamed a blood-curdling scream, stopping only when she was struck again.

"Nobody is coming to your rescue. We could kill you here, and nobody would ever find you." He shook her head violently and said, "Do I have your attention?"

"Yes. What are you going to do to me?" She thought about being sold into prostitution — or worse — and sniffled back some tears. They tasted of blood.

"My friends have a business" he started. "One of your co-workers used to work for us, but she decided to…ah… quit." He smiled a grotesque smile, standing there, bending over her, and it sent a shiver down Isabella's spine in a 90-degree barn. She could now make out a very big man standing at her feet; she thought he was a giant. Right now he was licking his lips and rubbing his crotch.

Goatee continued. "She used to bring us some drugs from your pharmacy, so a position is open, and we arranged this meeting so that you could apply." He smiled at his joke.

"No, I could never…"

The big man stooped down and tore her blouse off very easily. He grasped her bra and yanked it off her shoulders. She screamed and tried to roll away, but the other man held her hair tightly.

"Wow! Check out them tits," the big man said. "Forget the drugs — let's just fuck this bitch now." She heard a zipper behind her. The other man, goatee, spoke close to her ear, but she couldn't see him as she was now on her knees, her face in the dirt and straw.

"Maybe you should rethink, or maybe you would rather be a prostitute at one of our clubs?"

The big man began yanking at her jeans again; she tried to fold up placing one foot behind the other, keeping her knees together.

"No, no. I can get you whatever you need!" She had to spit out some dirt.

"Are you sure? You sure are a sweet piece of meat. I could change my mind."

"No. I'll get you whatever you need. I promise — I promise I'll do it."

"Pull your pants up, Tauro. I think we have a deal here. Is that what I am hearing here, girlie? Because, let me tell you: If you don't follow through for us, we are going to come get you and take you to a place you will never return from. We will turn you out so bad, you will beg us all to fuck you for some more heroin. Do you understand? My friends on the police force will let me know if you try to run to them. So, understand: This is your one and only chance to continue to live like you once did, unless you want to kill yourself like your friend did." He reached down and grabbed her breast, handling her roughly. "That would be a waste."

He found her phone in the gloom of the barn and called himself. When we call, you will bring us 1000 tablets of Ketamine. Do you understand? Once a week from here on, we will contact you." They turned, and she immediately started feeling relieved. "See you soon" goatee turned and said on his exit.

She heard the Chevy roar to life; dirt and stones were thrown everywhere, pelting the side of the barn when they left in a hurry. She laid for several minutes looking about at the barn; light filtered in between ill-fitting and warped wood, and dust swirled and danced in that light. The smell of dirt, hay, straw, and even horse manure was something that usually made her happy. Now it was forever burned into her memory as something to fear. She began to weep, holding her torn garments to her chest. The door swung open, and Isabella let out another scream, trying to back up like a crab on the floor. It was the woman who had walked her to the barn. She apologized profusely, telling Isabella that her son somehow owed these men money and that she could not fight them. as they might hurt him.

Isabella just wanted to get away, and she scrambled to her feet, holding her torn clothing, heading to her jeep. She drove back to Hudde's house, tasting blood the whole way. She was proud of herself that she did not cry any more.

Chapter
Twenty-Six

Gordan Hudde burst through the front door of his house, excited by a day on the ocean, even more excited to see Isabella's Jeep in front of the home.

"Over here" she said, sitting cross-legged on the floor, a bottle of tequila and a beer nearby.

He could see the discoloration of her left cheek and eye, and then he noticed a washcloth and small puddle of water on the glass coffee table.

"What the hell happened? I didn't see any damage to your Jeep."

She took two deep breaths and then explained the assault at the farm in the countryside. Hudde knelt at her side and inspected her injuries. She was very proud of herself for not crying at all through her description of the events.

Hudde sat before her, hand going through his beard, occasionally asking her to elaborate, making her repeat the story over several times.

She looked at him almost with suspicion. "What are you trying to do?" she asked.

"I want to help." He shrugged his shoulders as if saying, "What else would I be trying to do?"

"You're not going to ask me to call the police?"

Hudde tilted his head, a little defeated. "If that makes you feel better, Isabella, why don't you call the police." He wasn't asking her. "You have seen the "head over heels Gordan," I understand. But that is just a part of me Isabella. I want to help. I can help. As a matter of fact, I may be the only answer you have."

"What are you talking about, Gordan? You are only one man — a guy who almost cried when I showed him some sick puppies."

"You can't call the police. This is most likely a gang affiliated with a local cartel, and they would have a certain amount of protection. I'm a Middle East conflict specialist; I've never studied your country's issues, although I know we have people here. You have two ways out if you handle this yourself: 1. Move. 2. Suicide. It worked for your former co-worker."

He studied her face.

She looked up at him through her hair, "What would you do? You can't pay them off. They would just take you for everything you have and still come after me." The first real tears began to form and flow down her face. He could see she wanted to believe he could help, but she just couldn't make it work in her head. She held his hand and looked up at him. "I loved what I was doing. I was so happy with you and work and everything. I just don't know what to do." She began to hyperventilate.

"OK, it's going to be OK. Now, just breathe. Can you get the Ketamine they want?" He rubbed the back of her neck.

"Of course, but I can't be stealing from the shelter — I just can't." She shook her head in defiance.

"Just one time, Isabella, and that is it. I will take care of this. I will fix it...I promise you." He sat down near her and took a pull of the tequila. "You have been so very brave. Can you be brave some more? Could you face these people one more time?"

"I think so." She still was confused, looking intently into Hudde's face.

Hudde kept eye contact with her. "When they contact you next week, you will direct them to the hotel parking lot. Tell them that you had to go to work and that you will get them whatever they want in the future — OK? It will be your job to convince them that everything is going according to their plan, so that they are not suspicious — understand? You are going undercover, as yourself."

"I think I can do that, but what will you do?" She was breathing normally and had stopped crying.

He could see the concern in her face. "I will follow them until I find their home base or headquarters or whatever."

"OK — and then?" She only knew this love-struck person; she hadn't seen anything — other than just his physical presence — that made her believe he could do anything about this.

Hudde looked at her without any hesitation. "I'll kill them all."

She pulled herself up to sitting on the couch. "Gordan! What the hell are you saying? Even if you could, you're not God! You can't do this. No, no, no. This isn't right; I couldn't help you get yourself killed!" She pushed him away from her.

He tried to give her a reassuring smile and then stood and began to pace, pulling down on his beard while speaking. "I follow them to their lair and then conduct two or three days' surveillance on them. Based on the information I collect, on the fourth or fifth day, I will go in. You never have to steal or meet with these people after that first time."

Isabella walked to the back patio sliding glass door and looked out at the darkening sky. "I know you said you were a soldier. I know maybe you've killed before — but in war, right? You can't just go around killing people."

"People have been doing it since forever." He shrugged his shoulders.

Yeah, but God, Gordan — you'll go to hell." Her Catholic faith kicked in.

"I'm not Catholic, but I believe in God as much as you do." He tried to reassure her with a smile.

"Well, then, how can you talk so casually about this. Vengeance is for God, not for you or me."

"Isabella, it's not vengeance; it's survival. Why do you fix sick and injured animals?" he asked.

Isabella stomped her foot on the floor and threw her hands into the air.

"Don't change the subject on me."

"I'm not; tell me: Why do you help injured and sick animals?"

"Because I care about them, because I can; so what?" She looked a little angry.

"Is it a gift from God that you are capable of learning and helping those animals?" His left eyebrow raised up a little.

She snapped back quickly. "Of course! The grace of God brings me to them, and, by His providence, they heal."

"Well, why do you interfere in God's plan? Isn't that exactly what you are doing? Just because you *can* help? Maybe you shouldn't." He didn't wait for an answer. "Our same God gave me a gift, Isabella. I have helped many people survive because of the things I have done. I was born with a talent as much as you were. Why can't God be acting through me? Why isn't it possible that God brought us together so that I can help you now?" He stood over her and pulled on his beard while waiting for a response.

"Wow! That's awfully presumptive of you. Are you *sure* God wants you to go out and kill people?" She couldn't believe this was the same man.

"No, not at all. But do you think God cares deeply about those gang members? Those men who would not worry about raping you or care that, due to their actions, your friend committed suicide? If he does, he can question them in Heaven, because I will give them a chance to speak directly."

He was deadly serious.

"I have to think that way. I have never killed anyone over a parking spot. You have known me for many months now.

When have I lost my temper or spoken ill of anyone — or anything, for that matter?"

"Just let me think about it for a little while. It seems crazy, I just have to have some quiet for a while."

"OK."

◆ ◆ ◆

Gordan showered off the salt water and frustrations of the current events. The only answer for him when injustice or criminal behavior was allowed to run rampant was direct action — "violence of action," they would call it in the Army. The Army's version of shock and awe; your initial assault was so strong and violent that the enemy would be rocked back onto their heels and unable to continue a fight. Gordan found no reason that military tactics could not be the correct response for gangs, cartels, or mobs anywhere in any country. Somewhere, deep in his memory, he remembered a news exposé where a Los Angeles gang member was telling an anchor that his gang was at war with the police. He paid it no mind at the time but now wondered: *If a group declares war with the peaceful residents, why wouldn't we then bring the war to them? Send in some special forces groups; give them support with Delta and Rangers. Yeah — that would work.*

Isabella broke his thought process. "Could you get some help?"

He risked peeking out from under shampoo. "What? No — I shower all by myself, unless you're volunteering?"

She ignored his flippant remark. "Could you get help?, Would some of your army friends come help you?"

"It's possible, but why don't we stick with my simple plan? I will find out where these roaches go at night and see what I can come up with after that. Isabella, I have been deep behind enemy lines before. Don't worry. I know what I'm doing." He smiled and then got back under the water, finishing cleaning up.

He grabbed a towel hanging off a hook on the wall, running it over his head before wrapping it around his waist. Isabella sat at the mirror in the vanity chair not needing to turn to look at Hudde.

"I'm scared." Tears welled up in her eyes.

"How's that bruise?" Hudde pulled her hair away from her face. Standing behind her, he bent and kissed her very lightly near her eye. "Don't be scared, Isabella. You think about being an actress, and play your part. I will take care of mine. Everything will be OK. You'll see."

"OK, Gordan. I don't want to move, and I have too much to live for right now." She smiled up at him. "I can't lose you, either."

"You're not that lucky," he joked.

Chapter
Twenty-Seven

Isabella's phone rang. It was the following Friday, eight days since the assault. She was at her bar at the La Playa Hermoso Grande, and she didn't recognize the number.

"Yes?" she said uneasily.

"Do you have what we asked you for?"

"Yes. It is in my car."

"You will drive to…"

She interrupted: "I am at work at the Hermoso Grande. I got you what you wanted. I will keep trying to get whatever you ask for, but, please, don't make me lose this job, too. I can't leave. I can take a break and give them to you."

There was silence. Isabella was getting worried, but Hudde had told her not to speak after she told them this.

Finally, the silence was broken by whoever was on the other end. "I know this place; we will be there in 15 minutes, and you will be outside, waiting by your car."

"Yes, yes — I will be there." The call was over.

Isabella went out to the lobby, where Gordan was sitting, reading, wearing a deep-blue golf shirt and dark-grey khaki pants.

"15 minutes, Gordan." She was getting a huge adrenaline surge, and it made her nervous.

"Everything will be OK. Don't you worry. Stick to the plan; remember, if you must try to run away, I will be there in 30 seconds, so fight like hell if you have to."

"OK. Be safe, Gordan."

"You, too. I will be very late. I may not get home until early tomorrow afternoon, so don't worry."

"I wish you would get a cell phone." She hugged him, and then he was off.

Gordan went out to his rental, a nondescript older Ford Taurus of a dark-grey color. He pulled out of the parking lot and drove just past the hotel, looking South. He pulled over where many did due to access to the beach. Gordan had checked this spot out earlier in the week. When he got out and walked North, the sidewalk ended at the edge of the hotel parking lot. From there, he could see Isabella's jeep and could be there in 20 to 30 seconds in a sprint. When the tangos left the hotel, he could easily pick them up.

Hudde spotted the green Chevy pull off the main street into the parking-lot drive. He understood that they would need to drive up, past the hotel, before making it into the parking area.

He watched and saw Isabella suddenly stiffen, and he knew she had seen them as well. "Easy, Isabella," he whispered to himself.

Isabella reached into her Jeep and pulled out a large white bottle with a yellow label. She hoped that if she just gave them the bottle through the window, they would drive off.

She was wrong.

The Chevy came to a stop near her; she forced herself not to look for Gordan. She pushed the bottle into the passenger window, where Goatee was sitting. He took the bottle and set it at his feet after checking the label quickly.

"Holy shit, man — you weren't kidding me," the driver said. He threw the car in park and jumped out. He was a short, muscular man in a multi-colored tank top.

"Just take the drug and go," Hudde whispered to himself approximately 100 yards away.

"Mama, let me look at you!" Tank top called out to Isabella as he walked around the front of the car. He took her right wrist and pulled at her, making her turn around so that he could ogle her.

He didn't release her wrist but bent a little, looking into the passenger window. "You weren't fucking with me! I say fuck the drugs, boss — let's take her."

Goatee leaned out the window a little. "What do you think Mama? You want to make some money with us. My men all agree. I'm sure the next person can get us the stuff."

Tank Top grabbed the ruffled long skirt that was the color of the uniform worn by the girls in the restaurant. He pulled it up and away, exposing all of her legs and underwear. Isabella swatted at his arm to try to get him to drop the skirt; she was unsuccessful.

He did drop the skirt, but he grabbed her by the throat and squeezed until she couldn't breathe. "Don't you ever raise your hand to me, woman." He took the moment to look down into her cleavage that the uniform also revealed. "You are put together!" He released her throat only to reach into her blouse and grab her right breast, cupping it as if he was weighing it. "I am going to use you for two or three days before we sell you off," he said into her face.

"Let's go," Goatee said from within the car.

Isabella was so proud that she fought her first desire to run or call out for help. They pulled away as she readjusted her outfit; she even fought off the tears that wanted to flow.

Tank Top pulled out into traffic, turning South along the beach. He turned to his boss.

"We can't let that go without getting a taste." He smiled hungrily.

"Don't worry. When the time comes, we know where she works. We have her phone number. When she tries to stop supplying our drugs or becomes difficult, I will give her to you." He slapped Tank Top on the thigh, and they shared a laugh.

Gordan Hudde was three cars back; he had just added another nickname to his list of future dead men.

Gordan thought they would drive miles into the wilderness. He worried that tailing such a vehicle might be difficult. But they wound up about three miles away, in an abandoned warehouse area. There was about a block of empty buildings — some low, looking like storage buildings, and some others two and three stories tall. They currently were heading South. There were no through streets heading East. When the green Chevy pulled East into a side street, Hudde slowed, pulling up cautiously, ensuring that it, too, was a dead end.

He drove past the Western drive and pulled into the next parking lot on his right. He ensured that it was an empty building, and then he got out and walked back North. Directly across the street from the dead end, the Chevy had gone down was a three-story building. Hudde checked the windows. It seemed to be full of trash. There were no signs that it had any life, including homeless people. In the back of this building, Hudde saw an emergency escape ladder with a security fence built around it. But there was no need to use the ladder. Hudde ran and jumped, pushing off the building itself, propelling himself high enough to grab the security fence. Pulling himself hand over hand until his feet could get a hold, he easily gained access to the roof.

Looking about, Gordan could see some cement blocks, a few pieces of pipe, glass bottles, an old broom, and about a half-dozen bricks, probably all left by the original construction crews. Gordan knelt, frog-walked, and then low-crawled to the front edge of the building. He could see the green Chevy parked in front of two buildings on the end of the dead end street before him. The two buildings were identical — three stories tall, with large roll-up doors. On the left, there was a man door. On the right, there were no windows visible.

Hudde slid back and then reversed himself until he was safely on the ground. He returned to his vehicle and took one slow trip around the area. It turned out that the East was blocked by a golf course on the other side of a large brick fence. Gordan turned back to the West and drove into a thriving business area, adjacent to a tourist area and the beach. He headed back to see Isabella. She was fine, and he assured her that everything would be OK.

Chapter Twenty-Eight

Gordan found the clothing store that Isabella had taken him to earlier for funeral-service clothes. He bought himself a dark hoodie, a new pair of sneakers, and some new khaki pants — exactly the same as he was wearing. Stuffing them in a paper bag, he pushed the items into his back seat floor.

Across the street at the camping and outdoor store, he found himself a dark-grey lightweight tarp, a camping mat, a good pair of leather gloves, and a K-bar knife. He started to drive back to his place when he spotted a dirt-bike and motorcycle store. He jerked the wheel, parking and heading into the location. He looked at some helmets and found some face masks and balaclava-style racing hoods that suited him. He found a punisher skull balaclava and couldn't help himself; he bought it. The punisher logo was a symbol for many military units in the Army. He headed home and got some additional sleep; he was going to need it.

He awoke when Isabella sat on the bed near him. He reached out and pulled himself to her, laying his head in her lap. She caressed his head and ran her fingers through his hair.

"Gordan, are you sure this is the right thing to do?" She looked down at him; the concern showed in her face.

He knew she had worried the rest of the day.

"I am positive; there is no chance of anything happening the next couple of nights, OK? I am just going to go and watch; no need to worry." He began pulling her down so that he could kiss her.

"I can't relax; not now, Gordan." She pushed at him. "You're incorrigible."

"Well, the only other thing I am thinking about is food; did you bring anything home with you?"

"No, I'm sorry."

"Well let's see what we can have." And he swung his legs off the bed and started off to the kitchen. She laid her work outfit on his bed and found one of his t-shirts to put on, following him out to the living room.

"How about if I fry up some potatoes, onions, peppers and some eggs?" He was staring into the refrigerator.

"That's OK. I'm not that hungry" she said.

He started pulling out the ingredients; she pulled up a barstool to watch.

"How can you be so calm? Aren't you afraid of what might happen?"

"No need to worry about what might happen, I made a plan, and now I'm go to carry it out. Most plans need to be changed once you start but less so when all I'm trying to do is surveillance." He just said it matter of factly, like when she said, "I'm going to work." Isabella thought that maybe this man was much more than she knew.

The sun went down just past 7 pm, or 1900hrs; at 2000hrs, Hudde got up and stretched.

"I guess it's about time to go." He went over and hugged her. "Don't worry. I am not sure when I will get back. I am guessing sometime after the sun comes up tomorrow — OK?"

"OK." She wanted to be strong for him. "Promise you will be safe."

He smiled down at her. "Always" was his one-word reply.

Jumping into the rental, Hudde headed South until he was sure he was past the block he needed to get to. He turned East and then North, and he came across the proper street. Just as the area had done before, coming from the North, the homes gave way to small business and then some larger buildings that all were empty. Some business plan had gone bust, and several blocks of buildings sat empty and decaying — perfect for the dirt bags he was looking for.

Hudde found the same building he'd parked at before. Again he ensurthat there were no signs of life. He parked his car and rolled a 55-gallon steel drum and a wood pallet in front of it so that it was not visible from the street. He walked North to the next building, made sure his ruck was fitted properly on his shoulders, and leapt and climbed to the roof as he had done earlier. Looking into the sky, he saw that there was little light from the surrounding community and that it had turned dark quickly. Stars were plentiful in the Eastern sky, with no ground light and the moon not yet risen. Looking back to the West, toward the beach and the hotels that attracted tourists, an ambient light reached into the sky. It was good for Hudde to remember that he could be silhouetted in this light when he was at the front of the building.

First Hudde grabbed the five cement blocks and the six bricks and placed them closer to the Northeast corner of the roof. He then laid out his tarp and rolled it lengthwise. Taking the tarp, he laid it at the front of the building, with the end pointing at him. He rolled it out toward the four-inch ledge of the building so that there was a solid foot of the tarp exposed. He placed two of the cement blocks on each front corner and added a second block on top. He rolled the tarp out, up over the blocks and back toward the center of the building. When it was completely rolled out, he laid the remaining block and bricks onto the back end of the tarp so that it would not catch air.

Hudde crawled under the tarp, laying out the camping mat so that he could lie in a shooter's position pointing East toward the suspects' HQ. He took out the knife and sliced a horizontal slit in the tarp right in front of his face. He cut a four-inch vertical cut at each end so that he had a flap that he could look out of. He crawled out from under his blind to retrieve the ruck. Looking back at this setup, he knew nobody would notice him even if someone came out on the roof. He doubted they would make him out unless they stepped on him.

Hudde crawled back under and got into position and told himself that this was a long-term position and to just get used to it. He glanced at his watch and noted it was just before 2100hrs.

After the first hour, Hudde began to think that he had the wrong street and would have been sure of it if not for the green Chevy parked 200 yards away at the end of the street. He closed his eyes and got used to the noises. Just two blocks East, a main drag produced a lot of traffic noise, which drifted into his ears. Somewhere, a dog barked. When the wind stiffened just a few miles an hour faster, a steady noise indicated that a door was open and working back and forth on some squeaky hinges.

Hudde practiced breathing slowly, deeply, and steadily. He also worked on isometric exercises to flex and relax muscle groups in his back and shoulders. He didn't want to keep getting in and out from underneath the tarp and increase his chances of being observed. The night air dropped into the high 70s, and as it was an ocean wind. He actually was happy to have something over him — this would be impossible during the day. He would have been forced into looking into the surrounding buildings for a different point of view.

And then it began. At 2215hrs, several strings of Christmas lights came on, and music started blaring from the enemy HQ. Hudde shook his head at his own stupidity: Green, red, and white were the colors of the Mexican flag. The roll-up door started up, it stopped when it was high enough for your average man. The guy who walked under it was not average height. He ducked to keep from hitting his head. He must be the "giant" Isabella had identified, Hudde thought. He looked to be about 6'6" and about 330 lbs., Hudde guessed. He wasn't going to win a body-building competition, as he was big and fat. In Hudde's estimation, he should probably be looking to lose about 60 to 70 lbs. Still, he was a big, imposing man. Isabella had said that Goatee had called him "Bull," and that sounded like it fit him to a "T." "Bull" dragged a stool out to the Chevy, currently parked sideways in front of the roll-up door, and took a seat.

Hudde couldn't observe anything going on inside. Lights were on, and that was all he knew. A car approached slowly and steadyily. Hudde imagined that this street got no traffic except for this crew's activities and the occasional person who was slightly lost. And then Hudde observed a light bar and understood that it was cop car. It made the turn down the dead end and hit the lights and sirens for two seconds. "Bull" jumped off his stool and walked toward the police vehicle. When the car rolled to a stop, "Bull" gave two one-finger salutes to whoever was in the car. A uniformed passenger got out and pointed into the building. "Bull" just waved him in and then ducked down, speaking to the driver. The cop came back out in moments with a rolled-up brown paper bag. The trunk popped, and he placed the bag in the back before getting into the patrol car. When the cop car did a K-turn to get back out the street, "Bull" kicked it in the back side panel and gave the universal hand gesture in their direction for masturbating.

That was friendly enough, Hudde noted. Closer to 2300hrs, a skinny, little long-haired guy came out, dragging a backpack. He jawed with "Bull" for a few minutes and then headed down a side alley. Moment later, an older-model Honda Civic pulled out of the alley and turned toward Hudde; it was red or light brown. The Honda's small engine screamed when the skinny guy hit the gas, taking the corner without looking. When he let off the gas down the street, the Honda backfired during a downshift. Hudde christened skinny guy "Rat," and he wondered how big this crew was. Another car came down the street. Hudde was not sure of the make and model; it turned gingerly down toward "Club Mexico."

"Bull" walked over and ducked down, looking into the car. A conversation ensued, but Hudde could not make it out, and, if it was in Spanish, it wouldn't have mattered anyway. "Bull" reached into the car, and bent at the roll-up door, and appeared to call in.

Tank Top came out, he and "Bull" shook hands, and he headed back inside. "Bull" reached out into the car, and transaction was over; the car drove off.

This scene was repeated over and over for several hours before anything different happened. At 0200hrs, a newer-model Chrysler four-door sedan pulled into the street. "Bull" stood and walked to the driver's-side door. After a conversation, he pointed to the North side of the street, and the car pulled over and parked. Five young males came out of the vehicle, hooting and hollering. They danced and drank for a few minutes, and then two of them went into the HQ building. Tank Top came out and gave the new guys something that they began smoking. There was no need for quiet, and these rowdy actions did not seen to be frowned on at all.

One of the rowdy young men began walking to the HQ door, and "Bull" stepped in front of him. There was an exchange of words, and "Bull" shoved the young man, who went stumbling backwards; "Bull" suddenly had a machete in his big right hand. The other guys were making the "hands up" sign to "Bull" and pulling back their overly ambitious member of their group. It appeared to Hudde that, whatever was happening inside, there was a "two-at-a-time" limit. "Bull" slid the machete into a sheath inside the back of his pants and sat back down. The rowdy group continued to dance and drink and stomp around. Another vehicle came and parked; just two men got out and waited. They appeared to know "Bull." Tank Top came out and shook hands with these two. The rowdy team's two missing members exited the building and met with their pals. They huddled up and began talking and yelling. The other two men went inside. Team Rowdy got in their sedan and left.

Versions of this happened until approximately 0430hrs, when the lights went off and "Bull" dragged his stool inside. The rolling door went down, and other than possibly adding some more broken bottles to the street, you would never have known that anything out of the ordinary had happened here at all.

Hudde watched the sun begin to climb into the sky; he guessed that by 0900hrs the sun would hit his blind and begin to heat it up very quickly. The thing was, he had lain there for many hours and needed to piss badly. He slid out of his tarp and crawled, stooped, and then walked to the Southwest corner of the building, relieving himself over the edge. Of course, that's when he heard a backfire; he quickly reversed the process and came back to his position. The light-red Honda screamed down the dead end and backed back into the alley it had left from earlier. Moments later Rat and his duffle bag reappeared into view. He walked to the man door and wrapped twice, hard, on the door. "Bull" opened the door, and the two disappeared inside. Hudde's watch said 0705hrs. Nothing happened until the sun started heating the building's roof, making it unbearable. Hudde backed out and crawled to the rear of the roof. He stretched before climbing down and freeing his car from the debris he had hidden it with. It was 0920hrs.

"Oh, thank God!" Isabella made the sign of the cross when he entered the house.

Chapter
Twenty-Nine

Ricardo Cruz had his man drop him off near the security gates of the new docks in Heroica Veracruz. Cruz was unsure why Carlos Morales wanted this meeting at the facilities he had built here. Cruz figured he wanted to show off a new speed-boat or yacht he had purchased and was more than a little pissed that he had to take a two-hour drive to appease the ego of the *Jefe*.

It was much different than Cruz had envisioned; there was a large metal warehouse that seemed to hover over the water on the east edge. Nothing flashy — not the cruise liner that Cruz had envisioned parked at the docks. Marco Vargas stood near a heavy-looking metal door. He nodded at Ricardo and said "Good morning." He was wearing a shit-eating grin that made Cruz even more suspicious. He decided that he should engage Vargas to determine what the *Jefe*'s intentions were in bringing him here.

"Have you convinced Carlos to kill that moron Gonzales yet?" He knew that this was a *cause celebre* for Vargas.

"No good news on that front, but I appreciate your support on that." Vargas seemed to focus over the shoulder of

Cruz, and he nodded; Cruz turned to see fellow lieutenant Adrian Campos walking toward them.

Campos was young, a dark and flashy man, right in the mold of Morales himself. He was a lieutenant with a reputation for fast cars, fast boats, fast women, and fast with a knife. He looked like he could be Morales' kid, and secretly Cruz hated him.

"Adrian — good morning." Cruz extended his hand. "Do you know why we are here this morning?"

Campos shook his head. "No, my friend. I do not, but I hope it is to play on a new yacht or something as exciting."

Vargas interrupted: "Now that you both are here, let's go see the boss." He motioned to the South, where a few shipping containers sat near a construction trailer. A large generator hummed nearby, and security Jeeps crisscrossed before them as the three men made the three steps into the cooler air of the trailer.

A Chinese man bowed to Carlos Morales, turned, and nodded at the three men as they entered and he exited; he was dressed in nondescript coveralls and black work boots. He was wearing a white construction helmet.

Cruz watched the man walk toward the warehouse as he shut the door; he had a confused look on his face as he turned back to the others.

Morales was standing over a drafting table. He pointed to some stools in the room, and everyone took a seat. Morales was as excited as Cruz had ever seen him.

"Tell us how much losses you have been having on your border operations, Ricardo."

What the fuck? Cruz thought to himself. *Am I in trouble?* "Nothing new," he said calmly.

"What percentage do we lose right now over land?" Morales asked, waiting for the correct answer.

Campos stiffened, knowing what question he might get next; he started thinking about his answer.

"*Jefe*, nothing has changed for the last couple of years. I guess that we are holding at about 12 to 15 percent losses."

"And you, Adrian — what about our water operations?" Morales now turned his gaze at Campos.

Campos felt better about his answer. "10 percent, *El Jefe*."

"And each time our product is interdicted, I watch these smug bastards across the border run to the TV and talk about their big victory. They catch peanuts and party like they have scored a big victory." Morales stood behind the table. "If I could find the right people, I would just give them $250 million as a gift to get them to stop and leave us to our business. You know they are not serious about stopping us; we are the engine that drives a huge portion of their economy. DEA, CIA, IRS, TSA, ATF, and the Department of Homeland security — we keep them all employed, do we not?"

Everyone nodded their heads in agreement.

"My plan is to continue to give the Americans the little taste they get from us, but I will now just give them what I want to, anytime I want to deliver our goods unmolested; I have a new secret weapon. Come and look at this map." He waved them up to the tilted, oversized drafting table.

Vargas already knew what was going on and hung back, pouring himself another coffee. Campos and Cruz stood near Morales, looking at the map of the Gulf of Mexico and the surrounding land masses.

"Either of you two see what I saw when I looked at this same map?"

He looked left at Cruz and then back to his right at Campos.

Cruz had nothing; Campos said, "Lots of water and thousands of miles of coastline." Campos punctuated his comment with a shrug of his shoulders.

"Look at the water." Morales thought it was obvious, but neither of the other men offered anything else.

"Look at the deep water of the Gulf. There is a trench that leads from just off the coast here to the Alabama-Pensacola, Florida, coast. Do you see this deep blue area here?" Morales pointed at the map.

Both men agreed, but neither understood.

"Follow me." Morales wheeled and headed outside, making a beeline to the warehouse and the large steel fire door.

The four men entered and found themselves in a small, eight-by-ten office-like room, with a drop ceiling over a concrete floor. There were no chairs or desk, only a door straight ahead and one to their right.

Morales turned and addressed the others. "I have enough money, and my children will be well taken care of. You men may think you could do better, but you do quite well — way better than whatever day we met." He waved a finger at each in turn. "For me, now, it is the game." He smiled as if they would immediately understand, yet it was obvious they did not. "I need to win the game; I need to beat the Americans every time we play. We have bought the Mexican government, but the Americans never will be so bold. Sure, they take our money, but, outwardly, they continue to try to win. I had a dream, and today I show you my queen on the chessboard."

He opened the door in front of them and ushered them through, smiling broadly the whole time.

"What the fuck! Are you kidding me?" Campos stood dumfounded.

Cruz's mouth hung open. Morales was excited and happy to see their reaction.

Chapter Thirty

Gordan grabbed a couple of small bottles of water and a few energy bars. He kissed Isabella and headed out for another night of lying on the roof of an abandoned building. He repeated the circular rout to get to his hiding spot and repeated the climb to the three-story roof. He stood breathing and taking in the night sounds with his eyes closed. Nothing out of the ordinary came to his senses. He crept to the envelope that was his blind and slid underneath, taking up the same position as the night before. A quick glance at his watch showed that he'd arrived there about an hour later than last night, about 2130hrs.

Upon looking out the flap in the tarp, Hudde immediately noticed that the green Chevy was not parked in front as it had been last night. The Christmas lights came on at 2210hrs. Hudde noted everything that had occurred the previous evening. Rat left with his little Honda, and cars started slowly coming into the area, increasing in number near midnight. Hudde didn't see Tank Top, but he did observe Goatee come out and assist "Bull" with some of the transactions. He was most pleased that no new players had shown up for this so far. For five or six people, he could come up with a quick and easy plan. Anything more than that, he would worry about logistics and errors and would need much more time to come up with a plan that might require help.

Gordan began thinking about maybe following one or two of these guys away from the HQ, removing them from the equation, and then returning to the HQ to finish the job. He wanted to run his hand through his beard while he thought but was currently resting on his elbows while lying in a prone position.

The next vehicle that pulled down the street was the green Chevy. Hudde glanced at his watch; it was near 0200hrs. The Chevy pulled up to the roll-up door as it had the previous night. Tank Top jumped out and yelled out a "Whhhoooha!" raising his hands in victory.

"Bull" stood and stretched, and Goatee walked out from under the door. The passenger door opened, and a blonde female poured out the door, falling to her knees. She looked to Hudde as if she had been out at a bar or party. She wore a festive yellow dress with very high heels. She climbed uneasily to a standing position and looked to be assessing her environment.

The blonde screamed, "Somebody help me!" She walked uneasily around the hood of the car.

Hudde took note that she sounded American.

Tank Top screamed out, "Somebody help me!" in broken English, obviously mocking the girl.

Tank Top high-fived Goatee and then shoved "Bull" as he walked past him toward the girl. She appeared very uneasy on her feet, and he kicked — no, more like *shoved* her — in the ass with his foot. The girl stumbled forward and then fell again to her knees. Tank Top walked over and grabbed a handful of blond locks; he rubbed her face into his crotch. She screamed out again and started flailing at him. He leaned back and laughed; grabbing her wrists, he dragged her under the door.

Goatee shared a word with "Bull," and then he, too, disappeared into the HQ building.

Hudde knew that everything had just changed, and he now understood why several men were allowed into the enemy HQ building two at a time.

Nothing but a few drug deals appeared to take place from then until 0400hrs, when the lights went off and the door came down; Hudde figured the HQ would be locked up until 0700hrs, when Rat would return.

Hudde pulled the blocks and bricks from his tarp and dragged it to the back of the roof, where he folded it up and packed up his duffle bag. He climbed down the outside of the emergency ladder and made his way to the Ford.

He drove out and headed South and then West, until heading North. Turning East, he returned to the area from the North: A big half-circle. He pulled into one of the East dead ends a block from the target and backed into an alley between abandoned building, much the same as Rat had done yesterday morning. He took time to quietly walk from building to building, attempting to determine if any were still being used or were currently occupied. Everything seemed completely abandoned; he returned to the Ford and slipped the punisher balaclava onto his head. He reached around to the small of his back and felt the K-bar firmly and comfortably in place.

Without any artificial light and very little moonlight, Hudde picked his way very slowly past the sides of the building, stepping toe to heel, ensuring that nobody close by would hear him moving past. He found his way to the back edge of the two buildings that Rat had parked in between the morning before and had pulled out from on two consecutive nights. The back had some garbage and pallets, and three 55-gallon drums with an assortment of trash inside. One appeared to have had a fire in it at one time or another. A quick glance at his watch showed that he had a least an hour and a half to wait; he leaned against the brick and closed his eyes.

Hudde kept track of the time in his head, keeping his eyes closed for nearly thirty minutes; when he next opened them, he could see that the sun was starting to lighten the Eastern skies and stars were dimming. When he was on the roof, the direct sun didn't begin hitting the East corner until later in the morning, due to the mountains in the East, so he knew that, at 0700hrs in this alley, there would still be deep shadows.

At 0630hrs Hudde moved away from the building he had been leaning against and started stretching, rotating his arms to loosen up his shoulders and doing some deep knee bends. Lying on a roof for two nights and standing still for the last two hours was detrimental to suddenly having to react quickly.

A backfire just before 0700hrs was the perfect sound for the start of a violent morning.

Chapter Thirty-One

"Tell me, Miguel — what news about the Gulf Coast boys?" Eduardo Gonzales said while picking at some toast and turning the page of the local newspaper. The sun was just starting to peek over the mountain to the East, just like it was for Gordan Hudde, approximately 150 miles to the South.

"Nothing new, Cowboy. They pretend that the attack on your fields never occurred. I am convinced that it was Marco Vargas, on direct orders from Morales." Miguel Lopez walked toward the breakfast spread that had been laid out on the 3rd-floor patio of the Gonzales estate.

Gonzales made a gesture at the table, offering anything there to Lopez. "Let me ask you: What we could take away from Morales that would hurt him the most? Something that would make him decide to never again attack any of our operations?"

Lopez took a deep breath and then sighed. "Cowboy, everyone knows that you have the most military support. Everyone in this hemisphere understands that you will take great vengeance if anyone crosses you or tries to hurt your business. I have been the man you send many times to ensure these things get handled correctly."

"But what?" Gonzales interrupted.

"On the East coast, they believe in their own power. This will never end for us until our own untimely death...or theirs." Lopez looked expectantly at The Cowboy.

"You want to kill Morales, or you want me to take their money?" Gonzales reached for his coffee.

Lopez walked to the edge of the roof and breathed in the morning air. It was heavy with moisture and earth. "It does not matter to me; it is for you to direct me which it will be: More war or temporary peace? Sometimes when I lie in bed at night and think of all the men I have killed, I feel like the hero from Rome or Greece — do you know the one? The strong man." He rolled his right hand several times out in front of his chest; he looked at Gonzales for help.

Gonzales tapped the table. "Ah yes, um...Hercules!" he said, proud of his memory.

"Yes, yes — that's the guy. He fought the giant reptile, and, every time he cut off a head, two more grew in its place." Lopez nodded approvingly at his own reference.

"So what answer do you have?" Gonzales asked.

Lopez walked back toward Gonzales. "That is it. I do not know. Maybe it ends for me when I am no longer as quick with a knife." He accentuated this by pulling his knife out and flicking it out before him. "Or maybe one day you grow tired of my witty conversation." He held up his knife and then put it away.

"Sit. Have something for your belly." Gonzales pointed at the good food spread out on the table. "Today is not that day."

This was not exactly the most comforting way to turn a phrase for Lopez.

Chapter Thirty-Two

The Rat shot past the alley just to the North and West of their base. He threw the Honda into reverse and backed in too fast, as was his usual method. He jumped out and flipped up the seat to pull out the duffle bag, now filled with coke and marijuana, resupplied for the next night or two.

Gordan Hudde grabbed him from behind by the throat, his oversized hands firmly choking off the yell that Rat tried to utter — and also the breath he wanted to take. Hudde slammed him like a rag doll onto the frame of the small car, knocking Rat unconscious before snapping his neck. Hudde pushed his lifeless body into the back seat of the vehicle and closed the door. He quickly crossed the street and stood before the large steel door. Placing his back onto the brick just to the right of the door, Hudde back-handed two large raps to the door with his left hand, loosening his K-bar with his right.

The door was thrown open, and "Bull" took a half step outside. Hudde noticed the surprise registering on "Bull's" face while he drove the K-bar repeatedly between his third and fourth ribs, looking for his heart and puncturing his lungs. "Bull" collapsed quietly, half of his body inside and half out;

bright-red blood bubbled out his lips as he quietly spoke his last words.

Gordan dragged him into the building and closed the door. A quick glance showed that a makeshift bar had been set up in the back of the room; a steel stairway was to Hudde's right. He headed to the second floor, where three doors could be observed. Two of the doors faced Hudde directly, a steel railing running along a steel-grated hallway. A large room at the back of the second floor had one door at the end of the steel walkway, facing the same way as the door Hudde had just walked through — North.

Hudde sprang up the 10 steps. He yanked open the first door, bloody knife in hand; it was empty. Most likely, it had been used by Rat or "Bull." Hudde closed the door and was about to yank on the second door on his right when the door at the end of the walkway opened. Goatee was standing, sleepily staggering forward, rubbing his face, stopping when he saw the skull-masked-clad man before him.

Hudde ran directly at Goatee and kicked him in the chest as hard as he could, sending him flying backwards into the room he had just exited. Suddenly Tank Top threw open his door, flicking a Japanese *katana* at Hudde as Gordan turned toward the noise. Tank Top was off balance and, fortunately for Hudde, not a swordsman. But he got close enough that Hudde felt a flow of blood over his left eye. Hudde feinted toward Tank Top and then jumped back into the main room, where Goatee was extracting himself from a coffee table and lamp that he had tumbled into. Hudde kicked him in the face, intending to knock him out — not to kill; he then turned to the door where Tank Top had followed him. Tank Top was standing just before the frame of the door; his only real option was to thrust at Hudde while he was turning from the kick that Gordan was delivering.

Again, Tank Top over-extended, and Hudde stepped forward, getting a big hand on the man's right wrist. He pushed down further, getting Tank Top further off balance, and then twisted his wrist inward while using his left leg to kick at his knee. Tank Top went to his knees; falling forward; he let go of the blade. Hudde spun 360, getting a grip on the sword handle. When he stepped back into Tank Top, he found out that the blade was real when it slid easily from just in front of Tank Top's collar bone down until it protruded from the small of his back, just above the kidney. Hudde let go and stepped back. Tank Top fell on his face.

Turning his gaze back to Goatee, he was back to his knees and starting to rise. He appeared to want to get to a desk just out of arm's length. Like he had been heavily drinking, Goatee staggered behind the desk. He was used to being in charge and began speaking-in Spanish.

Hudde told him, "English."

"Oh, English. Did you come for the American girl?" Goatee was beginning to feel strength come back to his legs. His hands hung before him, shaking, and he tried desperately to get control. Goatee was very used to violence that he directed at others; he was not used to violence being done to him.

"Where is she?"

"She is fine. She is downstairs… you can have her." Goatee looked at the skull face.

"I know." was Hudde's only response.

"Do you know who I work for?" A weak sounding veiled threat.

Hudde looked at a black duffle bag filled with cash in the corner, and Goatee took that moment to reach for a handgun in the front right drawer of the desk. Hudde was fully expecting something like this, and he grabbed the offending arm pulling it down first and turning the wrist over, Hudde stepped over and snapped Goatee's elbow across his knee.

Goatee dropped to his knees, screaming in pain. "Take the money, take the drugs and the girls, and please just leave me alone!" Goatee pleaded.

Gordan stepped up to Goatee. "I have killed your friends. I will take anything I want from here, and I am going to kill you for threatening my girlfriend."

Goatee looked up, momentarily defiant. "The Cowboy will kill you!" Goatee screamed out, spittle flying from his mouth.

Hudde pulled off the skull balaclava and looked down at the man at his feet.

"It's a free world. He can try."

He reached down and placed both of his big hands around the throat of Goatee. He pulled him to his feet at the same time his hands began to squeeze. Tendons and ligament in Hudde's arms pulled his fingers and thumbs together, hands crushing everything between them. Tendons, ligaments, and cartilage in Goatee's neck snapped and crushed, and he died, dropping to the floor like the trash he was.

Gordan stepped over Tank Top and headed downstairs. He walked to the back. There were two padlocked plain wooden doors. He found an oversized screwdriver and worked off the hasp on the first door. Before opening the door, he pulled the balaclava back down over his face. The blonde from earlier in the night cowered in a corner. Not much larger than four feet by eight feet, she was sitting near a bucket and a sleeping bag on the floor; she looked up and screamed.

"I'm the cavalry" Hudde said. "You want to get out of here?"

"Yes, oh yes! Hell, yes!" she said.

Hudde stepped out and yanked off the hasp on the next room. It was slightly larger. Two young women were lying on dirty mattresses on each side of the room; it smelled of sweat and urine.

"Freedom?" Hudde asked.

Neither of the girls reacted. The blonde behind Hudde said, "I know Spanish," and she began talking with the two girls. After several moments, she turned to Hudde. "They have been here for days, given drugs and forced to perform sex."

Hudde reached up and rubbed his chin through the mask. "Alright. You are all safe now. Please sit here for a moment. I will be back to help you. OK?"

The blonde translated and turned back to Hudde. "Thank you," she said.

Hudde turned and headed upstairs. He brought down a duffle bag full of cash and took it outside to the Honda. He started the car up and pulled up next to the Chevy out in front of the door. He dragged Rat into the building and piled him onto "Bull." He called back, "Can any of you drive a stick shift?"

"Yes," the blonde replied.

"OK. Come forward to the front now."

The girls came forward slowly, scared of what might be happening; one began whimpering when they came upon the dead bodies.

"That is why you are safe now," Hudde stated flatly.

The two Mexican girls spoke briefly; one stepped up and kicked "Bull" in the face, spitting on him as they passed.

Hudde smiled, knowing that she would turn out OK. He led them to the Honda; he showed them the cash and took the bag of drugs, throwing it inside the building.

"Listen: Go to one of the resorts, and get ahold of your families. Get a room if you have to. Do not go off on your own. You, especially, American girl, will be not safe until you are out of the country."

There was some Spanish banter, and then the blonde turned to him and said, "We thank you."

"You can thank me by taking your time getting to the resorts."

He turned and headed back inside; he grabbed several bottles of alcohol and headed back up the stairs. He had noticed a short ladder to a roof hatch in Goatee's office. He climbed the ladder and poked his head and shoulders out the hatch. He observed that there was a direct route to the building to the North and then the alley behind it leading to his vehicle. With two of the bottles, he made Molotov cocktails with a piece of Goatee's shirt. The other bottles he poured all over the bodies and the walls. He found a lighter on the desk and lit the first bottle. Stepping onto the steel walkway, he threw it at the far corner of the first floor. Blue and yellow flames shot out quickly, and Hudde returned to the roof. Looking down into the hatch, he lit the other bottle and threw it back into the office. Hudde turned and ran, jumping the eight feet between buildings easily. He ran to the back corner of this building and climbed down to the alley below.

In ten minutes, he was already heading North to his house closer to the coast. In twenty minutes, he was in his bathroom using superglue to close the cut over his left eye. He was in the shower when Isabella padded in and asked him how this evening went.

"I'll be out, and we can talk about it," was all he said in response.

"What!? Nothing about how I should come in there to find out?" she asked. She suddenly noticed that the clothing he had on the night before was not strewn about the floor but in a paper bag. There was a couple of bloody gauze bandages on the counter. She ran into the shower.

"Gordan, are you alright?"

"Well, that's one way I can get you in the shower" he noted.

"I'm serious — you were bleeding." He was warmed by the obvious concern. She made him turn around, and she inspected him.

"Just a small cut over my eye," he said and showed her. "I'll live." He tried to smile reassuringly at her. "I'm done. How about coffee and breakfast, and I will fill you in."

He came out and dried off quickly with a towel, wrapping it around him when he was done. He threw out the bandages and then rolled the paper bag down, adding, "I will get rid of this in a little bit."

Over some super-black coffee, eggs, and toast, Gordan continued.

"Understand that you can live your life without ever fearing that these men will ever bother you again. Please, no matter if you and I are together or not, never speak of this to anyone. If you must confess to God, please do it here in your prayers, not to a priest. I am not joking. No one must ever know, or you will immediately be in danger again."

"OK, Gordan. I get it."

She sat quietly, looking at him. He didn't go into details, but she just couldn't believe this was the same man who'd been putty in her hands. He'd been a goofy puppy, fumbling all over himself whenever she was near, but now he somehow made this evil go away? She understood that he was a strong man, but he never seemed to take himself very seriously. He was always quick to smile and laugh. Could it be true that he stopped those men all by himself? She swore to him her silence and then told him she needed to go to work.

He was a little worried that she looked at him a little differently this morning. But she was safe, and nothing else mattered.

Chapter Thirty-Three

"You bought a fucking submarine!" Cruz blurted out.

"Fuck Crockett and Tubbs! Yes, I have a submarine." Morales was grinning ear to ear.

They climbed the conning tower and looked over the sub and surrounding concrete pier. A miniature railway ran the length of the pier and headed to two large rolling doors at the back of the facility. A crane that appeared to have about a forty-foot reach was on the rails; Cruz could see where an operator would sit at the controls. Pipes ran to the back end of the pier, and stiff hoses lay alongside.

"That would be the diesel fuel lines." Morales saw that the men were taking in this amazing site. "This is a Russian-made model from the Cold War era, a Quebec class, but well kept and maintained by the Chinese, from whom I purchased it and the expertise to train our men."

Morales held both his arms into the air and turned a full 360 degrees:

"An amazing sight, is it not?"

"Do you have torpedoes?" Campos asked.

"No, there is no need for such. The Americans don't patrol the Gulf for subs, and they look for idiots in small craft with their Coast Guard. They wouldn't know what to do with a submarine if they saw it."

"My Lord," Cruz suddenly said. "How much weight in product can you fill this thing with?"

"Ha, ha, ha!" Morales did a small jig atop the tower like something from *Fiddler on the Roof*. "Now you see my genius! One successful trip a month will equal everything you do for six months, Adrian." He continued to laugh and spin both arms above his head.

Chapter
Thirty-Four

Isabella Santiago stood at the end of the bar, looking up at the news playing on the TV overhead. She was feeling lightheaded as she learned some details not shared by Gordan earlier.

"You don't look well, my dear." The assistant manager pushed her to a stool.

A local anchor was talking to the fire chief, who was praising his men and the good fortune that only two buildings burned in what they thought was an abandoned area. He noted that four badly burned bodies had been found and that the police would be investigating — it did not appear, after a preliminary review that they had been killed by fire. Next, a police captain said that he believed this had something to do with gang violence and the three women who had been found at a local hotel right down the street.

"Maybe you should go home, Isabella. Here, have some water. You are white as a ghost." Her manager was sincerely concerned.

"You know, I think I should go." Isabella walked out.

◆ ◆ ◆

Gordan opened one eye and saw Isabella standing over him, still in her work outfit.

"My God, did I sleep that long?"

"I don't know what to think; you didn't tell me anything this morning. You did all those things they said on the news?"

"I made the news?" He sat up, rubbing his head.

Isabella turned on the TV, finding the local channel; a soap opera was on. She muted the volume, put her hands on her hips, turned, and looked at him.

Hudde couldn't discern what the attitude was; neither could Isabella at the moment.

She sat at the end of the bed, her back to Gordan. "You saved a girl?"

"Nope, I saved three girls. They were kidnapping them from some kind of party or bar scene and then doping them up and pimping them out, from what I could tell." He lay back and folded his arms behind his head, just waiting for the follow-up questions.

"That's what they said they would do to me," she said, almost to herself.

"I know — not anymore."

"You burned four men?" She placed her hand to her throat.

"No. I burned up four dead bodies."

"That you killed?" She looked at her feet.

"Yes."

"'The Bull'?"

"Gone."

"Goatee?"

"No longer with us."

"Tank Top?"

"Deceased."

"And one other?"

"I called him 'Rat'; emphasis on 'called.'" Hudde paused. She wasn't judging him; she was just processing the info. "I found a spot and burned up my clothes. Nothing will come back to you or me, and it probably will get little attention other than trying to figure out which rival gang did it."

"That's what the police said on TV." She turned now and walked to the middle of the bed, sitting closer to him. She reached out and ran a petite finger across his brow and the bandage over his left eye. She stopped her hand on his cheek and studied his face. He smiled up at her and reached up, rubbing the back of her arm.

"Isabella, everything is alright. You are safe, and the world is a better place." He grabbed her hand, slid it to his mouth, and kissed it gently.

She put her other hand up to her face. Covering her mouth, she began to cry. "You cried looking at sick puppies?! How could the man I love be capable of such a thing?"

Gordan noted that she said she loved him but chose to ignore it right now. He sat up and wrapped both arms around her. "Nothing could stop me from trying to keep you safe; we talked, and I saw no other viable option."

"I know." Those arms about her felt a little different now; still a safe place for her and yet… dangerous. She let her head drop down, resting on one of his oversized biceps. "I know."

Chapter Thirty-Five

Miguel Lopez was walking the stairs to the third-floor "office" of "The Cowboy" Gonzales. He had seen the news and had no illusions that this would be a comfortable conversation. Lopez already had men driving to Mazatlán to find out what the police knew about the loss to The Cowboy's people and operation there. He stepped into the glass-enclosed office and observed Gonzales standing, looking out the window, as he often did when he appeared to be thinking.

Gonzales saw Lopez's reflection in the thick window. He turned to him and pointed to a bottle of tequila.

"If you tell me that this is the work of Morales, then I will kill them all myself."

Lopez was shocked that Gonzales wasn't yelling, and then he was surprised that this scared him more than usual.

"Boss, I have a team of men on the road now. I just can't guess what the fuck happened." He poured himself a drink and offered the bottle to Gonzales, who declined. "Mazatlán is an area with no opposing gangs; we have no history of any rivals there."

"Which is exactly why I believe this to be Morales. That bastard wants to drive home that we aren't safe in our own territory." Gonzales was using his glass to drive home his point, liquid nearly splashing over each time he accentuated a point. "He is trying to force me to take a cash offer or pay through these attacks."

"My men will know more tomorrow, Cowboy. Until then I would…"

Gonzales interrupted: "You should prepare for war is what you should do. We will attack that bastard with such ferocity that he will beg us for an end to hostilities."

Gonzales didn't even raise his voice; he turned and returned to staring out the window.

Lopez knew this conversation was over. He just said "We will" as he left the office and headed down both flights of stairs and out to his vehicle.

Chapter Thirty-Six

Gordan couldn't help but notice that Isabella seemed to take some extra shifts and was working long hours at the shelter. He understood that she would need time to full comprehend what had happened over the last few weeks. He did not ask anything out of the ordinary and did not broach the subject. If she had an issue she wished to discuss with him, she would find him.

He used this time to run the beach and hang out at the scuba shop, looking for more adventures on the high sea with Cristova.

One night, Hudde lay alone on his bed, looking up at the ceiling. Just when he was beginning to think that maybe they had crossed some kind of line that Isabella could not come back from, there was the sound of an engine and then a knock at his door.

Hudde padded quietly to the window and looked out, observing Isabella's Jeep parked out front. He opened the door.

She stood before him in a rain slick, holding it tightly up around her throat. Her hair was wavy and wild about her face.

Hudde couldn't tell you what a woman did with make-up, but he could see she that had extra-accentuated her eyes and that her lips were a deep red. He took time to notice that her tone and tanned legs were visible running out from under the bright yellow coat. They looked shiny and smooth, down to a pair of very-high-heeled white shoes.

Hudde whistled. "Wow! I was just thinking about my girlfriend."

"Your girlfriend left you alone when maybe you needed her most," Isabella said. "I am here to make it up to you." She slipped the slicker off her shoulders and stood before him in a white piece of lingerie.

Hudde always had confused a teddy and a baby-doll. Whatever. She was radiant in the nearly sheer, white flowing garment.

"*Oh*, my Lord!" Gordan started to say more, but she reached up and placed a finger across his lips.

"No more talking." She slipped past him, dropping the coat on the floor as she went by.

He locked the door and saw her drag her hand across the wall as she disappeared into the bedroom.

There was no talking.

The sun came up on a perfect world, according to Gordan Hudde; Isabella looked up through black thick locks.

"Lunch at Mama's today." Her eyes narrowed.

"Yeah — that sounds great; why the concern?" He was now sitting up in bed, leaning back against the headboard.

"I need to get into the bathroom, which means getting past you while I'm naked." She slapped his arm.

"Impossible task," Hudde said. "You'll need reinforcements, maybe an air campaign."

She frowned at him. "What?"

"Never mind — military humor. OK, I'll close my eyes"

"OK." She slipped out of bed and walked around the foot toward the bathroom. She caught him peeking and wagged a disapproving finger at him.

Chapter
Thirty-Seven

Carlos Morales was looking at one of his lieutenants in a manner that should have concerned him. "I had nothing to do with the unpleasantness in Mazatlán, and if The Cowboy doesn't believe it, I don't care. If he is paying you to ask, by all means let them know: I don't know about this and don't care." He looked across the table. "And if he is paying you, I suggest you stay on the West coast."

"No, no *Jefe*. It is just information I have heard on the street." The lieutenant bowed down in deference.

Morales dismissed him with a wave of his hand and called out for Marco Vargas to enter his office.

"Yes, sir." Vargas was quick to stand before him.

"Marco, you don't know anything about the incident in Mazatlán, do you?"

"No, Carlos. We didn't have anything to do with this. I haven't heard anyone bragging so far. It's probably some local beef Gonzales isn't even aware of; I can't imagine that bastard is able to get anyone dedicated to him."

"Even so, we need to be cautious. I haven't heard anything regarding our Phoenix trip."

"I'll fix this for you forever, *El Jefe* — just say the word."
Vargas flexed his shoulders.

"Of this I have no doubt, my friend. But we will wait,
for now; in the meantime, I need to you to reach out to the
Secretariat of the Navy. I hear he is frowning on my having
a submarine." He smiled up at Vargas, tapping on the desk
before him. "Find out if this is just a play for more money or if
there are concerns we do not know about yet."

"I will find out."

Chapter Thirty-Eight

Hudde looked over Gabriela Santiago's shoulder at the onions and peppers steaming in a frying pan.

"That smells delicious!" He took a swig of the beer in his right hand and walked past Isabella, sitting at the kitchen table. He allowed his left hand to run over her shoulder as he walked out to the back patio.

"Some men have insatiable appetites," Gabriela said over her shoulder at her daughter.

"That one sure does!" Isabella giggled at her own joke. She pulled her right leg up to her chest and hugged it, laying her head onto her own thigh. She closed her eyes; she was a good kind of sleepy today.

"So, everything is good?" Gabriela looked over at her daughter. She could see that she was very happy, and, therefore, so was she.

"I don't think it can get better, Mama. I am afraid that it can't be so good."

"Just enjoy it, baby. That's the way life is sometimes. Best enjoy the good moments when they are happening, and then be able to think back fondly about them when times are bad.

That's what keeps you going through those difficult times." She handed the fork to Isabella and said, "I'll go see what that man of yours is doing."

She found him looking about the desert scrub in her back yard.

"Looking for my 'dog' because I don't ever know when he will show up." She stood next to Gordan and slipped her arm around his waist.

"I always wanted a big dog or maybe two," Gordan said wistfully, looking down at Gabriela and smiling.

She pulled at his arm, and he bent at the waist so that she could whisper to him. "Somebody is in love!" she said quietly.

He was obviously so happy and proud that he had earned her daughter's love that Gabriela was gushing with joy.

"I want to take her away for a while and ask her to marry me. I just need her to know that is how serious my feelings are for her." He looked deeply into Gabriela's eyes. "I don't care if we marry quickly or if she needs time, but she just has to know that this is real for me."

"Well, that will do it, son. I don't know what she will say, if that's what you're asking. But she will know you're serious." She started to turn back into the house but spun back and hugged him. "I think it will be 'Yes,'" she said into his chest.

"Hey! What are you two up to out here?" Isabella suddenly appeared on the patio. "You better watch out, Mama. He said he would ask you out if I dumped him."

"I may say 'Yes' if you dump this man!" Gabriela grabbed Gordan's ass as she went back to the house, and she growled lustfully.

"Mama!" Isabella blushed for her.

Gabriela slapped Isabella's bottom as she headed past her on her way back to the kitchen.

Isabella walked up and nudged her head under Gordan's arm, much the same as Gabriela had just been standing.

"I was just suggesting that you and I take a trip and get away for a while. I was checking to make sure it was OK with her."

"So what did my Mama say?" Isabella said, looking up at him, her chin on his chest.

"It's OK with her; she admitted that she kind of liked me." He smiled down at her. Reaching down, he grabbed her hip with a big hand. Leaning into her, he kissed those big full lips; he growled a deep, low growl — hungry and feral — into her mouth.

"Do you want me?" she said, her eyes never leaving his. Her hand slid down his chest across his flat stomach, grasping his manhood through his shorts. "Oh, I think you do!" she giggled.

He reached down around her lower back and picked her up; she instinctively wrapped her legs around his waist, and his hand slid down, cupping her ass, holding her against him.

"I've wanted you every minute since the moment I first saw you."

"I thought that went away for men after they get what they want," she pointed out, from what he perceived was past experience.

"It's only gotten worse for me; I want you so bad it hurts." His other hand went into her hair at the back of her neck. He grasp a large handful and pulled it back so that her neck was exposed. "I want to be a vampire or werewolf so that I can eat you." He started biting her neck and kissing her exposed collarbone.

She giggled and started squirming in his arms so that she turned, and he was carrying her more like a child in his arms. She grabbed a handful of Gordan's beard and pulled his face close to hers. "I thought that's what you were doing last night." She licked his lips up to and across his nose.

"Come on in, kids. Let's eat!" Gabriela called out from inside.

"Put me down, you big ogre!" Isabella said and wiggled to her feet. She reached out and grasped his hand, pulling him in the direction of the back door.

"I'm gonna have to wait for a minute," he said to her.

"I'm really hungry. Why?" she asked, turning to look at him.

She followed his gaze down to his tented shorts.

"Oh, sorry," she laughed and headed into the house.

Hudde began some deep-breathing exercises, thinking about ballistics of 7.62 rounds, trying to change the current blood flow.

Chapter Thirty-Nine

Gordan opened the door to his home. As it was approaching September, he was afraid he might have to look for another place if the owners contacted him soon.

"So what do you think about getting away?" he asked Isabella as she walked under his arm and into the house.

"They would hate to have me gone as the tourist season is getting into full swing," Isabella thought out loud about the hotel.

"If you continue following your dreams about a veterinarian practice, you would have to quit anyway," Hudde pointed out.

"No, no. I want to go; I think it's a good idea." She went to the fridge and pulled out a beer. Looking over at Hudde, she held it up and raised an eyebrow.

"Yes, please" Hudde said. "Well, what would it be? Would you like to see the Statue of Liberty, or the Eiffel Tower, or the Leaning Tower of Pisa — maybe go to Disney World?"

She handed him the beer and plopped down on the other end of the couch, putting her legs up between his legs, which reached well past her hips.

Without seeming to even think about it, Hudde reached down with his free hand and began to use his thumb to massage Isabella's petite left foot.

"Well? What are you thinking?" Hudde asked.

Isabella allowed her head to fall back to the armrest and momentarily closed her eyes; she let out a tiny moan. "You can do that forever," she said.

"Just that?" he said playfully.

"Well, for now," she sighed.

"Come on. Where are we going?" he asked.

"I always wanted to go see the pyramids?" she said, with a hint of a question.

"I wouldn't feel right taking you to Egypt. It isn't safe right now for tourists."

"I mean the ones right here — and maybe Machu Picchu. Have you ever been there?"

"Nope. Can't say I have. I'm sorry. I don't know where the pyramids and other sites are, but Peru is where Machu Picchu is — right?" he said.

She looked a little disapprovingly at him. "Have you ever heard of the Internet?"

"Ha, ha!" His sarcasm couldn't be missed. "OK. That sounds interesting to me. Next week?"

"Sure," she said, still enjoying his hand on her foot.

He set his beer on the floor and really began giving a foot message with both hands, enjoying the obvious effect this was having on her. She drained the rest of her beer, setting the empty nonchalantly on the floor, and slid down, closing her eyes and relaxing completely. Hudde pulled up on his left leg, which was the inside leg, giving her additional room on her end of the couch.

"Maybe I should have invested in a bigger couch," he said out loud.

"Nope. This is perfect," she cooed.

He stopped working on the left foot and reached down and grasped her right ankle, allowing her left foot to rest between his legs. He began focusing on this foot, allowing his hands to travel up her calf as well, which caused him to pull her further toward him. He also noticed that this caused her shorts to ride up at an angle. Now that her legs were further spread, the crotch of her panties was visible. He began kissing the bottom of her foot, and she giggled and laughed, saying, "Ooh — that tickles!"

This caused two unexpected actions to take place: Her panties now were wedged firmly between her sex, and her writhing actions were so sexy, he was as hard as a rock — her left foot began sliding up and down the length of him.

"Oooh, somebody is happy!" she exclaimed, peeking out from under her black locks.

"Maybe he's angry at how you treated him this afternoon," Gordan whispered.

"What are you looking at?" she said, knowing full well that her baggy shorts had slid over, exposing herself to him. She stopped rubbing her foot over him and slid that foot over to the floor while he still held her other foot to his face, kissing her toes.

She reached down, running a finger run along her thigh and across her sex. She allowed her hand to go under her t-shirt and began messaging a large breast. "Somebody is a bad, bad boy." She smiled as she arched her back and sighed, never allowing her eyes to leave his.

"You haven't seen anything yet," he said.

She began a slow, rhythmic thrusting of her pelvis, her other hand returning to her own crotch.

"You are a bad girl!" Hudde said louder than he intended.

"Are you going to punish me?" she said, smiling wickedly.

"Yes, I am." He stood and began to lose his clothes.

"Hard?" she asked.

"Very! You are going to beg me to stop!" He reached down and grabbed a handful of that lustrous hair, pulling her to her knees, pushing her head over the top of the sofa.

"Prove it!"

Chapter Forty

Approximately 100 miles south of Mazatlán, about 20 minutes past the small town of Teacapan, Miguel Lopez stopped the Humvee when they ran out of road at a beach on the Pacific. Eduardo Gonzales jumped out of the passenger side and surveyed the area.

"You are fairly sure this is the spot?" he asked Lopez.

"Eh, Cowboy. I have asked everyone and placed a bounty on information about other cartel organizations; this is all I have come up with." He shrugged his shoulders and threw up his hands in a moment of admitting to not having enough information.

"Why the fuck would Carlos buy property here, on the Pacific coast? He has the entire Gulf coast?" Gonzales said it out loud, but it was not a question he or Lopez could answer.

The two men walked back the way they came uphill and off the short beach. They continued upward until they were seventy-five feet above the Humvee below.

"It's a shitty beach for a tourist destination," Lopez noted.

"Yes, you are correct," The Cowboy agreed, "but look at how this area juts out from the rest of the beach, and it appears that the water deepens quickly here."

Lopez placed his hands over his sunglasses to prevent glare and looked out into the ocean; the dark blue of deeper water came almost to the beach. "For larger boats?"

"Could it be that Carlos believes he can move some operations to our coast?" The Cowboy mulled it over and began walking back to the ride. "Let's get back."

Lopez backed the Humvee up the hill, into the high grass and packed earth of the high ground. He turned the vehicle back to the East and gunned the big diesel.

"Let's stop in Mazatlán. I wish to see the building where we lost our men." The Cowboy stayed in deep thought the entire time.

Lopez had never seen The Cowboy so quiet and thoughtful. He was more used to the rants and bouts of extreme violence. This new Cowboy currently scared Lopez more. When they arrived at the burned-out buildings in Mazatlán, the sun was going down. Lopez turned the Humvee so that the headlights shone directly on the man door of the now-half-standing building. He fired up the off-road lights across the top of the Humvee that they had installed, which lit up the area brilliantly. The Cowboy dropped out of the passenger side. Gonzales walked over to the man door and looked at the door frame, still intact.

"This looks as if there was no damage, no?" Gonzales looked over at Lopez.

"No, but half the time, their doors were open; we have no history of any issues here. There was no sign of bandits. Everything but the women seemed to be here."

"Have we interviewed the women?"

"Yes. They all say they saw no one — that there was a commotion and they heard their locks removed. But they were too scared to open the doors until they smelled the fire; then no one was around."

Suddenly a police cruiser's lights and siren lit up the dead-end street. An officer jumped out the driver's-side door and pulled a service revolver, pointing it back and forth between the two men.

"Stay where you are, and show me your hands!" he screamed at them.

Lopez slowly approached the officer with his hands at shoulder level. "Do you know who that is?" he asked bitingly.

"I will shoot you both!" the officer yelled. "Stay where you are!"

"This is The Cowboy Gonzales, you fool!" Lopez couldn't believe this.

The Cowboy swept past Lopez and got into the face of the officer. "Do you work this area often?" he asked.

"Yes, this is my area," the officer responded. After a moment, he said, "I'm sorry, *El Jefe*. I did not recognize you." He began to holster his weapon.

Gonzales snatched the handgun from the officer. "Have you ever killed anyone with this weapon?"

"No, sir."

"Do you accept money from anyone else?" Gonzales was seething and speaking through clenched teeth.

"No, no. I come here and pick up money from the men here. That is all..." the officer started.

"My money, eh?" Gonzales pointed out. "Where were you the morning of the fire?"

"I was the first one here, *El Jefe*. The building was totally engulfed in flames. There was nothing I could do." The officer looked over at Lopez, searching for acceptance.

"Worthless mother-fucker!" Gonzales shot him between the eyes with his own service weapon. Red blood and pink-grey brains splattered the driver's-side back passenger window and door. The officer fell straight back. What was left of his head slapped wetly near the back tire, one eye hanging from a broken socket. Gonzales dropped the gun onto the officer's chest.

"It looks like the poor guy was so incompetent that he committed suicide."

Lopez knew this version of The Cowboy and was glad everything had returned to normal.

Gonzales jumped into the Humvee, and, when Lopez was firmly behind the wheel, he turned to him. "We are going to strike that Carlos with such ferocity that he will leave Mexico!"

He said nothing more for the entire trip home.

Chapter Forty-One

"OK."

Gordan was staring at a laptop screen.

"I think we could head to just Northeast of Mexico City to check out the pyramid and historic site there, and then we could head down near Cancun and check out the pyramid down there. Hey, this is pretty exciting — don't you think?" He turned to see if Isabella was still looking over his shoulder.

"Yes, but…" She bit her lower lip and then scrunched up her nose, making a funny face. "I kind of lied to my mom once that I went to the Pyramid of the Sun."

Gordan started to speak, but Isabella shut him down. "I also said I went to the Basilica of our Lady of Guadalupe, so maybe we could go there, too, and then I could stop feeling as bad." She raised her eyebrows high, looking for a response.

"But why…" Gordan started, but Isabella knew what would come out next.

"My girlfriends and I wanted to go to a big party, and I lied about where we were going and where we would be staying. It was a mistake, but here we are today." She continued to look at him, questioningly.

"Certainly, dear. We can revisit those places." He hit the word *"revisit"* with as much sarcasm as he could. "Now I think

Peru will be a bigger trip and take more planning, but we can start right here."

She ripped off a stream of quick Spanish that he did not understand, and then she laid a huge wet kiss on his cheek before heading to the back window and looking at a currently overcast day.

"I think stories of your youth may be much more exciting than anything I have to tell," he called out after her.

Chapter Forty-Two

Miguel Lopez stood looking out the same window as Eduardo Gonzales.

"This is everything I know." He'd just finished up with his update of current information about the Gulf cartel and the Mexican navy.

"So the question becomes: 'Why would Morales feel the need to give additional money to the Secretariat of the Navy if he already bribes him monthly?' No?" The Cowboy looked at Lopez for an answer.

"What else could it be but something to do with the property just South of here?" Lopez walked over to the Westward window and continued looking off into the distance.

"And your sources are sure that Marco Vargas will deliver that money personally, next week?"

"They are positive."

"Well, I propose that you disrupt that meeting with a message that will be heard loud and clear across Mexico. Anyone who wishes to extend their territory into my lands will not live past the planning stage." The Cowboy turned and pointed at Lopez to make his point. "Make sure it is well known that we disagree with their current direction."

"It will be well known, Cowboy, trust me. People will know your position." Lopez smiled and nodded at the Cowboy before he turned and left the third floor.

Chapter Forty-Three

The following week found Gordan and Isabella standing before the Temple of the Sun, approximately 30 miles to the Northeast of Mexico City. The September weather was holding at 75 degrees — a bit breezy, with large patches of white, fluffy clouds. It looked safe to hike to the top of the Pyramid. Gordan was looking forward to watching those black yoga pants a few steps in front of him. Her oversized football jersey (the Raiders) had probably been selected for the color scheme and hung low enough that, sometimes, it covered her behind, and it was just tight enough across her chest for one to understand that she was very shapely.

She hugged him tight, standing at the bottom of the giant structure, looking up and her arms wrapped tightly around his waist.

"You can't stand here without asking 'Why?'" she said to him.

He, too, was looking up. "The amount of manpower back then to do not just this but the others in the area." He made a sweeping gesture with his loose left arm as the other was around Isabella's back.

He looked back down at her and said, "Ready?"

"Let's go!" She began walking forward.

There were hundreds of fellow tourists walking about the area. Somewhere around fifty people were either walking up or coming down the pyramid at the moment. Two hundred feet wasn't the most monumental task for people in Gordan or Isabella's age range, and there were many elderly people in the mix. An Oriental couple here, an Italian over there — it was a really multi-ethnic mix of people interested in the historical site. The steps were chiseled out and very well kept, considering that, unlike the pyramids in the Middle East, these were cobbled from much smaller stone. There was no mystery on how the stone had been moved, but it still must have taken an amazing amount of manpower. They stopped at each of the different levels, and Isabella took pictures with her cell phone. They took their time, lingering, touching each other and enjoying each moment.

The top was slightly two-tiered. The stone was raised, and it made for the need to pay attention to each place you set your foot down. Hudde wondered out loud to Isabella what would happen if any of the elderly folks twisted an ankle up here. Isabella continued up to the pinnacle, about four feet higher than Hudde was standing. He watched her stop at the direct center and then conduct a 360-degree turn, scanning the horizon.

Just as she returned his glance, the sun came out from behind the clouds. Isabella placed her forearm across her forehead; a breeze pulled her hair back, and it danced about her face. The wind pushed the loose top across her body, and her figure was no mystery to anyone watching. She was the most beautiful thing Hudde had ever seen — like a scene from a movie with the heroine taking the breath away from every male in the audience.

He went to her and told her so.

"Tell me more." She smiled at him and then pulled his shirt until he stooped to kiss her.

"I have to tell you something," he said to her.

"OK?"

"I've told you before about traveling for the government and never feeling like I had a home or that I ever stopped to…" he searched for the words "…smell the roses."

"Yes, Gordan. I understand." She frowned sad at his story.

"Don't frown." He smiled down at her and rubbed a thumb across her raised brow. "I've never been happier, and it's fitting that we are here, because you are my sun. I can't wait to wake up and see that you are near me, and I am so impatient if you go to work. I can't imagine a world without you."

Isabella cocked her head to the side and continued to look at him questioningly.

He reached into his pocket and then dropped to a knee. "Isabella, I think we make an incredible team, and I don't want to do it without you. Would you marry me?"

While the crowd was thinner here at the top, some people were paying attention, and they had a small audience.

"Forget about everything else except the way you feel and how we are when we're together." He looked up at her, not wanting to show his growing concern.

She took the ring and looked at it and then at him. It was a small moment for her, an eternity for him.

"Oh, my God, Gordan! I'm sorry — of course!" She kissed him, and their lips remained together as he stood. He picked her up, and she wrapped her legs around him when he did.

"I'll admit that I've thought about it," she said, "but you caught me a little off guard." She nuzzled into his neck and whispered into his ear, "You need to take me somewhere and make love to me right now."

He set her on her feet and took her hand, leading the way. People cheered nearby when they understood she'd said, "Yes."

"Wait, Gordan." Isabella suddenly pulled back on his hand. She approached another young couple and spoke. Handing them her phone, she returned and put an arm around Hudde. "Let's get a picture"

They posed for a moment, and the young woman returned Isabella's phone to her. Hudde heard her say, "Congratulations."

Isabella, grinning ear to ear, hugged him again before turning and leading him off the pyramid.

Chapter Forty-Four

The Mexico City Hilton was less than an hour away, and Gordan had already set up a two-day stay there in case the plans changed at all. The entire time he was driving the rental from the historic site to the heart of the city, Isabella stayed on the phone, speaking first to her mom and then emailing some of her girlfriends. While she mostly spoke in Spanish, he understood this was all happy talk, and her joy brought an additional happiness to him that he had no idea would permeate his own spirit. He enjoyed looking over at her while she obviously was speaking about their relationship to someone else, and she eyed him back and smiled slyly back at him. He placed a big hand onto her thigh, and she placed her small hand on top of his, pulling it up into her crotch, where he could feel her warmth. He got the idea, and he found this to be a special kind of driving distraction that he'd never trained for in the agency. She kept her hand over his and continued to "help" him find the right places that needed attention.

Gordan tried to focus on the road and getting them safely to the hotel. She began to almost purr, and she leaned into his strong fingers, her hair cascading across his arm. She placed her forehead onto his triceps and bit into his elbow; she said his name softly over and over before breathing out deeply and sitting back in her seat.

She took his hand and held it with both her own little hands. "Tell me what you thought the first time you saw me."

"You were easily the most beautiful woman I had ever seen," he said.

She began to lick his fingers, allowing them next to slowly push past her lips; her tongue darted out to lick them first.

"More," she requested.

"I thought you should be in movies or, at a minimum, maybe a weather girl on TV — you know: They always find attractive women for that." He was afraid to take his eyes off the road.

"Uh huh…and…" She took his thumb into her mouth; she squirmed forward and placed her hand into his lap.

"I wanted to ask you out, but I was afraid that you would be tired of vacationers bothering you."

"Wow! Somebody is dying to get out!" she whispered into his ear.

They pulled up to the circular drive of the hotel, and she giggled, jumping right out. Gordan found an excuse to fidget in the car for a few minutes before popping the trunk, getting out, and giving the valet a tip. He untucked his shirt to hide the obvious.

Isabella stood near the doorman with her hands together and between her legs. She twisted back and forth, her head tilted down while she looked up through dark locks. She was acting like an impatient young girl but looked like the sexiest thing Gordan had ever seen. The hotel staff was paying full attention.

"What's taking you so long, honey?" she said, smiling devilishly.

"The door was broken or stuck," he said, playing along.

Gordan had requested a suite, and it was large and luxurious, a giant king bed in the middle of the room; floor-to-ceiling windows gave them a great view if they were interested. The bellhop pulled the dolly near the door and placed their bags onto the floor; Gordan turned and gave him a tip. The kid turned for one last look before closing the door.

"OK. I'm hungry," she said.

"Oh, no. You need to finish what you started, ya smart ass!" Gordan started toward her.

"Wait" she said using both hands to push against his stomach as he continued walking toward her. Her feet slid across the carpet, pushing her back to the bed. "How about we meet in the middle?" She grabbed his belt and began to loosen it up. "I get a snack, and you get happy." She started pulling his pants over his hips as she sat back onto the high bed.

They ended up ordering room service.

At about 0620am, Gordan was lying on his back, arms folded behind his head; he was awake and thinking. Isabella rolled over. Now facing him, she looked up at him.

"Is everything OK?" She momentarily propped herself up onto her elbows.

"I think that that's the problem." He brushed the hair from her face. "It's not just the absence of problems — it's that

everything is perfect; I've never experienced anything like it."
He smiled at her. "I can't believe a lug like me is with a woman
like you."

"Wake me up in a little bit, and I'll prove it" she said, lying
back down, her head on his chest. She draped a leg across
his. She was making little "cooing" noises in just a minute,
and he knew she was back under.

He didn't know how, after so many years of life, he could
find so much happiness.

Chapter Forty-Five

Miguel Lopez inspected his soldiers one by one, making sure each was sure of his weapon and the target. Six two-man teams were trained, practiced, and ready to go.

Marco Vargas inspected the briefcase full of money. Carlos Morales was on the phone with him now, explaining that this was the final additional sum of money the Secretariat of the Navy was going to see. Vargas understood.

Chapter Forty-Six

"We could head to the States, where I have to do something with my townhouse — at a minimum, throw out everything in my fridge." Gordan walked into the bathroom, where Isabella was finishing up her hair and makeup. "You need to decide where we are going to live anyway. We should see a bit of the world before we make up our minds." He leaned against the door frame while speaking.

Isabella was turning her face from one side to the other, inspecting her work on her eyes. "I have to see the church, and we might as well continue to the Mayan ruins, as you planned. We can discuss the other stuff while we take the drive, right?" She started to pack up her makeup, satisfied she was done.

"OK, then — to the Lady of Guadalupe it is." He turned, heading back to his map on the coffee table near the window. He was old fashioned and didn't believe in using GPS devices. His duffle bag was packed and ready to go; she needed to finish packing up two larger bags.

She came out of the bathroom and announced she was done. She had on a loose-fitting white blouse that hung off her shoulders a little and seemed very tame and respectable. Her slacks were black and baggy, and she had some black flats that looked very comfortable and acceptable for a little walking.

"Look at you. Put on a pair of glasses, and you would pass for a librarian." He reached up and ran his hand over his beard a couple of times and then grunted. "And I think we would have to stay another hour." He smiled.

"Men: Food and sex, and nothing else." She reached high and smacked him upside the head with her palm as she walked to the door. "Are you finally ready?"

"Yes, dear," he said sarcastically.

Their car was ready, and the young man was loading the luggage into the trunk. Gordan handed out the proper tips and looked up at the sky. Mixes of white and grey clouds were racing across the sky, the morning sun unable to break through but for a few moments here and there. The wind seemed to be a steady brisk breeze; Hudde thought that they would be driving in rain after lunch for sure.

The valet shut the door for Isabella, and Hudde stood at the passenger side, looking down through the window for an extra moment, taking in Isabella's beauty for an instant without her knowing. The sun broke out; she closed her eyes and lifted her face to the warmth. When the sun disappeared, she opened her eyes and turned to look at Gordan, staring down and smiling at her. She just winked and looked back down at her lap and the map Gordan had given her. Gordan put his palm out and spread his hand flat against the window for a moment before getting into the car himself.

Hudde felt he was a good driver but was frustrated at the amount of one-way streets they came across in Mexico City. They ended up a block south and west of the Basilica of our Lady of Guadalupe. Where Hudde had wanted to turn North, the traffic flowed one way South.

He growled out loud, yanking the wheel to the right, and headed South, thinking that he could do a big circle, landing them closer. Isabella leaned forward as he made the right and looked left; she reached out and placed a small hand on his forearm

"Honey, it's right there. I can see it. Go ahead and pull over. We're young — we can walk." She smiled at him, knowing he was growing frustrated. "It's OK." She gripped his forearm hard enough that he knew she was there.

Gordan found a place to his right where there was parking on the street. On the East side of the street, there was no parking, and a large building that had that big-concrete-and-official look took up an entire block. He pulled over and took a deep breath. "I really hate cities." He looked over at her. "I hope you will continue to enjoy country life?"

"I've never wanted anything else," she said and got out of the rental car.

Gordan climbed out, and they headed North upon a well-kept and large sidewalk. There were shops all along the West side of the street — one-story and two-story buildings painted in many colors. Gordan figured each was trying to get the tourist attention, and it made the street seem festive. They were going to need to cross the street and continue. Another block North, they took a moment and jogged across the three lanes. Getting to the East side, they turned North again, and Hudde felt a large raindrop splatter across his forehead. He looked up; the clouds had thickened, and further West, it appeared ominous. In the Army, this was liquid sunshine, and he chose to ignore it until Isabella suddenly pulled on his arm.

"I just felt a raindrop." She looked up at him. She turned on the charm, placing her hands against his chest, she leaned into him, creating contact from thigh to stomach. "Honey, would you go get the umbrella?"

He looked back at the five hundred yards they had already traveled and then back up at the clouds.

"I think this top will just about be transparent if it gets sopped," she said. She smiled an evil little grin.

"I'd enjoy that," he said but turned and started back to the rental car.

"Thank you, honey!" she called out sweetly after him.

He took big strides and walked quickly. He really didn't want her to get wet.

She continued walking toward the North, stopping near the next intersection, looking back and waiting for Gordan to catch up. A few more drops hit her; they were big and felt cool. The wind started gusting a little more, and she thought maybe they had picked the wrong day for a sightseeing trip.

A large dark Mercedes slowed and stopped just fifteen feet from where Isabella was standing; it sat idling for a moment. A large black Cadillac Escalade parked directly behind it moments later. Two men climbed from the Cadillac's back seats — one with a long raincoat, which was not odd at all to Isabella — and the other with a large briefcase. Isabella took note that it was leather and looked somewhat like saddlebags. She guessed that it was a very expensive piece of luggage.

Two men got out of the Mercedes and met with the other two, who were already standing near Isabella. They were close enough that Isabella could hear the voices but could not make out the words in the wind. They stood very close together, and Isabella felt that these were important men about to have a meeting in the federal building just behind her.

A block away to the North, Miguel Lopez called out on a radio, "Now!"

Gordan didn't see the umbrella in the trunk; he went around and unlocked the driver's-side door. He leaned in and saw the shiny, pointy end of the umbrella sticking out from under the passenger seat in the back. He reached and grabbed the umbrella and began wrestling to get it out from under the seat. It was hung up on the seat-adjusting mechanisms, and he leaned further into the car, finally yanking it free.

It was a natural move for him as he reached back with his left hand, looking up a little and to the right, out the back window. He'd spent his entire adult life training and being careful.

Electricity shot through his body when he saw men on the roof, one of whom held an RPG-7, he was sure.

Charging up the center of the street back toward Isabella, Hudde stole a glance up and to the left to the rooftops. He observed men on several roofs all along the street.

Gordan didn't realize that he was carrying the umbrella like a rifle across his body as he ran, yelling for Isabella. The wind and her curiosity of the meeting taking place near her left, Isabella did not hear Gordan bellowing until both she and the man in the raincoat heard him. The man knelt and pulled an Uzi from under his arm, letting loose with a volley of rounds at the big man charging them. Isabella screamed and ducked. Six men on roofs across the street fired their RPGs at the two vehicles just fifty to one hundred yards away. None of them were going to miss by much.

Gordan felt stinging pain shooting up his entire left side and heard the familiar snapping of rounds going past his head. He began to stumble now, about seventy yards from Isabella. He heard the sound of the RPGs firing. He fell forward onto his face, as his left side was no longer keeping up with his right. The first blast went off, and he tried to get to his feet and look up.

That's when the lights went out for him.

Chapter Forty-Seven

Gordan was able to lift his left eyelid, but even this slight movement caused him pain; he realized he was in a hospital bed. He was not on a respirator. That was a good sign.

His left arm was bandaged near the shoulder. He tried to pick up his right arm, and he realized that that arm was attached to an IV. He began to click the nurse's call button that his right hand had found nearby. His head was wrapped, covering his right eye. He needed to find out if Isabella was OK.

He didn't hear her come in. Suddenly a nurse was standing at the foot of his bed, reading a chart. He tried to speak but only a hoarse, crackling noise escaped his lips.

"Oh, you are awake. The doctor will be pleased," she said.

His right thumb still clicked away at the call button, and the nurse looked into his one eye.

"I'm glad you found the morphine drip, but you can only get so much per hour." She laid her hand over his.

He fought his left eye closing, but lost.

Suddenly it was light. A doctor hovered over him, inspecting the bandages around his face and head.

"I'm the doctor who operated on your eye socket. Dr. Esteban Perez."

"Isabella?" Hudde couldn't make his voice work.

"The doctor who took care of the bullet wounds said you were very lucky that nothing found any vital organs and that you should be fine." Perez stopped momentarily to look into Gordan's left eye with a small flashlight. "I think you will be 100% in three months or so." He smiled, happy with his work.

"Isabella?" Gordan tried again.

The doctor turned, and Gordan could hear water and ice being poured into a cup. When the doctor turned back to Gordan, he offered a straw to him to drink.

"Go slow, sir; you haven't had anything for more than ten days. When you prove you can hold it down, we will remove the IV."

"Girl." Hudde got the word out so that it could be understood.

"I'm sorry," the doctor said. "I'm not aware of any female survivors of this terrorist attack." He paused, placing a gentle hand on Gordan's chest. "I am sorry if there was a woman with you, but we have only one other male who survived the incident." He started to walk away but turned back. "Speaking of other men, there is a man waiting for you ever since they found out you were awake. I believe he is from your embassy."

Gordan fought the urge to close his eye. A tall, thin man in a dark suit entered the room and approached quietly.

"Water," Gordan croaked out.

The American grabbed the cup and offered the straw to Gordan; he took what felt like a long pull and allowed his head to sink back into the pillow. The cool water felt hot across the back of Gordan's throat.

"I'm Peter Buryshkin, US diplomatic attaché. The directors been busting my balls for a week to figure out what you were doing down here."

"Isabella Santiago," Gordan said, rather forcefully; it surprised even him.

"What?" Buryshkin was right over him. He had to have heard.

"A woman was with me?" Gordan questioned.

"We have twelve dead, four cartel guys, three government officials, two civilian men, two civilian women, and one child. You and another male civilian were the only survivors. If somebody belonged to you, I'm sorry. Our big question is: 'Why you were the only one shot?'"

Gordan closed his eye and cried, before falling back to sleep.

When he next opened his eye, it was dark. No light came in from behind the hospital blinds. Gordan made sure he could reach the cup off to his left and that it still had water in it. Then he tore the IV from his right arm.

The next morning when he opened his eye, there was light and pain — a headache that was beyond anything he ever had before. The light caused pain, sound too, but he was less groggy without the painkillers.

"Hey, I never got an answer yesterday." Peter Buryshkin hovered over him.

"Don't tell me you've been babysitting all night? Not official business. Actually, I just got engaged." Gordan opened the eye to see Buryshkin's response.

"Oh, brother. Sorry, man. Obviously nobody in the States knows anything about it, but they want to get you back and give you a once-over from our medical staffs — to make sure you got put back together right."

"Cartel," Gordan said.

Buryshkin turned and stood close over Hudde. "Shut the fuck up," he said slowly and enunciated each word as if it would stand alone. "I understand you are some kind of war hero and all, but I'm telling you that the cartel boys would have their own air force bomb this entire hospital down to rubble just to shut you up, if that's what they wanted." He placed a hand on Gordan's chest, much like the doctor had before, but this had none of the caring feeling. "For your own good, man: Never say that out loud to anyone. Let's just get you the fuck out of here."

"Why don't you guys do something?" Gordan asked.

"What are you, some kind of Boy Scout? Are you a virgin, too? These people don't give a fuck about anything or anybody. The only way anyone will ever make a difference is to kill them all or just take over the business ourselves." He shook his head. "Look, I'm sorry. Let's get you out of here ASAP." He patted Hudde's chest a couple of times. "Oh, yeah: There's a good-looking MILF out there wanting to see you." He said as he exited the room.

Gabriela Santiago came in. "Oh, my poor boy," she cried.

"I'm sorry, Gabriela. I let you all down." His tears began to flow again.

"No, no, my son. How could you ever have suspected anything? Of course, you have done nothing wrong." She didn't bother wiping her tears, and they fell on Hudde's left arm. She did dab at her nose with a tissue. "My daughter was so happy — never forget that. In her last call, she said that the two of you would give me beautiful grand-babies!" She put her hand up to her mouth and sobbed and took a couple of deep breaths.

Gordan reached for her arm with his left hand, and he squeezed. He wanted to be strong for her, but he had never felt such a loss before.

"Gordan, nothing can be done for Isabella now. She is at peace. But for you and me, something should be done to the men who did this."

"Gabriela," Hudde whispered, and she leaned closer. "The men who did this had something to do with the drug cartels."

"So, do they get a pass?" She frowned down at him.

"No, it's just that both our countries have tried to take them on for thirty-plus years, and I don't think they have had any success." He hadn't let go of her arm "Much of your country is like a war zone."

She leaned in even closer, until he could feel her hot breath on the side of his face.

"I know what you did to those gangsters who threatened Isabella a couple months back," she whispered.

"What?" Gordan was having a difficult time getting his one eye to focus on her face so close.

"I told her you were a dangerous man the first time we met, Gordan Hudde. I told her to leave you be, but she fell in love, and so did you. I thought maybe it would be OK, and I think it would have been if not for this freak thing. You did love my daughter?"

"I'll never love anyone like that again." It was just a fact, and she understood it.

"She's gone. We can do nothing. But you and I still live. You can do something for us."

"Gabriela, what can one man do that our countries could not? I would want to do something, but this — this is impossible."

"Not for you — I know it. Come find me when you are done, and we will visit Isabella together." She leaned slightly forward and kissed his bandaged forehead. "Get well first." She turned and left.

Chapter
Forty-Eight

"You pig-headed stupid son-of-a-bitch! Do you know what you have done to me?" Carlos Morales yelled at Eduardo Gonzales on a seldom-heard-of *El Jefe* to *El Jefe* phone call.

"I take your call so that I can be disrespected?" The Cowboy asked.

Morales stood alone in the long conference room at his offices that he often used for meetings of his business.

"You wanted ten million dollars for the mining of your fields, for a million worth of product and a few farmers. You just cost me tens of millions of dollars, in actual cash, not made-up figures, you moron!"

The Cowboy looked out his own window to the West, at the mountain just behind his home, and he imagined the beach that he could not see, further to the West. "But yet you still began setting up an operation on my coast line without asking *me* for permission." The Cowboy pointed his right thumb at his own chest to accentuate the moment.

Morales banged the table with his fist. "You don't own the oceans, Cowboy."

"Ah, yes — but I do own the land that you tried to sneak into. Just what were your plans — you and your Navy lackeys? ...What? No snappy comeback? You think I don't know what my enemies are doing on my own lands?"

Morales took a deep breath, he didn't want to admit that the loss of the Navy Secretariat and Marco Vargas was a huge blow to his operations. "Listen, Cowboy, if what I plan on the East coast works, I will cut you in for access to the West coast — I promise. Just please stand down; allow me to regroup."

Gonzales was pleased that he had Morales pleading. "OK, for now, I am done. Do not think that I will not find out if you cross to the West coast."

"I understand, and I will search out for your counsel if it comes to that." Morales hung up.

The Cowboy hit the speaker button to hang up the line; he patted Miguel Lopez on the shoulder as he walked past him. "You, my friend, have earned a bonus. I never expected your mission to net such results!"

"I thought he was going to cry for a moment there, Cowboy," Lopez said.

Chapter Forty-Nine

Dr. Perez was called after the nurse had removed the bandage from Gordan's head. She'd returned to Gordan's side and was cleaning the wound when the doctor entered the room.

"How's the pain?" he said to Gordan.

"I'm waiting for this headache to go away so I can figure out if the gunshots hurt," Gordan replied sarcastically.

"OK — the wound and stitches look fine. No sign of infection. The swelling has subsided considerably, and it appears that there will be no need for cosmetic surgery — unless, of course, you're going to continue with a modeling career?" the doctor said, in an attempt at some humor.

It wasn't lost on Hudde. "No modeling — just Hollywood blockbusters."

"Mr. Hudde, I want you to close your eye while I remove the bandage over it. We're going to introduce light very slowly." The doctor gestured to the nurse, who shut the blinds and turned off the lights.

"OK, now keep your eye closed; I will be wiping your eyelid with some disinfectant and water."

Hudde felt the cool liquid across his eye and cheek.

Dr. Perez spoke to him: "Mr. Hudde, very slowly, begin to open your eye."

Gordan closed his left eye and slowly began to open his right; it seemed stuck closed for a second and, then, like a slightly broken garage door, slowly began to rise. At first, everything was badly out of focus, but when he had opened it completely and blinked several times, he could see fine.

"I think you did a great job, Doc," Gordan said.

The doctor began looking with a small pen light, asking Gordan to look up and down, left and then right. "Well, it does look very good right now. In a couple of days, we can get an optometrist in for a complete eye exam, but I foresee no problems."

"That's great, Doc. Thank you." Gordan was pleased to hear the news. "Can I see what it looks like?"

The nurse brought over a hand mirror and held it out to Gordan. He took it in his left hand and began looking at the right side of his face for the first time in two weeks.

"I think I'm glad I didn't see it two weeks ago," Gordan said as he looked at the fading purple and yellow of obvious major bruising. The wound was a lazy "U" around the eye socket; hundreds of stitches were tender and pink looking.

"I did good work. You may look like an old boxer, but your face is going to heal, and you will need to look hard even to see the wound." He smiled and patted Hudde on the chest again before taking away the mirror and exiting the room.

Chapter Fifty

Two of the bullet wounds were more like gouges from the soft tissue of his thigh and upper arm. The wound in his hip seemed to be a little more difficult, causing some pain, and Gordan found himself limping down the hallway with the use of a wooden cane.

A dapper-looking Peter Buryshkin stepped out of the elevator just in time to see Hudde resting in place, eyes closed, face pointed up at the ceiling.

"That's what we want to see. Ready to get out of here?" Buryshkin said to Gordan as he walked past him.

"They said three more days," Hudde responded.

Gordan turned the corner and gingerly sat on the edge of his bed. Convalescing was something that he had not experienced before; he didn't appreciate how suddenly he felt so vulnerable to all threats.

"We have anyone on the tail of the assassins?" Hudde asked.

"When you were an altar boy, did you believe in Santa Claus, too?" Buryshkin shut the door and walked to the window, looking back at Hudde. "You're going to fly back to DC and tell everyone you have no idea who or what happened to you and your girlfriend…"

"Fiancée," Gordan interrupted.

"...Whatever. Do you understand what I'm telling you, son? I've been around a long time and am about near retiring. You're not ruining my plans. If that isn't enough, there are others out there, too. Nobody's ready and willing to throw a monkey wrench into things." Buryshkln raised his hands as if he'd had enough. "Listen, Boy Scout: Everybody, right to the top, knows what's going on, and we don't need you riding in to save the day. Go home, grieve, and get over yourself. Listen, if you want a piece, or you need money to go to family, we'll take care of that. But, otherwise, cut the shit." He looked at Hudde, waiting for a response.

Gordan sat running his hand down the length of his beard, deep in thought.

"I'll send you up a little homework if you need it tonight. It's a movie called *Serpico*. Ever seen it?" Obviously, Buryshkin was a bit uneasy with silence.

"First of all, I'm no Boy Scout, and I believe you about the system and how it works just fine. I also believe you that there is money here for everyone, so I need some "insurance" money to get to the mother." Hudde was finding some strength from moving and thinking.

"OK, we will take care of it for you." Buryshkin started to relax and seemed happy to get a response from Gordan that was positive to the situation, as he saw it.

"Second," Gordan continued, "I don't like feeling weak, I don't appreciate being threatened, and you missed your chance to remove me from the equation when I was unconscious. Every minute I get stronger, your chances to make good on your threat dwindle."

Gordan took a deep breath.

"I'll go back to the States and get better, and then I will come back here. I'll be back with a company or a squad or by myself — it won't matter. I just want you to know that, when that day comes, you'd better stay under your rock." Gordan couldn't quite get a smile out, but the grimace worked just fine.

"I get it; we're not quite on the same team." Buryshkin nodded. "That does alright as long as you don't upset my applecart. Go ahead and piss in everybody else's cornflakes." He smiled at Gordan and stepped in close to him. "What do you want the MILF to get?"

"Two hundred and fifty thousand dollars should cover it. Make sure it appears totally upfront; tell her I put insurance on her daughter when we got engaged." Gordan noticed that Buryshkin was about to add something. "Don't argue with me, Peter." He kept a steely-eyed stare into Buryshkin's face.

Buryshkin thought twice, shook his head, and left the room.

Chapter Fifty-One

Gordan Hudde was still moving gingerly as he walked to pick up his luggage a week later at Dulles International airport. He hailed a taxi that took him to his one-bedroom townhome in Gainesville, Virginia.

He set the two bags he returned from Mexico with onto the driveway and walked over to the keypad to access his garage door. It had been more than eleven months since he had left there. He stood at the side of the garage. Leaning on the damp siding, he looked about. The sky was a typical November grey, with temperatures hovering somewhere near 40 degrees; it looked like the sky might open up at any given time and produce a steady downpour. Horizon to horizon was different shades of grey, and it matched Gordan's mood.

The garage door opened swiftly and smoothly. Gordan conducted his normal procedure to detect trip wires and booby-traps; he had made many enemies over the years, and he didn't delude himself. He didn't feel like getting down onto all fours to finish by checking the undercarriage of the dark blue Toyota pickup, still parked stoically in its place, so he set a reminder to do that tomorrow before driving up to Dolly Madison Ave. He checked the garage door and entered the kitchen. He was hit immediately with the odors of rotting food; he never intended to be gone so long and had not thrown out perishables.

At least there was still beer in the fridge.

He awoke early the next morning and cleaned out the refrigerator, throwing out the brown vegetables and the green lunchmeats. He thoroughly checked out the pickup, and then he showered and drove toward the CIA headquarters building.

CIA director John Stevens looked the same — a grizzly bear of a man, with a lot of energy and sharp eyes. He pumped Gordan's hand enthusiastically, pointing at him to sit down.

"I've got some specialist lined up to check you out — see when you can return to duty." Stevens's eyes gave away some legitimate concern.

"I've watched many men go through some kind of medical recovery," Gordan started, "but I feel a like a brittle old man. I keep using this cane as a mental crutch, I think, and as much as I understand it, here I am with my cane."

Stevens was studying Hudde as he spoke. "It's the head wound, I'm told, that could be the real issue." Stevens paused. "I mean, the loss of your girlfriend — I'm truly sorry, Gordan. I wish there was more I could say or do."

"When she was killed, she was my fiancée," Gordan corrected him, "When I'm back to one hundred percent, I'm going back."

Stevens looked away when he started speaking, and Gordan knew that whatever was coming was going to be a lie.

"Gordan, we've been fighting that mess down there for 30 to40 years; what can you do?"

Gordan wasn't mad that his former boss would continue spewing the Company line. "I understand you and the government make a tidy sum by continuing this…charade; I don't have any desire to fuck up whatever your plans are for the area, but I will get revenge. The US government, through the drug war, makes for quite a large number of jobs and additional budget expenditures. I'm very aware, but please: Spare me any patriotic bullshit to keep me silent. I'll remain silent because of what I'll do with your help in the future. " He thought about whether he wanted to bring up some of the conversation with Buryshkin or not and decided it might help. "Your boy, Pete, in Mexico, explained it to me well. I didn't appreciate the tone the message was delivered with, but I understand the message just fine."

"I didn't give him a message to deliver — just to get you back here in as good a condition as he could."

Gordan believed that.

"Listen, John: Whatever I plan, I will let you know first. Hell, I'll probably need some help, and, frankly, our past relationship requites that. Right now I do need to just get better first. I honestly can't tell you right now that I'll be back in the saddle here; I'm sorry, but I haven't thought that much about the agency for a while."

The big man rose from his chair. "I hope Buryshkin didn't bother you that much, but I understand. Call me if there is anything I can do." He extended a big hand.

Maybe his old boss didn't want an argument. Maybe everything Buryshkin said was true. Gordan needed to think this one through.

Chapter Fifty-Two

Rafael Torres surprised his men when he and Piero Campos stepped off the tuna boat in San Diego. As a lieutenant in the Calderon Durango cartel, maybe this was not something that a man in charge would do — follow his drug run into America to check on operations. But as an officer in the CIA, it was something he had to do to get the memory stick in his pocket placed at the drop in Vegas.

Torres was beginning to believe that staying in Mexico would be easier than going back to the States. He had risen to a high-ranking position, with dozens now working for him directly — Luis Calderon calling on him sometimes for advice, even! If he were to return to the agency, he would probably get promoted to a desk somewhere, barely making a six-figure salary. Torres just didn't see where the end point was to his current position, and he had heard no feedback in months. He honestly was feeling more like a team member to the cartel than to the CIA.

Deep in his own thoughts, he suddenly realized that his men were waiting on him. He stole one last glance at the *USS Midway* just to the North and then gave a hand signal to get rolling to the two men driving the panel van to Vegas. He shook off the invitation to sit in the front and climbed into the back with Piero and his drugs.

The trip to Vegas, while uncomfortable, was uneventful. Both Campos and Torres stretched and walked about the auto-repair shop once they arrived.

Campos smiled and nodded his head at Torres while they watched the older Chevy pickup truck get prepped for their return trip to Mexico. The bed to the pickup truck had been modified. Nothing could be observed by any casual observer, but there was a four-inch-deep compartment under the bed packed with cash. A $14,000 truck was now worth something near ten million. Torres smiled back at Campos.

Torres walked out the back of the auto-repair shop and to the front sidewalk. It was an industrial area, and, early on a Saturday morning, there was no traffic, Torres saw the mail-box on the corner that was his drop. He walked up and leaned nonchalantly on the side. A three-inch gold-star sticker was near the top center of the side of the big blue box, Torres picked at it and tore it off. Then he dropped the memory stick into the slot. Job done. This stick had all of his operations over the past several months, including some of the other Calderon operations he was sure of and much rumor and speculation about the other cartels' operations, including some rumors about the major bombing and assault on the Mexican Naval Secretariat. He adjusted the .45 in his waistband and contin-ued to walk about, stretching his legs before he and Campos continued their journey.

"Everything OK, boss?" Campos peeked around the corner of the shop and startled Torres from his thoughts.

"Yeah — almost *too* good, I keep thinking." He patted Piero on the shoulder. "Are you ready for the ride back?" He headed into the back work area of the shop.

"I'll drive to Kingman if you do the rest," Torres said to Campos and then jumped in behind the wheel. Firing up the big engine, they took off — another successful trip. "I don't think I'll ever do this again, Piero." He looked over at his passenger.

"Nobody expects you to be out doing such things, boss; Jose or I can handle it if you need us to."

"I know. Things are going so well, I didn't trust it — just a feeling. But, in the future, either one of you can take the trip once in a while; keep people on their toes." Torres kept his eyes on the road as he spoke.

Nothing out of the ordinary happened all the way until they filled up in Tucson. The winter sun had overheated the cab as they drove the desert highways, but the cool air was too much once they rolled the windows down — a strange desert dichotomy. It was easier to control the cabin temperature with the air conditioning.

They continued their journey South to Tombstone, planning a crossing at Naco. They couldn't have been two miles from the border when they were lit up by a sheriff's vehicle. Any casual observer could see the bed of the truck was empty. Torres knew that they hadn't been speeding, so he was unsure of the reason for the stop.

The sheriff walked easily to the driver's-side window, just slightly behind the driver, able to keep an eye on the passenger as well. The truck's extended cab made the officer a little uneasy, but he did observe the empty bed. If he could get a glance into the truck, he would let them off with a "warning" — no harm no foul. He hadn't even called it in yet, something that was common for officers to do when conducting a "fishing" stop.

As the window was already down, the officer asked, "How's everything today?" in English.

Piero responded in Spanish that they were fine and wanted to know what was wrong. The officer ended up pretty fluent in Spanish and asked them if they knew that one of their taillights appeared to be out. He requested the paperwork, which was Mexican and all in order.

The deputy, an old-timer, had been around the block more than a few times. He glanced at the back wheel well and then back at the scruffy men in the truck. Nothing seemed out of the ordinary — probably a couple of lawn workers heading home for a weekend. But, suddenly, something seemed to be bothering the deputy. He glanced back down at the wheel well and knew that there was some visual discrepancy there. He looked into the bed and back out at the wheel well.

"I think your tailgate is loose," he lied and walked to the back after handing the paperwork to the driver.

The deputy was so focused on the bed of the truck that he didn't notice Torres get out of the vehicle until he'd been shot twice in the chest. Torres immediately followed up with a double tap to the radiator of the officer's vehicle. He stepped on the deputy's hand and yanked his radio out of his belt, smashing it on the ground and then stepping on it to finish it off. Torres checked quickly, ensuring that the officer was wearing his vest and whispered, "Stay down." He yanked the service weapon out and threw that into the field. Then he checked to see if he had a backup. He found none. He checked if any traffic was paying undue attention before emptying his clip into the vehicle's electronics from the passenger-side door.

"Across the border — quick," Torres said, and they were moving before he was fully in his seat. Torres was perspiring, and his heart rate was high. He concentrated on dropping his breathing and turned up the AC until they hit the border.

"Holy fuck, boss — I had no idea that was about to go down!" Piero was jacked, the adrenaline flowing.

They were across the border in moments, free and clear in a half-hour, driving much faster now that they were in their own, controlled area.

That might be difficult to explain away to the CIA, Torres thought. He knew that, after hours of interviews and detention, they would have gotten released by federal agents in the know — and after they skimmed some cash. But, honestly, Torres just didn't want the hassle. It frightened him that he was thinking this way.

Campos got them to Durango in record time. They dropped off the vehicle and then went and shared a couple of drinks together before heading to see Luis Calderon. He, too, wanted to share a drink at their victory over the Americans. Torres had no idea how this would add to his reputation going forward.

Chapter Fifty-Three

Gordan Hudde received a final doctor's release to return to duty just six weeks after the assassination plot that he and Isabella had walked into. He even stopped getting headaches each time he exercised or elevated his blood pressure. John Stevens requested a meeting the next day, a wet and cold December Wednesday.

Gordan not only had returned to training and exercising his body, but he had been going over scenarios and plans that Stevens would possibly sign off on. He sat in the dark in his favorite chair, staring at a darker TV screen and allowed the plan to play out in his mind. He stroked his beard as he was lost in the scenes playing out before him, projected from his own mind. He found what could be called successful and made it happen through determination and violent, swift, and terrible action. He began packing for the scenarios that he planned for. Finding the scull balaclava, he packed it last.

Yes. Punishment was what he sought.

Stevens appeared sincerely happy to see him, and he pointed at a chair while closing the door. "I can't put it off any longer, Gordan; I need to know what your plans are."

Gordan slid forward in his chair and ran his hand once through his beard before locking eyes with the director. "When I left here a year ago, I resigned. You need to back date that first for the day I turned it in."

Stevens reacted like he had just been shot in the chest. "Well, that's not where I envisioned this starting."

Gordan held up his hand as if to stop an approaching vehicle. "Stop and listen to my entire plan before you say anything…"

Approximately twenty minutes later, Stevens was saying, "You're fucking crazy, Hudde; has anyone ever told you that?" Stevens shook his head like he had just smelled something awful.

"Wait one minute" Gordan requested. "Let it all sink in, play out the downside, and think of the possibilities of the upside." Gordan started to slide back in his seat for the first time since starting. "You can't find any reason to stop me, can you?" Hudde nodded in the affirmative knowing that Stevens was playing out the same equations he had already gone over thousands of time. "It's all upside for you and several other agencies if they want to play." And that was it. He sat back, finished selling.

"I can't believe I'm saying this, but I'll get back to you after I reach out to a few people and check out some information." Stevens started to get up and show Hudde to the door.

"Talk to you soon," Gordan said as he walked out the door.

Chapter Fifty-Four

"The Ellanor Lawrence Park 0930hrs Tuesday morning" was all Stevens said on the call Friday morning.

Tuesday morning was brisk. The park was near enough that Gordan didn't have to leave early, yet he did and scouted the area well before dawn. He then left and found a plaza with a donut shop, grabbing himself something to eat and another coffee. He drove back and settled in until the big black Cadillac Escalade slid in next to him and his Toyota.

Gordan knew enough to get out and into the Caddy. The back seat seemed to be the only empty spot, as an unknown person was in the front passenger seat. Stevens's big body was behind the wheel.

"Gordan, this is Paul Westerville, Administrator of the DEA. Paul, that there is one Gordan Hudde."

The two shook hands between the seats, and Westerville said, "So you're the crazy son-of-a-bitch that Stevens has been bragging about."

Stevens added, "We had an off-the-books meeting, discussing the plan you have proposed. It took Paul a day and a half before he got back to me, but he's in, Gordan." Stevens held a big paw up and said, "Wait. I've got to tell you: This is a death sentence you're selling us on. We both agreed that, before we needed to handle our part, you will be a dead man. So stop looking satisfied."

Westerville handed a large, thick manila file back to Gordan. "Here are the two men we think are best positioned to help you, one from each agency. There is a letter enclosed to give to the agent in charge in Phoenix for the vehicle you requested. They don't need anything from you — understand? Don't worry: If you make it to our part of the operation, we'll be there for you. I guarantee it." He smiled at Gordan. "I understand you want nothing afterwards?"

"Nope." And Gordan slid from the seat and back into the cold. He leaned back in and asked, "Do you want the files returned, or can I burn them before I head South?"

"Burn them." Stevens said. He followed up with "When are you leaving?"

"Tonight." Gordan closed the door.

The big dark-blue pickup roared to life and backed up before leaving the parking area. Stevens looked over at Westerville. "You've heard of the 'immovable object'; well, you just met the 'unstoppable force.' I would never bet against the guy before, and, with his current motivation, I wouldn't want to be a cartel member right now." And they, too, left.

Chapter Fifty-Five

Gordan lay back on the canvas straps of the seating offered in an Air Force C141-Starlifter. It was like old times in the Army, and, just like back then, it made him want to sleep, which was OK under the circumstances. He had caught the flight from Andrews to Luke Air Force Base in Arizona. His two large canvas duffle bags were at his feet; neither would have gotten through any airport in America, no matter how incompetent the security staff or operations were.

After taxiing for a few minutes, the large carrier came to a halt, and the load masters began moving to get several large skids of unknown items out of the tailgate. Gordan walked out and immediately identified a large dark sedan, with the trunk up, off to the side gate, with a young, well-dressed female agent standing by in sensible shoes. He set off in her direction with one bag over his shoulder and the other in his hand. The C141-Starlifter roared behind him as it taxied to a different location.

Hudde placed the bags into the trunk, and, without any conversation, the DEA agent threw him a set of keys and jumped into the driver's seat after opening the back driver's-side door. Hudde took the hint and climbed into the back seat. The car was already running, inaudible over the roar of the base's aircraft. She threw the car into drive and took off. There was no conversation, and, after an hour, the agent pulled into a gas station just outside a small town called Gila Bend.

The female agent threw the sedan into park and popped the trunk; without speaking she exited the car and headed into the small quick mart attached to the station, she never looked back.

Gordan hopped out and grabbed his bags. There was one early '80s brown Chevy pickup parked nearby. Gordan tried the keys, and it opened. He placed his bags on the passenger side and tried the ignition. The truck came to life, rocking with anticipation of being used. Gordan threw it into drive and took off heading South.

About an hour into his drive, with everything going just fine, Gordan pulled off the main road and popped the hood of the old truck. Other than the body, nothing was "old" about this vehicle. It had obviously been recovered in some drug operation, and the DEA had been using it for whatever purposes they deemed fitting. The engine was outfitted with top off-road racing equipment, and Hudde, while not familiar with car and truck racing, knew the undercarriage had been outfitted with superior shocks and struts. He wasn't an expert by any means on engine maintenance or off-road racing, but he was very familiar with the GPS unit, and that was what he was looking for. Hudde removed it and placed it into the cab with him to dispose of elsewhere. Nothing else was out of the ordinary. Hudde returned to the road and continued his mission.

On the way to the town of Durango, in the center of Mexico, Gordan pulled off at a gas station and topped off the tank. He spied some kind of soda-vendor trucks parked to the side of the building; a man with a uniformed shirt was filling a wall of refrigerated items in the back of the small shop. Gordan shuffled past the vendor's truck and placed the magnetic GPS device firmly onto the truck's frame. He hoped that the man had a large, vast route to keep everyone at home busy.

Gordan pulled into the new development, complete with townhomes that were almost exact replicas of the townhouse he had rented in Mazatlán. This in an area just South of Durango, with quick access to the main roads in and out of town. Durango was central enough to fit Gordan's travel plans; it was also the base for head the Durango cartel's Luis Calderon and one of his newest lieutenants, Rafael Torres.

In fact, Gordan drove past Torres' own townhome on his way to the rental agency/model home. He had driven through the night, and the sun was just rising to the East. Gordan knew that he would have to wait for an agent to show up, but this didn't bother him a bit. He cracked the window and got some sleep.

Four hours later, Gordan pretended to be satisfied with the townhome he was inspecting with a 40-ish Mexican woman. "Yes, this will work out just fine." Gordan nodded and tried to smile. "Will a three- or six-month rental agreement work out for you?" They walked out the front door and strolled back to the renal office.

"*Si*. Do you wish to pay with a credit card or a check, Martin…? I'm sorry — I forgot your last name."

"I don't think I gave it." Again Gordan gave his best smile "You know, I'm not sure I fully introduced myself. I'm sorry. Martin Riggs, but my friends just call me 'Marty.'" He stuck his big hand out at the slightly overweight businesswoman. As the two shook hands, he continued, "The company gave me an envelope with some get-started money. Maybe I have enough to get started?" He started looking into the manila envelope he was carrying.

"Who do you work for?" The woman had very little accent, and Hudde was impressed.

"It's a big-name company you would recognize immediately," Gordan said "But company HQ doesn't have all the land rights yet. I'm here to do some research. Oh, well. I may have already said too much, and they don't like a lot of publicity." He tried to smile sheepishly.

"You'll need $2500 to move in now," the agent said.

"What if I give you $3000? Could you see that the electricity is on and everything? I need to get to work first thing tomorrow, and I'm not sure I'll have time." Gordan knew it was a "soft" bribe, but it worked, and she took the money, coming back in a few minutes with a receipt and keys.

"Good luck with your research, Mr. Riggs." The agent smiled as she walked Hudde to the door.

"With all the satellite capabilities, one day my job will be gone — but thank you." Gordan thought back on how Isabella and her friends believed him to be an oil-company man or looking to exploit the country's minerals, and he hoped that's exactly what this woman would believe. He turned and waved as he headed back to his rental townhome.

He stored his gear in a walk-in closet in the master bedroom and then went out and looked about the town. He found a bakery and walked in. When it was his turn to be waited on, he inquired about a half-sheet cake that said "Congratulations!" and ordered it for two days from then.

The truck turned South, and Gordan wasted no time continuing with his mission.

In Mexico City, Gordan got a room in the same Hilton as he and Isabella had shared just about three months before. Then he traced his drive to the exact location he had parked at on the day of her murder.

Gordan parked his truck and climbed out. He looked at the sky, which was light blue with small patches of completely white clouds, and they matched his mood not at all. At the peak of tourist season, as they all were escaping cold weather from the North, he was surrounded by throngs of people, yet he was alone. The storefront, painted brightly, no longer made him feel festive. He was angry.

He walked North and stopped on the corner where Isabella had lost her life. He tried to find the exact spot he last saw her and stopped there. He knelt and said a silent prayer. The concrete was obviously new, and Gordan could see the vast amount that needed to be replaced after the massive attack. Looking back across the street, he instinctively understood that much of the glass in the surrounding stores was only three months old as well.

Gordan strode into the chapel area at the church of the Lady of Guadalupe and found a seat on the worn wooden and uncomfortable pews. The rich, deep-reddish stain of the wood, the brass, the ornate carvings, and the brick and stonework gave the hushed high ceilings the feel that Hudde understood the builders had desired.

This is what you took her for, huh? Gordan began an internal conversation that he didn't know was going to happen until he sat down.

You know I believe in you. I know I'm a sinner and I'm supposed to try hard to live and love. So the question is: Why take her? You know my heart. Lord. If the path I am about to take is wrong, take me before I lose any chance of finding your kingdom. He paused and added, *If I'm about to do the right thing, give me the strength to finish.* Gordan stood up and took a couple steps towards the exit. He looked back at a picture of Christ and said out loud, "Amen!" and walked back to his truck.

Chapter Fifty-Six

Gordan looked out his townhome side window and observed the black Land Rover pull into the driveway of Rafael Torres. Only one man got out, and Hudde thought he could positively identify Torres. He grabbed the cake and walked up the street. It was a sunny, yet cool, early evening. The workers at the construction sites had packed up and gone home. No other traffic came or went. Gordan thought he and Torres must be the only people on this block.

He rang the doorbell and took a step back, holding the cake box out in front of him, and smiled. The door cracked, and Rafael Torres opened the door, his right arm behind his back.

"Don't shoot me; it's just a cake, man." Gordan smiled through his beard.

"Who the fuck are you, and what do you want?" Torres said in Spanish.

Gordan just stood and continued smiling a goofy grin. "Oh, I know they taught you English at the Texas high school you went to."

Torres took a step back and allowed Hudde to enter; he closed the door and then lifted the box top. "It is a cake. 'Congratulations'? For what?"

Gordan walked over to a high counter top and set the cake down. "I guess that depends on if I read your file correctly."

"And just what did you read?" Torres shot back.

"Same kind of reports I was writing two years ago. Gordan Hudde" Gordan stuck out a big hand.

Torres took it. "Hey, I read about you." He studied Gordan's face for a moment "Yeah, they patched you up pretty good. Sorry about the girl."

Gordan let go the hand and just said, "Yeah, that's all this is for me — about the girl. But I need help."

"First tell me what you read in my file." Torres started to sit down.

"What, no coffee?" Gordan seemed perturbed.

"You want a beer?" Torres asked.

"Who eats cake and drinks beer? That's like ketchup on a hot dog."

"Whatever, man." Torres got up and started making coffee "The agency sure has some strange people on the payroll."

"I'm a free agent, not on any payroll, and I like cake." Gordan shrugged his shoulders. He continued, "Your reports, between the lines, were screaming, 'Isn't anyone going to do anything?' and that's exactly how mine read. Let me tell you: The boys in Washington are in a circle jerk telling people how much extra cash the departments need and telling each other how wonderful they are. The boys in all the agencies you or I have ever worked for are all busy trying to figure out how they can look successful, all the while skimming as much cash from the cartels." Gordan stopped and waited for Torres to say something.

Torres stepped over with two plates and a couple of forks. "You can eat the whole damn cake for that assessment."

Gordan waited until Torres was looking at him to continue. "I can't help you with the agency; they aren't ever going to take an action that would make you happy. You know the Mexican government is never helping. But I think I can help you in the Durango cartel."

Torres sat back in his seat. "How and why? I don't understand at all. I've been here for years and haven't figured out how I could make an impact."

"I was influenced by two people." He took a bite of cake. "Something Peter Buryshkin and my future mother-in-law said to me while I was laid up. This is good stuff." Gordan gestured with his fork at the cake and then again at the coffee pot.

Torres got a simple stone mug and filled it. He looked over at Hudde.

"Black," Gordan said.

Torres finished and set the cup before Gordan. "Yeah, so what are you going to do to help me, and what do you think I want to do?"

"I think you want to be an impact player; I think Washington wants some victories. I think the agencies want a steady flow of cash. I think the cartels want to believe they are doing what they do successfully, without interference." He wolfed down another big piece of cake. The frosting hung up in his mustache. He took a pull from the mug. He pointed at the cake with his fork. "Good shit. I'm sorry I never ate this stuff before; I didn't know what I was missing." He nodded his head at the cake as if it should acknowledge his feelings.

"Alright, I think you got us all pegged, but what are you going to do to help me?" Torres stopped everything, waiting for the big reveal.

"Get you promoted." Gordan took another large bite; yellow crumbs fell into his beard. He grinned.

"I'm as high as I can go in the Durango cartel. I have no family ties that go back like the others. I think I have been doing pretty well. The agency isn't ever going to promote me, either..."

"But what?" Gordan asked.

Torres hesitated.

"You're my guy. Don't worry about it," Gordan said.

"I had to shoot a border agent recently." Torres looked down.

"He live?" Gordan asked.

"Yeah, he was wearing a vest, but I wasn't sure of that when I pulled the trigger." Torres ran his hand through his hair, obviously concerned.

"Cartel know about it?" Gordan seemed almost excited.

"Yeah, it's really added to my reputation." Again, he hesitated for a moment. "I didn't report it on my last report."

Gordan smiled, green frosting in his teeth. "Good — this will work even better. How would you like to be the *Jefe* of the Sinaloa Cartel?"

"What? What the fuck are you talking about?

Hudde just sat chewing, smiling back at Torres.

"You're bat-shit fucking crazy — you know that, right?" Torres dropped the fork and moved away from Gordan like he could catch it.

"Seems to be the universal consensus of everyone I speak to lately. May have something to do with the massive head wound." Gordan winked at Torres; it didn't give Torres any additional comfort.

The two went back and forth for about another hour before Gordan refreshed his coffee and made sure it was OK for him to take the mug, "You know you're not getting it back," he said as Torres walked him to the door.

"Stay alive, and I won't let you down," Torres said as Hudde disappeared into the night air.

Chapter
Fifty-Seven

Gordan's truck was perfect for driving the rough roads or for taking off-road routes. It was comforting not to have to care how something looked as long as it ran well — sort of how Gordan thought of himself.

He headed North out of Culiacan, looking for a route that took him more Easterly. The land all the way from the Pacific beach 15 to 20 miles west of here to this point was very flat until you could begin to see large outcroppings of large boulders — not mountains, but bigger than a hill. The land also started rising in elevation until, just another 5 to 10 miles North and East, you began to get into the mountains. Looking out his side window as he turned East, he could see the mountain on which Eduardo "The Cowboy" Gonzales had built his mansion, on the eastern side. Gordan couldn't see the mansion, but he knew it was only another mile to his North. He pulled over into the shrub and grass and climbed out onto the bed of the truck. Scanning the area, he saw what he needed about a mile Southeast of his current position, and he located a wash that appeared to head in that direction and took off.

He found a spot to pull up and out of the bank of the wash to the East and not do too much damage to the side of the truck. He pushed through some small Palo Verde trees and desert sage brush until he found himself at the Western edge of a steep rise. Gordan climbed back out and hopped back up onto the bed of the truck to scan the area. He could look back to the Northwest and see the high point of the mountain that the Cowboy called home. It rose about 10 to 12 stories high and appeared to be made of granite and cactus. The hill he stood at the base of now appeared to be about four or five stories high. Gordan slid a walking stick out from behind the seat and pulled the backpack out from the passenger side of the truck. He slid it over his shoulders and started to slowly pick his way through the cactus, creosote brush, and mesquite, taking his time climbing over the large rock formations, looking for the top.

A jackrabbit ran from its hiding spot and startled Gordan as he hadn't seen it before it dashed through the brush. Gordan payed more attention to the area near his feet, not wanting to disturb a snake looking for the sun in the late December light; he had no anti-venom. The larger plant life began to dwindle, and Gordan made it to the top of his hill, sitting down on a boulder that was fairly flat, about eight and a half feet wide and twelve feet long, Gordan thought this boulder may have been standing at one time and then split and fell in two halves. This one was perfect for his plan; the other had broken into more pieces, some of which appeared to have fallen off a cliff just behind him to the Southeast.

Gordan used his binoculars to scan The Cowboy's home. He could see the large ornate gates at the road and the twisting driveway, which he lost sight of about halfway from the road. But then, it reappeared, meeting up with the circular drive near the large double front doors. Two large barns were situated between the road and the main house. Gordan could see some men milling around one of them and guessed that some of The Cowboy's men would always be stationed there. Gordan could make out three of the six garage doors, as the garage was orientated more to the North. The home was two stories, and Gordan estimated that it was twenty to twenty-five thousand square feet. Perfectly visible was the third-floor glass "office" that was so often bragged about. Its ability to stop .50 caliber rounds was well known by everyone in all of Mexico.

Gordan scanned slowly up to the top of the mountain, just behind The Cowboy's estate. He figured that two men with a .308, an M79 .40mm grenade launcher, and a couple crates of ammo could ruin The Cowboy's day up on that mountaintop. Anyone who conducted that mission would never make it back alive, but it would be fun while it lasted. Gordan shrugged his shoulders because that wasn't his plan. He liked this spot, and he picked his way back down to his vehicle, clearing the rout of branches and fallen debris so that he could navigate without problem in low light. He then retraced his rout and used a spray can of neon orange paint to put spots on rocks or branches to mark his route from below to the top. Satisfied, he went back to his truck.

Back in Durango, Gordan packed a day pack and placed it near the door. Next week Tuesday, the Morales Pacific Coast cartel would have the last meeting of the year. Gordan packed the rucksack for that trip and placed the full ruck into the closet near the front door. He pulled out one of his throwaway phones and contacted John Stevens. "Please send the package" was the simple message, and he hung up and removed the battery, placing the phone on the table to be thrown out on his next trip.

Gordan went to bed early, setting his internal alarm to 00:01hrs for the next part of his plan.

Chapter Fifty-Eight

Gordan opened his eyes and turned his right palm toward his face so that he could see the illuminated watch dial. He had overslept; it was 00:10hrs. He slugged down some coffee and dressed in his dark camouflage Vietnam-style, tiger-striped BDU bottoms and a dark long-sleeved turtleneck. He crammed the skull balaclava into a large thigh cargo pocket; he laced up his black tactical boots and picked up his hard-knuckled combat gloves while getting the backpack.

He had studied the Calderon home from aerial photo and satellite images while in the States and now drove past the home to the North until he found a spot to pull off road. As Calderon had not been participating in the cartel wars over the last 10-12 years, they had become a little more relaxed with overall security operations. They only had some men at the gates and in the front of the home at the main gate; a 10-foot wall that surrounded the home seemed to be the main line of defense.

Gordan picked his way South and West until he came upon the back portion of the fence, where a slight rise gave him an advantage to running, jumping off the wall, and grasping the top of the wall. He pulled himself up and lay flat on the wall for about 10 minutes, waiting to observe movement or hear anything. Nothing — all quiet. Gordan walked the top of the fence until he was in position to run the last few feet and jump for the flat roof of the multicar garage. Just as he was about to leap the 10-foot span, a twinge of pain shot through his left hip, some remnant of the bullet that was removed not all that long ago. Gordan saw that he was going to land on the edge of the roof — not several feet in, as he had planned. His right foot touched the edge of the wall and slid out onto the gravelly mix of roofing materials and shot out in front of him. He found himself falling backwards and had little to no control; his head smacked the edge of the roof, and he heard himself exhale as he slapped down on the roof — hard.

Hudde reached back and massaged his head for a moment while he tried to listen for activity. His balaclava didn't appear to be wet, so he guessed he wasn't bleeding. As long as he was down, he low-crawled to the front edge of the roof and looked over the slightly elevated edge. He could see a man standing in the middle of the driveway, looking around, while another called him back over to a card game at a small table near the front gate.

Feeling that his mistake was going to go unnoticed, Gordan crawled back to the back side of the garage, to the back edge of the veranda that was the only part of the home with a second floor and balcony. A quiet and easy jump landed Gordan onto the balcony, and he walked quickly into the bedroom of Luis Fernando Calderon. He stood quietly in a shadow and listened to the deep breathing of the *Jefe* and his wife.

Gordan knelt down and place a gloved hand over Calderon's mouth. He whispered into his ear, "I'm not here to hurt anyone; I am not interested in even waking your wife. Could we speak in private?"

A jolt of lightning went through Luis Calderon as he was shocked at the intrusion. He opened his eyes and listened to the voice of this dead man. His skull face did not make him feel comfortable. Yet if an assassination was what this man intended, would he not already be dead? Calderon nodded his acceptance, and he began to slide out of bed. His feet went automatically into slippers near the bed, and he walked the intruder into his kitchen on the first floor.

"No lights," Gordan whispered to Calderon as he walked in and leaned against a large granite island.

"Why do you slip into my home in the dead of night with a death mask if you do not intend me or my wife harm?" Calderon couldn't help but ask.

"I'm a desperate man, and I need help." Hudde was being honest.

Calderon wasn't comfortable. "So come here tomorrow through the front gate. This is not how a man asks for a favor."

"You missed the 'desperate' part, and I don't think that you would see me if I were to ask. I also don't think you would accept my predicament if I walked up to your front door one day." Gordan slipped off the backpack from his back and set it on the granite counter before the two men. "Do you have some glasses?" he asked and reached into the small bag.

Calderon stepped back and raised his hand to defend himself.

Gordan pulled out a bottle of Alquimia Reserva de Don Adolfo Extra Añejo Tequila, setting it on the counter after removing it from the towel he had wrapped it in. "Relax. I'm here with a proposition." Gordan said. "I'm looking for revenge, Mr. Calderon, and I need some men for support. I plan on doing the dirty work, but I need some numbers to a least look stronger than I am."

"With whom are you looking to extract this revenge, um, ah 'Mr. Skull'?" Calderon had a sense of humor.

"The two men who had something to do with killing my fiancée: Eduardo "The Cowboy" Gonzales and Carlos Morales," Gordan said, matter-of-factly. He finished unwrapping the tequila and pulled on the top. He held up the bottle as a question.

Calderon turned and removed two thick and heavy shot glasses onto the counter. "Then your hood is fitting, Señor, for surely I am about to share a drink with a dead man." Calderon waited for Gordan to down a shot before he allowed his glass to touch his lips. "Mr. Hudde, your man at the embassy told me your tale." And then he held up the glass and downed it.

Shocked, Gordan removed the balaclava. Instantly, he ran his hand over his head afterwards, like his hair could be messed up. "What…"

Calderon interrupted him: "I understand what has befallen you, sir. I respect that you would risk your life to revenge your loss. I, however, have spent many years extracting my group from the petty squabbles of the other *Jefes*, and I have no interest in starting up now as I approach my last years." He paused and poured them both another shot. "I do have to admit that I am interested in knowing your plan and why you would believe that I would assist you."

Gordan took another shot. "Buryshkln is on your payroll; figures."

"Don't be disappointed Mr. Hudde — many, many men are 'on my payroll,' as you say."

"There is going to be much violence with or without you, Mr. Calderon. I am not going to be swayed from my labors. You can help me and enrich yourself in the process, or you can stand idle and be suspected by the others. I snuck in here so that you could continue to try to remain neutral whatever your answer to me is."

"What would happen if I would go to the others behind your back after you leave here?"

Calderon immediately regretted asking that question.

"You, sir, are known to be a man of honor, and I do not think that would be the case. I could have killed everyone on your staff getting to you tonight if I thought you were a threat to me or my plan — and I still can. But you are no friend to those others, and I believe you will like to hear what I have to say."

The two men spoke quietly for more than an hour. Gordan pulled a map from his pack and showed the Xs that he had placed onto it Northeast of The Cowboy's estate about two and a half miles and approximately a half-mile from the Calderon estate in Ciudad Victoria.

"The two men you have mentioned are young and eager but still dedicated to you?" Gordan asked again.

"*Si*. Yes, these two men are my best, youngest talent, and I have much confidence in both."

"Then have this Torres and 50 men at this point here, near The Cowboy's estate when I tell you. And the other man, Sanchez — ready with 25 men at this point." Hudde looked at Calderon, and Calderon nodded at him. "Torres will be the *Jefe* of the newly organized Sinaloa cartel, and Sanchez will be second in command on the Pacific coast."

"It is agreed." Calderon held out his hand and shook Hudde's large mitt. "You are out of your mind if you think you will pull this off."

"Well, I'm betting my life. What do you want to bet?" Hudde said through a smile.

"And how will my men know when they should move?" Calderon ignored Hudde's wager.

"Tell your man outside The Cowboy's estate that he will have four very distinct signs to let him know." Hudde could see the confusion in Calderon's face. "Your other man will know when the occupants of the Morales estates come out to give up."

"That simple?" Calderon asked.

"I think so, for your men. You may have to dole out some cash for additional bribe money, and there may be some smaller squabbles. But, I think, when the dust clears and with the additional income of two entire cartels at your disposal, you'll manage."

"And if you die before the sign of four is observed by Torres?" Calderon asked a good question.

"Then your men had better pack up, get back here, and pretend this conversation never happened. 'No harm, no foul,' they say in my country," Gordan said.

"And what else will you be needing from me in the future, Mr. Hudde?" A fair question.

"How about a favor if I find myself in Mexico again?"

Calderon looked hard at Hudde. "That's it?"

Gordan was sincere, for his motivation was just revenge; it was that simple. The men who had something to do with the death of his Isabella would not, could not, be allowed to live unscathed, and Gordan had no intentions of waiting for *karma*.

"I wish you good luck, Mr. Gordan Hudde. If you do what you have planned to do, what you have promised to do, please come back here to finish this bottle." He started to show Gordan to the front door.

"Um, I think I better leave the way I came in." Gordan pointed out. "Don't be too hard on your men."

"Well, yes, then — after you, please." Calderon held his hand out before him, allowing Gordan to go first up the stairs.

Gordan exited the big double-wide French doors onto the balcony and disappeared into the night. Calderon watched for as long as he could see Hudde and then made a mental note to improve his security nightwatch before heading back to bed. He lay back down and drifted off to sleep, dreaming of being the *Jefe* of all *Jefes* in Mexico soon.

Chapter Fifty-Nine

Early Saturday afternoon, Gordan met the FedEx man at the door; the obvious boxes of Dell product should not be left on porch stoops. Gordan signed for the boxes and waved good-bye, thanking the man. The driver, if anyone was paying attention, stopped at no other stops; no one was paying attention.

Gordan unpacked the American equipment and ran diagnostic tests to ensure they were working properly. He ensured that the batteries were at full power as well at the backup batteries. He packed the items away for later use.

Chapter Sixty

Monday found Gordan Hudde crossing the country to get to Ciudad Victoria to check out the area near the Carlos Morales HQ. The large rucksack was on the floor of the passenger seat and a backpack on the seat. He was comfortable that he had everything he would need.

He was happy to arrive at the Morales HQ well before dark. He drove around the building and observed the emergency exits, noticing the three stories, all-glass, modern-looking facility. A parking garage just to the West offered a perfect location for Gordan to get out and stretch his legs. He noticed a coffee and pastry shop kitty corner from the main doors of the Morales building. He went over and got a muffin and a large coffee, sitting outside approximately 130 yards from his target.

Patently waiting and watching, Gordan observed that every half-hour, a security guard would come out, walk West, and in approximately 15 to 20 minutes would come around the East side of the building and re-enter the main doors. In a two-hour period, Hudde observed three different men.

There was no security on the roof, no other security measures that Gordan could observe. But then, why would they? This was one of the most powerful men in all Mexico. You would have to be mad to make a direct assault on the Morales HQ; so everyone had told him so far.

A large black and heavy-looking Mercedes drove up to the front doors. A man got out of the passenger side and opened the back door. One of the uniformed security guys opened and held a main door open, and, right there in front of Hudde, Carlos Morales came out and enjoyed the same air that Gordan breathed — for now. He didn't realize it, but he was gritting his teeth.

Gordan suspected that tomorrow, five or six leaders of the Morales cartel would have their drivers and maybe a security man of their own drop them off at those same front doors. They would head upstairs for a meeting, and those men would park the vehicles in the same garage. Then, most likely, they would sit right there at that same coffee shop, waiting for their master's call. There would be somewhere up to a dozen armed and dangerous men, depending on a few things — and, of course, minus one, as Marco Vargas had been killed in the same attack that killed Isabella and injured Gordan.

Gordan sat running his hand through his beard for almost another hour. Once a plan solidified in his mind, he jumped up and headed for his truck. Pulling out from the garage, Gordan began doing concentric circles, using the Morales HQ as the center. About a mile as the crow flies to the North, Gordan found a quiet plaza with a small grocery and a laundromat — enough traffic at that end of the complex but a closed and boarded-up retail lot at the other. He also found another thing he was looking for just a little farther North and East from the plaza he liked. Gordan topped off his truck fuel tank and parked it near the boarded-up retail shop and quieter end of the plaza. He took off on foot to the Northeast for that other item he had decided he needed to successfully accomplish his mission.

Gordan circled wide and came up on the small-time drug dealer at the corner he had identified earlier. It was down the street from some small bars that had some good activities. If the dealers were setting up shop here, then they always did, and no one would pay much attention to them. Gordan staggered a little left and then over-corrected coming up on the 1995 Toyota Tercel that he had seen on his trip around town. Gordan leaned on the car for a moment.

Someone began barking at him in Spanish. He did pick up on a few swear words, and a little guy about 5'6" gave him a shove. Gordan backed up a step and then fell onto his ass in an attempt to appear drunk out of his mind.

"Guy said you'd have smokes," and he thumbed over his shoulder at the bars down the street.

"American? What the fuck do you want?" The little man danced around Gordan to the side.

Gordan formed the OK sign with his fingers and then brought them up to his lips in the universal sign language for "smoke."

"Five hundred," the Mexican drug dealer yelled at him.

Gordan shook his head and got up onto his knees, allowing him better access to his front pocket. He allowed a wad of bills to fall out onto the ground, and he began picking them up. "Only got about two hundred left." He slurred and began to get up.

"OK, OK. You wait here, and I'll get you two hundred worth." The dealer patted Gordan's chest several times.

The dealer went to the end of the street and made a hand gesture. A dark van came down the street, and the men had a conversation. The van turned and came into the empty lot; the driver shut off the engine, and the door to the side slid open. One other man jumped out from the back and the driver made three, more than enough to take money from a drunken American tourist.

Nowhere near enough to take anything from an angry soldier with years of hand-to-hand fighting training, *judo, karate,* and *krav maga*, which had been practiced by Gordan for as long as he could remember.

The man from the back of the van pulled a knife and immediately found it sticking out his own neck. The bigger man from behind the wheel had expected no such resistance, and Gordan's own Kay-bar slid between his third and fourth rib before he even uttered a word. Gordan wheeled around, hearing the stones behind him move. The dealer was heading for the driver's-side door of the Toyota. As he fumbled to get the keys in the ignition, Gordan reached through the open window with his two big hands and encircled the small man's neck. He dragged him from the vehicle and snapped his neck like a twig.

He shoved the three bodies into the van and then closed it up, locking the keys inside with the bodies. He picked up the Toyota keys from the floor and started the car; it had a half-tank of gas and appeared to be in good condition for a twenty-five-year old. Gordan was flying by the seat of his pants; he hoped things went right; he headed back to his pickup and began getting to work on the Toyota for tomorrow's short trip.

Gordan got a couple hours sleep in the cab of his truck and then got up and out near 0800hrs, stretching and pacing about, getting the blood flowing to all his extremities. The meetings at the Gulf coast HQ went from 0900 to 1300hrs regularly, and Hudde wanted to make his entrance near 1000hrs. The air was cool this late December morning, and Hudde thought he could see his breath. His nerves made him focus on the mission and what this most important part would accomplish for him to finish this and go visit Isabella with her mother. He visualized how the entire mission would play out. Then he visualized possible scenarios where things went wrong and how he would react.

At 0945hrs, Gordan touched the Colt .45 under his right shoulder with his left hand and then the K-bar at his waist. He had two extra mags for the handgun under his left shoulder and a Ruger .357 snubbie in an ankle holster. It had been ported but still roared and kicked pretty fierce, especially with the smaller grip. But Gordan had switched the grip for something larger, due to his big hands. It helped, but he hoped he wouldn't need it; it would mean things weren't going well. Gordan slipped the skull balaclava over his head and then rolled it up until it appeared to be a watch cap. He slipped on a light-grey windbreaker to cover the shoulder rig and jumped into the Tercel.

At 0955hrs, Gordan rolled out of the parking lot just a mile from his target. In less than three minutes, he turned the hard right onto the multi-purpose road into the business park just in time to see the guard begin a walk around the facility belonging to Carlos Morales. Gordan pulled into the circular drive and up onto the sidewalk, about 10 feet from the front doors. Gordan flipped a small switch he had run wires to late last night and observed a green light begin blinking on the console between the front seats.

Hudde quickly exited the car; one of the other guards began to exit the front doors just as Hudde was getting there. This was not part of the plan, but Hudde unfolded a map of Mexico and began waving it around, pointing at nothing, leading the guard back inside. A quick glance back at the coffee shop showed Hudde that no cartel men had made a move in the HQ's direction yet, and that was good.

Hudde quickly took the guard back to the guards' desk with a bank of phones and buttons. Hudde observed just a few cameras, which seemed to be focused on the elevators, stairwells, and a single office. The guard at the desk stood and placed his hand on the grip of his pistol, keeping a close eye on the "lost" American. Hudde understood that they desperately wanted him to leave and take the piece of junk parked on their sidewalk with him. Gordan spread the map across the table before them. As both guards took a moment to stop complaining and focus on the map, Gordan drove the

K-bar to the hilt into the chest of the guard's who was across the table. The blade dissected the man's heart, and he fell to the floor, bright-pink frothy blood gurgling from his lips.

Hudde whirled back, throwing a vicious elbow at the chin of the first guard that landed deep behind the man's ear and dropped him like a rag doll. Hudde finished by twisting the man's head around until his chin pointed at the ceiling while he lay flat on his chest. Hudde removed the big knife and wiped it on the uniform of the dead man. Hudde pulled both men behind the desk so that anyone stepping inside the front doors would not see them right away.

Gordan rolled the balaclava down over his face. Now the death skull would confront the Gulf coast cartel cadre on the third floor. Hudde ran up the three flights of the open-air stairwell that ran up the center of the business building. Hudde stopped outside the large, lightly stained oak doors. There should be six men inside. Five needed to die.

Chapter Sixty-One

CIA director John Stevens looked at his watch while twisting the cap to a water bottle in his Virginia office. 1200hrs was the designated time that Gordan Hudde said he would start his operation. He said a prayer for the man's success and safety, and then one for themselves, for this was the most controversial operation Stevens had ever been involved in. He didn't count the operation where the traitorous former administration had been killed, because he technically didn't know about that one until it had been over, and he would still deny everything if ever asked.

He slipped on a jacket and headed out to meet DEA administrator Westerville at a diner. Westerville was already seated in a booth with a window. The cold grey of a late December day could be felt a foot away from the window, so Stevens sat out near the end of the bench inside the restaurant.

"Nothing like some good greasy food and coffee when you're waiting on important information — eh, director?" Westerville seemed a little nervous.

"Nothing to be nervous about," Stevens said as he perused the slick and shiny four-page menu.

A waitress came over, in a skirt too short for her age but in sensible shoes and asked what he wanted to drink.

"Coffee, dear, and I'll take one of those breakfast skillets with the sausage, thank you." Stevens looked over at Westerville to see what he was going to have.

Westerville saw the look and replied, "Already ordered a BLT and some fries." He grinned.

The waitress smiled and left. Westerville looked out the window and spoke: "Stevens, I have never felt like I was about to be before a congressional hearing more than right now."

Stevens sipped his coffee. "Just imagine that the violence on both sides of the border goes down..." he shrugged his big shoulders, "...say, fifty percent, and your interdictions increase twenty percent over the next year. You think you're going to get grilled over that? And how foolish would anyone be even trying to take you on with those numbers, and it could be greater. Who knows?"

"Fuck, man." Westerville shook his head several times.

"We did the math on this. Today's worst case scenario: I end up with a former agent dead who was looking for revenge. Nothing comes back to us, period. So, relax."

"I guess I'm just not as comfortable straddling the lines as you 'spooks' are," Westerville said.

"Well, you're just as good at lying if you think you're just 'straddling the line' on this deal." Stevens sipped his coffee.

Chapter Sixty-Two

Hudde took a long, deep breath and then looked over the wooden railing out the front expanse of windows. He could see the men still seated at the coffee shop across the circular drive of the office building he was in; the tinting did not allow them to see him in return.

Hudde returned to the large doors and opened them both up, walking in as big as life. The first target Hudde identified was Carlos Morales himself, standing at the end of the table. It looked like Gordan had interrupted a speech. The second man Gordan identified was the DEA man Ricardo Cruz, whom Gordan punched in the stomach, dropping him to the floor. Gordan then turned and cut the throat of the third man before he even saw who it was. Gordan leapt across the table and drove the knife deep into the chest of the fourth man, who had just stood up from the table. Hudde believed he may have missed the heart on that one.

Turning quickly, Gordan struck the fifth man in the face with the hilt of the big blade, dropping that man in his place. Gordan did not take the time to finish him, as Morales was just coming to his senses and reaching for his cell phone. Gordan charged, driving into the man, picking him up and forcing him back into the wall, crushing all the wind from his chest; the phone went flying. Gordan drove the K-bar multiple times into his chest, killing the Gulf coast *El Jefe* without any fanfare or witty banter. Gordan stopped, turned, and listened, hearing his own breathing for the first time since he crashed through the doors.

Also breathing — well, coughing — was Ricardo Cruz, still sitting on the floor where Gordan had first encountered him. Gordan walked over and grabbed a handful of his suit, dragging him over and picking him up and dropping him onto the big meeting table. Cruz didn't like feeling like a rag doll and the ease with which he was being tossed around.

"English?" Gordan asked, knowing damn full well the guy spoke English.

"*Si*, er, yes. What do you want? Please just don't kill me."

"If you want to live, then gather up the remaining cartel members and hole up in the Morales estate until I contact you again." Hudde was looking into the man's eyes to see if this was registering.

The man Gordan had stunned with the hilt of the blade started to moan and get to his feet.

Gordan looked at Cruz, who was now sitting on the table. "Who's that guy?" Hudde asked.

"He's our maritime operations expert," Cruz said, flatly.

"Does he speak English?" Hudde asked.

"Sure."

Gordan walked over and grabbed the man roughly, checking for weapons. He found none, and he dragged the man over to the door.

"Listen up: I need you to go downstairs, open the front doors, and call for help. If you do this and do not run away, I will not kill you. Do you understand?" Gordan shook the man. "If you try to run away I will kill you." Gordan slid the knife back in its sheath and pulled out his .45 with his left hand. He followed the man to the door and said, "Remember" and pointed his gun at him.

Gordan gestured with the gun barrel for Cruz to follow him, and they walked to the railing, looking over.

"Do you want to be the *Jefe*, Mr. Cruz?" Gordan asked.

Cruz was shocked at the death skull before him now telling him he could be *Jefe*.

"What?"

"Your DEA bosses think you should be *Jefe*," Gordan said, flatly.

"You're DEA?" Cruz was glad he hadn't been punched in the head. He added, "Those guys are going to kill you," and he nodded in the direction of the coffee shop.

Just then, Gordan looked over the railing. The man from the meeting room, the maritime expert, had gotten to the door; he stopped, looked up, and opened the door. He started screaming in Spanish; it sounded very convincing. All the men at the coffee shop were on their feet and heading in the direction of the front doors. The door man then decided to make a break for it.

Gordan fired off one very loud round at the runner. The glass on the door starred but did not break.

"All bulletproof," Cruz noted and added, "I knew he would run."

"Me, too," Gordan said.

Then Hudde turned to Cruz and said, "So round up the cartel people at the Morales mansion, and make a good decision. The next time we speak, you just might have lived to be *Jefe* — understand?" Gordan stole a glance at his face.

"You ain't going to live through this, skull man," Cruz said, and he pointed at the 10 or 11 men outside the doors, now a little more cautious after a gun had been fired. In fact, most of the men were standing back at the Toyota parked on the sidewalk, listening to the man Gordan had released. The man yelled and screamed, all the while pointing up at the office building.

Gordan shook his head and reached into his jacket and pulled out a flip phone; he hit the single number listed and the dial button. The Toyota went up in a ball of flames. Gordan was surprised later to hear that only three men had died. None of the survivors were in any condition to give chase. though.

He turned back and poked Cruz in the chest. "It will be your decision, Cruz. Make a good one." Hudde turned and started to walk away. He stopped, turned, and said, "'Maritime expert.'" He laughed and said, "You guys crack me up."

Cruz seemed a little hurt. "We have a submarine, you know."

"Really?" Hudde paused in place "Nice." Then he turned and headed to the back of the building.

Hudde found the back stairwell and headed out the back door, hitting the fire alarm as he left. Crossing one grassy, park-like area, he rolled his balaclava back up, jumping a wall. With a quick jog, Gordan was driving in his truck, heading Northwest in less than 10 minutes.

Chapter Sixty-Three

John Stevens looked at his phone. "I have a text from Mr. Riggs."

"What's it say?" The excitement in Westerville's voice did not go unnoticed by Stevens.

"It says, 'This Thursday, Tango Oscar Tango 1800hrs local.'"

"That's it? What's it mean?" Westerville was trying to look at Stevens's phone — like maybe he was holding something back.

"One, it means that, today, he was successful. Two, it means we have to hold up our end for part three, which means time-on-target 2000hrs local here. This means we should get to work and then meet Thursday night for a drink to see if we are proud owners of the Mexican drug trade."

Chapter Sixty-Four

Standing on the bridge of the *USS Dixie*, an Arleigh Burke class US Navy destroyer, captain Lee Rolphes used his binoculars to keep an eye on the target vessel being towed to sea. His current task was to ensure that all sea-going vessels steer clear of the tugs dragging the old 564 feet worth of US Navy supply ship to its grave. The Air Force, he was told, wanted to test some new electronics on some ordnance designed for pinpoint accuracy. His other task would be to count the strikes and evaluate the accuracy of the eight bombs that would be dropped Thursday evening. The bombs would be basically concrete cone-shaped projectiles with tens of thousands of dollars of electronic equipment attached to guidance fins. Rolphes had seen it before.

Rolphes hoped that the good weather would persist, as he dreaded a loose "ghost ship" pitching and rolling in the Pacific 1000 miles from the mainland. He guessed the seas were at about eight feet right now and were forecast to be even lower tomorrow night; he knocked twice on the oak railing.

Currently, his ship was like a motorcycle following a bulldozer. They pulled giant loops around and around as the four ships made their way to the target area west of San Francisco.

Chapter Sixty-Five

Miguel Lopez carried the two packages just delivered to The Cowboy's estate upstairs to the third floor.

"You expecting something, boss?" he asked as he observed Eduardo Gonzales sitting in the oversized leather chair of the third-floor office.

"What you got?" Gonzales said as he saw the longer thin box and a small box the size of a brick. He nodded at Lopez to open them.

Lopez flicked out a knife from his back and slid it under the edge of the larger box; he pulled at the cardboard until he yanked out a laptop computer.

"You need a new laptop?" Lopez asked.

"I didn't order anything." The Cowboy picked it up and turned it over in his hands. "It looks normal."

He turned it on, and, after the systems ran, a flat black screen came up. One icon was displayed: A square, deep-blue box with a human skull emblem in the middle. A timer was counting down near it, and it currently was at 26:28:36, the seconds ticking off quickly.

"What the fuck!" The Cowboy said. "Is this some sick joke?" He turned to Lopez.

Both men jumped when the small box began ringing, like a phone. Gonzales nodded, and Lopez unwrapped it. It was a simple black flip phone.

Lopez picked it up, looking confused the whole time. "Yes," he said as he shrugged his shoulders and handed the phone to Gonzales. "He wants to talk to The Cowboy." He held the phone out.

"Is this The Cowboy?" the voice said.

"Who are you?" The Cowboy said. He was a little concerned and a little angry.

"Tomorrow night, at 17:30hrs, you will turn on the computer. We will have the ability to speak, using the laptop, and I will make you a business offer."

"Maybe I'm not looking for any new business deals," Gonzales said through clenched teeth.

"Well, then, sometime after 19:00hrs, I will walk up your driveway and kill you and anyone who tries to stop me — just as I did yesterday at Ciudad Victoria."

"That was you?" There was a crack in The Cowboy's voice.

"Carlos Morales didn't want to deal with me, either; it makes no difference to me," the voice said.

The Cowboy walked to the window and began scanning the wilderness near his home. "What makes you think you can walk into my home as you did the offices of Morales?" Gonzales spit it out.

"Defy me, and I will walk up your driveway, enter your home, find you, and piss on your corpse after I kill you," the voice shared, matter-of-factly.

"You call and threaten me?" Gonzales screamed into the phone, which he was holding above his head with two hands as if it had significant heft.

Lopez felt that The Cowboy might just die of a coronary if he didn't calm down.

"Well, you can accept my offer," the voice reminded him.

"You come here, and you will die, my friend; this I assure you." Gonzales closed the phone and was about to throw it when Lopez took it from him in case they needed it later.

Gonzales looked at Lopez. "I'm not running from my own home. If that freak wants to come to my own home and kill me, let him try, because he will need an army!"

They both started making phone calls and calling in their own army.

Gordan Hudde took apart the phone he had just used and destroyed it.

Chapter Sixty-Six

Two ominous B-2 bombers sat one in front of the other in a large metal hangar at Whiteman Air Force Base just southeast of Kansas City, Missouri. The heavy snows typical of the area had not yet blanketed the base, and the runways were wind-swept clean.

One ground crew from the 509th was prepping both aircraft for a training mission that was going to take place tomorrow morning. The electric bomb racks were nearing the undercarriage of the first bomber; eight 2000-lb. training JDAM munitions were on the racks, painted blue. These practice bombs were shells with concrete inside but still had the satellite or laser guidance systems to ensure accuracy.

The airman and senior airman loaded all eight "dummy" bombs into the first stealth bomber under the watchful eye of the crew chief, who was making notations onto a clipboard.

The second rack of munitions to be loaded on the other B-2 were fully armed and functional JDAM 2000-pounders with the most up-to-date, advanced guidance systems. Red flags hung from the end of the nose of each bomb. The bombs were equipped with systems that could communicate with satellites via secure communications as well as the plane, as each was temporarily connected via a USB connection attached to the plane's interior bomb rack.

After completing the task of loading each plane, the crew chief inspected the work and offered the clipboard to each airman to sign, confirming that they had completed the loading of the aircraft.

"Crew chief, this says we loaded four dummy bombs in each aircraft?" the senior airman noted.

"It's above our pay grade, son. Let's all just sign it and move on." The crew chief took the clip-board and signed his signature on the required line. "See — that was easy." He handed the clipboard back to the airman and stood with his arms folded, waiting.

The airman first class signed and handed it back. "I'll sleep OK — trust me." He had done some similar things in the past for covert operations, and he knew that he wouldn't remember anything other than the form if asked in the future.

Chapter Sixty-Seven

Ricardo Cruz carefully unwrapped the box that had been delivered to the former estate of Carlos Morales. It had a note attached to turn the device on at 17:30hrs that evening. Cruz was no computer wiz, but he had his own laptop, so he was comfortable that he could handle it.

Some of the men were very restless. Cruz had surrounded himself with the remaining heads of the Gulf coast cartel. They, in turn, had come with some of their own security men, and these hard people were often uncomfortable among their peers — like multiple lion prides sharing the same turf.

Cruz thought back to the man in the skull mask and his instructions. Was this a trick to get the remaining cartel men together in the same place, or was he telling the truth that, somehow, he could be the *Jefe* of the cartel when this was over? Was this a DEA operation?

Cruz was pulled from his thoughts when one of the men from the Belize border area slammed his hand down on the table.

"Why are we sitting here waiting for a man who has murdered the most senior men?" The man stood above Cruz, looking down at him in a disapproving way.

Cruz knew that there would be major strife among the surviving members and also knew this was an important moment, as many in the home were looking at him now.

Cruz took his time, slowly rising from the table and walking into the vast living room; on the way past, he patted several men on the back or placed a reassuring hand on their shoulder as he passed.

"Gentlemen." Cruz used his most authoritative voice. He placed both hands above his head, palms out, asking for both attention and silence.

"We have been attacked; I, personally, am lucky to have escaped with my life. I do not know who the perpetrator of this attack was. Does anyone here know? Being on the street may mean you have a target on your back, unlike anything that you have experienced before. I look around this room and across the property and see many tough and strong men. We are an army. We do not fear a frontal attack from anyone. So, why not wait and see what this communication is about? I know that we all will return to making money and controlling the Gulf coast as soon as we decide to do so. Is that not true, my friends?"

A murmur of approval went up from the room.

Cruz continued, "Any of you who wish to remain here and watch the video can do so. I have been promised it will start near 5:30 pm this afternoon. Then we will try to figure out where we go from here and how best to return our operations to our former glory."

Men were nodding in agreement all across the room.

"We must put back together a hierarchy. I imagine many promotions among you here, and some of your men will need to move up and accept added responsibilities. We need to assess our strengths..." Cruz waved his arms to be inclusive of everyone who was watching, "...and the men whom we employ. I, like many of you," he paused, looking as many men as possible in the eyes, " believe this attack to be something done by The Cowboy, but tonight we may know for sure, and then we can plan and return to business as usual."

Cruz exited the room much the same as he had entered, and he could tell his speech had earned him the support of almost everyone in the room, Many now patted him on the back or placed their hands on his shoulder as he milled about, looking to push his dominance. As they looked to gain his favor, none of the men left the premises.

Chapter
Sixty-Eight

At 38,000 feet, Lt. Col. Jim "Zeus" Tanner made his last radio communication with Whiteman "feet wet" as the B-2s passed the California coast. He then began the climb to the top operational ceiling — higher than 50,000 feet — and made his turn to the Southwest. His partner flew onward to the West, and they both disappeared from all civilian radar.

Chapter Sixty-Nine

Gordan Hudde finished loading his truck; he had no plans to return to this townhome. He was excited for the culmination of his plans. He was comforted by the Wilson combat 1911 under his right arm, the .38 Taurus ultralight in his left pocket, and the K-bar at the center of his back. He removed the K-bar for the drive, throwing it onto the seat near him. He jumped into the truck to make his way to his outcropping of rock two miles South from The Cowboy's estate.

First heading West to Mazatlán, Gordan couldn't help but think about Isabella and the reason that he had become the destroyer of cartels. He couldn't allow himself to be distracted, so he shook his head and started envisioning his plan step by step, going over every sequence. Then he started over and began to plan for every wrench that could thrown into his plans, and he made a mental contingency plan for those issues. He layered them in his head so that if any of these items unfolded, he would be prepared for them.

When he was finally able to turn to the Northeast and head back into the mountains, away from the relatively flat coastal area near Culiacan, he began to get excited again. Looking out his driver's-side window out to the West, out over the ocean, he saw that dark clouds were building, mixing with the orange of the dying sun.

It appeared that, this time, the sky would match Gordan's mood.

Gordan couldn't tell which direction the storms were traveling in, but he understood that they often moved East and North. About thirty minutes later, Gordan made the turn into the wash, heading toward the three-story outcropping of rock that gave him the vantage point to observe The Cowboy's property two miles to the North. There had been no rain since he discovered the area, and he followed his tracks back to the same, exact location.

He got out and stretched. The wind was coming harder from the West, maybe 20 miles an hour with some stronger gusts. He began the two trips to the top of his "mountain" with the equipment that he needed, hopefully, to finish this mission. The dots he had painted on the trees and rocks the last time he'd been there led him along the fastest, easiest approach. He stopped after the first trip up, looking down the cliff's East side and the desert scrub land 60-65 feet below.

After his second trip, Gordan glanced at his watch on the inside of his right wrist. He had 30 minutes to set up. The sun would set first on The Cowboy's estate, as his home was built on the East side of the 180 feet worth of rock and cactus that rose above his home. Gordan had a clear view to the East and the North, but the West and South were overgrown all the way down to his pickup. He climbed up onto the big chunk of flat boulder that gave him a perfect vantage point of The Cowboy's property and began to unpack and set up his equipment.

By 17:20hrs, Gordan was standing back, looking at his setup. A small camera was set up on a tripod looking at The Cowboy's estate. A small USB cable ran down to the suitcase-laptop sitting on the stone below it. The laptop was also connected to a small satellite antenna array about the size of two fully outstretched hands touching thumb to thumb. Another item connected to the laptop was the tripod-mounted laser identifier, a dark-green, boxy binocular-like item that Gordan was now kneeling behind. First, he glanced up to the West at the approaching storm, and then he looked through the laser identifier made by a large US corporation and used by the United States Special Forces.

Gordan could quickly identify the top-floor office of The Cowboy's home. Looking at the front of the house, he observed a Humvee with what appeared to be an M-60 on the turret. Then he took his eyes from the lens and rubbed them. Looking back, he saw what was probably a Russian-made tracked vehicle — maybe an anti-aircraft gun, a ZSU57-2, if he remembered his Vietnam area flashcards correctly — sitting in the center of The Cowboy's driveway. There were many men and several American-made M-113 armored personnel carriers heading down the driveway near the barn that The Cowboy used as a barracks. At the gate of the home, another tracked Russian infantry vehicle, a BMP, was parked across the opening of the gate, keeping any traffic from coming or going. Gordan was impressed; The Cowboy was taking his threat seriously.

Gordan slipped his communications headset on. It consisted of an earpiece and a slim mic sitting just to the right of his mouth. Then he stopped, closed his eyes, and listened. He swore he could hear an engine, but it was difficult with the current wind. Then he was sure and looked for a noise that was coming from the East and getting louder. Grabbing his field glasses, he scanned the scrub and rocks until he observed a small four-wheel-drive utility vehicle heading his way. The passenger had a rifle across his lap, and they were obviously looking for something. It wasn't an animal, because they would stop and glass if that was what they were up to.

"Fuck," Gordan said, out loud — he had no rifle. Gordan stooped down. He couldn't see them, and he knew he would be concealed as long as they remained on the angle they were coming at. It made sense that The Cowboy would send out some rovers to look for him.

Suddenly a voice entered his right ear. "Rogue, Rogue. This is Zeus. Over."

Gordan replied, "Zeus, this is Rogue. Reading you 5X5. Over."

"Roger that, Rogue. We are prepared to receive." Gordan knew the B-2 was somewhere over the Pacific and heading East, toward the Mexican coastline near Isla Altamura.

Gordan sneaked back to the edge of the cliff, the back of his perch. The small utility vehicle was now stopped about 100 yards off to the East. He prayed that they wouldn't head further west and come across his vehicle or the tracks that they could easily follow right back to it.

Gordan cupped his hands over the mic to cut the wind noise and spoke softly into the mic: "Roger, Zeus. Prepare to receive. Over."

Gordan crawled back to the laser finder and sighted in on the thick glass of The Cowboy's third-floor windows. He fired the laser and then looked down at the coordinates that lit up grey on the laptop screen. Gordan reached down and hit the "Send" button. Within seconds, the B-2 pilot made a call.

"Rogue, this is Zeus. Standing by for confirmation."

Gordan glanced back at the laptop screen and observed a second set of identical numbers to the original but now blinking red. Gordan once again hit the "Send" button, and, within another couple of seconds the first set of numbers disappeared, and the single set lit a solid green.

Gordan crawled to the back of his rock and peeked over the side. The two men in the vehicle were just sitting there and smoking. Gordan hoped it was weed; he would take any help he could get.

Crawling back to the laser identifier, Gordan selected the driveway anti-aircraft gun, the barracks, and the BMP armored vehicle as his other three targets, repeating the confirmation process for each of those targets.

Looking West, Gordan saw distant lightning, and the wind whipped and pulled at his clothing. He hoped it wouldn't knock over the camera tripod.

"Rogue, Rogue, we have positive identification for all four packages and are continuing to release point. Stand by" squelched into Gordan's ear.

Gordan crawled back and stole a glance at the two men he believed to be scouts for The Cowboy. One had his feet up, leaning back in the seat of the utility vehicle, still puffing on something. Gordan wasn't sure where the other one — the one with the rifle — was, but he couldn't wait to spot him.

Returning to the laptop, Gordan now began transmitting to the laptops that were on the desk of Eduardo Gonzales and in front of Ricardo Cruz, sitting in the Morales home. The cartel laptops would receive a skull picture instead of Gordan's face. Cruz would also see The Cowboy's office, but The Cowboy could not see and did not know that the Gulf cartel was currently watching.

Gordan spoke: "Cowboy — can you hear me?"

The cowboy's laptop camera was picking up part of the desk and a partial view out a window. The Cowboy's face suddenly filled the screen as he leaned over the desk. "I hear you, dead man," The Cowboy sneered into the mic.

From 30,000 feet above, out of the deep black and lightning-crisscrossed cumulonimbus clouds came Zeus's final call. "Rogue, Rogue. Package one away." There was a second pause between packages two, three, and then four.

Gordan pressed a button on the laptop, and a 10 minute timer popped up on everyone's video stream; the seconds immediately began ticking down.

"I have given you an opportunity to give me your drug-running operation or have me take it," Gordan said. "Your time is running out until I make the decision for you."

The Cowboy's face returned to the screen. "I have all my men here; I have Colonel Sanchez from the Mexican army and some of his men here. My own dangerous men are everywhere. Come and get me, assassin."

"Tell me, Cowboy; is there a 'Miguel Lopez' with you?" Gordan asked.

"That cold-blooded killer never leaves my side!" The Cowboy began laughing. "I am drinking to your last moments on Earth, bastard!"

Gordan again crept to the end of the rock and looked for the utility vehicle. One guy was pissing near the vehicle. Gordan still couldn't identify the location of the rifleman. A bullet whizzed past Gordan's head, and he had no idea where it had come from.

He had no time for this.

The timer had ticked down to three minutes. Gordan low-crawled back across the flat rock and turned off The Cowboy feed to the Cruz laptop and now sent them the video feed from the camera Gordan had set up on the tripod. It was a beautiful view of most of The Cowboy's estate.

"I need to see Lopez before I start," Gordan said.

Lopez stepped in front of the camera and said, "I hope our men allow you to enter the home so that I can kill you myself."

"You and that psychotic boss killed my fiancée, and I am going to kill you both before this is over. Look to the West,"

Gordan said. "My vengeance comes out of that angry orange sky!" He didn't mean to, but he screamed it out. Right on cue, the last sunlight competed with lightning to brilliantly light up the storm clouds. Gordan glanced at the time, which now read one minute and fifteen seconds.

He heard The Cowboy say that he would offer himself in the window and said, "Go ahead and take your best shot." The shot Gordan was concerned with had just come from somewhere near him, sending rock and dust into the air. Gordan had un-holstered his .45 and was crawling back to the cliff.

Chapter Seventy

Captain Rolphes stood with one foot up against the outer wall on the bridge of his destroyer, the *USS Dixie*, his naval glasses scanning the old frigate floating 1500 yards from his. The sky was still lit at this point 1000 miles from the California coast. The seas were light. He could have been fishing on the pond near his home, the craft was moving so little. No other vessels were in the AO, as required by Naval rules. He was interested in the munitions that would come and what they would do to the ocean-going ship out there and anyone waiting for his communication. His second, with his own binoculars tight against his face, was standing nearby.

"It should be any moment now, Captain," he said without taking his eyes off the ship.

Just then a shower of sparks and metal shot out of the deck of the cargo ship.

"Direct hit!" the second called out, followed by three more.

After a 30-second delay, four more strikes were observed on the ship. It was already listing badly.

Captain Rolphes turned to his second. "Send a message 4X4 followed by 4X4" 'All direct hits. Ship listing badly and sinking fast.'"

Rolphes kept his destroyer on station until the old vessel lifted temporarily out of the water and then went to its grave somewhere in the deep. He shook his head. It was so easy for a military to take out a ship these days. He didn't even know if these bombs had been released by an aircraft or maybe a satellite thousands of miles above earth. One day, his Navy would drastically change, and he thought the times were quickly approaching.

Chapter Seventy-One

Four thousand miles away, in Virginia, CIA Director John Stevens gulped down one more bourbon before getting up and looking out the window; nothing had changed from the last time. No street noise reached him here, and it seemed so peaceful to watch the snowflakes dance around the streetlamps on their way to the ground, where they joined force to wreak havoc on the traffic. He knew the snow on the ground here was nothing like the weather in Mexico. His neck was out there, big time, on this one, and it was a career changer. He hoped to God he never had to go before Congress and lie about this one.

Not far away, DEA administrator Paul Westerville was chewing another Tums, looking out at the same rotten weather and wishing he had never signed onto this operation. He knew that he would get no sleep tonight, and he jumped when his wife walked up behind him and put her arms around him.

Chapter
Seventy-Two

Gordan made out a man about halfway up the rocks behind him, trying to climb further up to gain the correct angle for a shot. Gordan lay flat and looked behind him just in time to see a giant plume of dust and rock blast up into the air as the first 2000-lb. explosion of "Package #1" struck The Cowboy's office perfectly. Gordan knew that the noise of the blast and the concussive shock wave would hit any moment, and he fired three quick shots at the rifleman as he stood, slack jawed, looking North. The first and third fat .45 slugs struck the man high in the chest and neck area, and the blast of the first bomb comingled with the quick trigger pulls. The concussive blast hit Hudde about the time the second blast was throwing up and powdering the vehicles in the driveway at The Cowboy's former estate.

Gordan jumped up and ran to the Easternmost edge of the cliff he was standing on. The driver of the utility vehicle was watching the fireworks to the North, and Gordan emptied his clip on the 100-yard shot, firing just above the man's head and allowing the barrel to rise slightly with each round. Gordan was not sure but believed he'd struck the guy with at least one round to the abdomen; it was terrible to gut shoot someone, but Gordan had no time to worry. He was wondering if there were other roving bands that this team could reach out to. So, when the man doubled over at the waist and fell to the ground, Gordan was somewhat satisfied.

Gordan ran back, dropped down to the laptop, and addressed Ricardo Cruz and his men on the East coast. "It looks as if a few positions have opened up in the Sinaloa drug cartel." Gordan hit a button, and a 15-minute timer came up on his screen for Cruz. "I have eliminated all those who have offended me. There is no need for more death this evening. However, this is your choice: Will you and your men continue to work and lead the Gulf coast cartel, or will your dust be spread about for miles in just less than 13 minutes now?"

"Wait…" Cruz started to ask a question, and Hudde interrupted.

"Are you the current leader of the Gulf coast cartel?"

Cruz looked at the men around him, who were all talking among themselves. "Currently, yes" he said.

"Well, I have no problem with you continuing in that position, with a little input from me, or…" he turned up the volume on the clock timer, and Gordan let the ticking noise make the final point.

"No, we will meet with you and continue to work this operation," Cruz said. He looked around the room, and no one seemed to be in open disagreement.

"Lay down your arms, and meet my men at the bottom of your driveway. We can start a peaceful resolution." Gordan spoke slowly and softly.

"What proof do we have that we will survive this meeting?" Cruz said.

"You will have no need for further proof in less than eight minutes." Gordan spoke matter-of-factly.

Cruz looked about the room, and there was agreement; he knew. "We are leaving now," Cruz said. Many men were on their way before Cruz had agreed. The floor of the home and the red cobblestone driveway ended up littered with military weapons and handguns of all makes and models.

Gordan turned off the laptop; he knew that there was now a flurry of activity taking place to set up the new unholy trinity between Luis Fernando Calderon, his cartel, the DEA, and the CIA. Gordan didn't care; he was probably now responsible for the deaths of everyone involved in the attack that had wounded him and taken Isabella from him.

Suddenly the wind howled, pulling him from a trance as hail began bouncing off the stone and making odd noises as it bounced off the plastic and metal equipment Gordan had hauled up to his stone hilltop. Gordan stood, turned his back to the winds and hail, and walked over to the cliff, looking East. It took several lightning bolts flashing across the sky before he confirmed that the two men he shot were lying in the same position and obviously were a threat no more. The wind howled and seemed to be trying to push him off his position.

Gordan turned back into the wind, looking up at the ominous dark clouds. He stood silhouetted in the lightning. He arched his back and lifted his fists just over shoulder height, spread to show his vast wingspan. He let loose a blood-curdling war cry to the sky.

If he had done wrong, let God take him now.

Lightning stuck, the wind howled, and the earth shook, but Gordan Hudde stood strong and alone up on his rock. He continued looking up, allowing the hail to sting his face until it turned to rain and no one would be able to tell whether it was heavenly water or tears.

Gordan turned off all the equipment and began to stow it. He thought he should hurry out from the wash in case this hard rain kept up and flooded his way out to the road.

♦ ♦ ♦

Approximately four miles from Gordan Hudde's position, Rafael Torres waited in a tree line with 25 men, including Sanchez and Campos. They had arrived in a half-dozen cars or trucks over the last half day to wait, like Luis Calderon had asked them to do. Torres knew of Hudde's plan but didn't know the signal to "go." So he waited for a sign that would involve the number "4"; Hudde had said he would not miss it. To make morale even worse, a huge storm looked like it was barreling toward them, and the wind had begun to pick up.

They stood and took turns watching the front gate of The Cowboy's estate, which now was being guarded by a military armored vehicle.

"We ain't got nothing to take that out, boss," Campos said to Torres, handing the binoculars to him as he turned and walked away. He held up his FNFAL .308 rifle and added, "I might as well throw rocks."

"I was told we would not have to worry and that, if we were unable to take them on, we are to return home." Torres tried to sound confident but was worried they would be returning with their tails tucked, as The Cowboy had called in half the army, it seemed.

At 5:45 pm, Torres rounded up his men. "Make sure you are ready to go. It should be any moment," he said to the anxious men.

"Listen, Captain," one of the men said, "I seen all the armor that drove up there today, and I'm not going up there with just a gun." He held up the AK-47 that he was carrying to drive home the point.

"I was told there would be a sign. The sign would repeat four times, and then we should go," Torres said to all the men. "If we do not recognize this sign, we will just go home."

Somebody yelled out, "What the fuck!" and everyone turned to look at a giant plume of smoke rising into the air. A large blast sounded, followed by the concussion of wind that moved their hair and pushed their clothing. This was repeated four times, the four individual plumes of smoke and dust quickly growing together into one giant cloud and blowing in their direction.

The men were all talking and excitedly pointing in the direction of The Cowboy's estate. Torres jumped into the bed of a pickup truck and yelled out to the men:

"Do any of you doubt that you just witnessed the sign to go? Do any of you doubt the power of *Jefe* Calderon over The Cowboy? Now get in your vehicles, and let's go see what's left of The Cowboy's famous estate!" He held his rifle up over his head and pumped it up and down.

The men cheered and ran to their cars and trucks. They took off South, just in time to drive into the hail and rain. No one could wait to see what had just happened.

Torrez was in the back of the big Chevy pickup they had brought to the assault. Campos was driving, and Sanchez was in the passenger seat.

"Fuck this! I don't think we're going to need guns, man," Sanchez said, looking out his passenger window.

Where there once was a large brick-and-iron gate with a Russian-made armored vehicle parked across the driveway, there now was a large, smoking crater. The truck hit and bounced over something. Sanchez reached across and smacked Campos across the shoulder.

"Dude — slow down, and watch where you're going!" Sanchez said.

The rain, wind, and growing darkness made it impossible to see very far, but there was no armored vehicle anywhere. They picked their way slowly now, allowing the other vehicles to follow easily. There was smoking wood and bodies or body parts littering the ground. Strangely, one wall of the two barns was still standing, but the other was all gone.

They slid slowly past a Humvee that was on its side and looked like it had been impacted from the top. Anyone who'd been inside was now entombed there. No one spoke now — just the wind and rain hitting the windshield as the wipers tried to keep up made any noise. They passed a part of another armored vehicle with a smoking large rubber wheel, and then they pulled up to a spot that once held the famous mansion of The Cowboy, Eduardo Gonzales. His often-bragged-about fortress on the roof was nowhere to be found. A burning, smoking ruin now lay at the base of the mountain behind it.

Torres knew that the Mexican government would investigate; he also knew that they would never get a satisfactory explanation for what had occurred here. Luis Calderon would "secretly" take full responsibility and gain a reputation that would solidify his position in the criminal underworld, and no one would ever challenge him during his lifetime.

Torres walked from car to truck and told all his men to go down into town and get rooms. He told them that they'd won without firing a single shot or losing a single man. "*Viva El Jefe Calderon*," they all said.

Epilogue

Gordan Hudde knelt in the grass, the early morning sun warming his upturned face. He closed his eyes and said a prayer. When he opened his eyes, he looked down at the three-foot-high white cross and small plaque that read, "A beautiful daughter and spirit — Isabella Santiago. RIP."

Gordan stood and put an arm around Gabriela Santiago, briefly squeezing her tightly.

"I don't see the beauty of the world anymore," he said to her. "I think it was through her eyes that I was able to do that."

"You made each other happy, and you never had time to find out if it would be forever. Honestly, that is the part that will haunt you." She squeezed him back. "What will you do now?"

"I'm going to find a country home and get a dog — forget about people if I can," he said. "And you?"

"I need to think about my spring garden and what I can feed that stray." She smiled up at him. "I don't know why, Gordan, and I guess it's not right, but it does give me peace knowing that all the men involved in her killing are gone. God forgive me."

"God forgive us all," Gordan said and hugged her one last time. Walking to his truck, he refused to look back; he was afraid she would look too much like her daughter.

I'm going to go have a drink with the new king, Gordan said to himself. He turned the key, and the truck roared to life.

He placed the truck in gear, and then he headed off to see Luis Fernando Calderon — this time, through the front door.

Gordan Hudde will return in: *A Hint of Silver.*

What is being said about **Gordan Hudde** novels?

A Deep Purple Hue-

"With an extraordinary conspiracy story, this book is perfect for fans of 24 as Hudde reminds me of a bearded Bauer - he doesn't always play by the rules and never bows to authority."   -The Book Magnet.

"The perfect conspiracy, well-suited characters, a beginning that hooks you right away..." – Serious Reading.

An Angry Orange Sky-

"With plenty of shocks and surprises, An Angry Orange Sky does not disappoint and I have no doubt that we will be hearing a lot more from Gordan Hudde, at least I certainly hope so!"- The Book Magnet.

"...Hudson expertly narrates what a single man driven by determination and courage can do to counter the evil forces around him." – Serious Reading.

"This violent, cinematic second entry in the Gordon Hudde Novel Series shows promise, with its surprisingly original plot, and despite a dauntingly large cast of characters..." – BookLife Prize in Fiction.

A Hint of Silver-

"...Graphic and violent, the gritty manuscript powers along relentlessly... it's hard not to root for a hero like Hudde." – BookLife Prize in Fiction.

Words being used by other reviewers-

"Addictive, interesting, dark, disturbing, brutal, brooding, and exciting.

One reviewer said: "This novel would make a great movie!"

A Retail Investigator- Many 5 star reviews!
"The book clearly outlines the excitement, risk, and exasperation that is part of the deal being in the investigation business. The stories narrated are fun to read and extremely informative for anyone who is currently serving or interested in anything related to the investigation industry." – Serious Reading.

Don't forget to leave your own review at the location you purchased this book!

Please visit me at my author's blog: http://www.markhudsonofficialsite.com/

You can also find me on Facebook: https://www.facebook.com/markhudsonauthor/

 Mark Hudson lives in Arizona with his wife Darlene and two rescued cats, Scotty and Chance. He spent his youth in the Army as a combat engineer and in the infantry with Bco 4/325 in the 82nd Airborne. In the civilian world, he became a professional in the retail security field, specializing in employee fraud and embezzlement.

The best gift you can give an author is a good review, please return to where you purchased this book and be positive! Thank you for respecting the hard work of this author.

www.ingramcontent.com/pod-product-compliance
Lightning Source LLC
Chambersburg PA
CBHW020249200626
46816CB00001BA/200